## HIS LIPS WERE FEATHER LIGHT AGAINST HERS

Kara kept her eyes open ever so slightly, stamping Peter's image into her memory. She knew she could not enjoy his touch for long, because she couldn't ever really forget who he was.

At last she tore her lips from his. "I'm sorry, Peter," she said, her gaze falling to the ground.

"What is it?" he asked, lifting her chin and scrutinizing her face. "You're hiding something. What is it you're afraid of?"

"I—I need time to get to know you," she ventured. "I need time to trust what you're doing with the kids at the group home." She knew her explanation was weak, but it was the best she could do. She couldn't tell him flat out that he was the one man she had reason to hate.

## ABOUT THE AUTHOR

Cinda Gault knows Guelph, the small Ontario city where she has set her first Superromance. While attending university there, she worked in a group home and met the man of her dreams (as does her story's hero). Cinda and her husband, Gary, now make their home in Toronto and recently had their first child. Gannon was born soon enough to help with the final draft of *Past Convictions*.

To Gary
with love and gratitude

**Cinda Gault**

# PAST CONVICTIONS

*Harlequin Books*

TORONTO • NEW YORK • LONDON
AMSTERDAM • PARIS • SYDNEY • HAMBURG
STOCKHOLM • ATHENS • TOKYO • MILAN

Published February 1988

First printing December 1987

ISBN 0-373-70296-5

# CHAPTER ONE

FROM HER NEATLY groomed fingernails to her crisply pressed tweed pantsuit, Kara Ridgeway looked like a woman who cared about details. She liked it that way. Kara had worked hard for her reputation as a careful, methodical juveniles officer. Her warm cinnamon-colored eyes and full friendly mouth made her appear approachable, but she tried to downplay this image. Kara felt it prudent for a policewoman to avoid makeup beyond a touch of lipstick and a light stroke of blush. This morning, however, even the blush was unnecessary. Her face bore the crimson glow of agitation.

"This is ridiculous!" Kara muttered as she slammed the telephone book into her desk drawer. She'd scoured the listings for group homes, hoping she'd overlooked a new or unfamiliar name. But magical solutions were rare in her line of work. Young offenders were frustrating, all right, but not only for the obvious reasons. There simply weren't enough rehabilitation services available for them.

Her partner, Stan, looked up with a start from his desk. "What's wrong?" he asked with concern.

"Group homes," she answered with a frustrated sigh. "There aren't enough of them. How can I do a decent job if I don't have the tools to work with?"

"Uh-oh." Stan smiled and glanced up at the large twenty-four-hour clock overhead. "I can see trouble ahead. Come on, it's time for a coffee break."

"I thought you'd never ask," she said, pushing back her chair.

Stan Manning had been her partner for three years, and Kara had come to rely on his sympathetic ear and practical advice. She always discussed her more troublesome cases with him. It was too bad, she'd often reflected, she couldn't have been attracted to a guy like Stan. Yet, even if she'd met him before he'd met his wife, Kara knew she would never have thought of him as anything more than a best friend. She didn't want more than a best friend.

Her interest in working with juveniles overrode everything else, which probably amounted to a problem in her life. The men she'd met in recent years had been pleasant and enjoyable company, but no one had managed to kindle a special spark in her heart.

Kara led the way to the lunchroom, which was unusually comfortable for a police station. Its polished oak floor and matching paneling contributed to a warm, friendly atmosphere.

Kara reached the back counter first and poured Stan a steaming cup of coffee, then filled one for herself.

"I really should cut down on this stuff," she commented, half to herself.

"For you, it's almost a healthy habit," Stan prescribed. "It relieves you of the burden of being perfect." He smiled as he poured cream into his mug, then added a couple of teaspoons of sugar. "My weakness," he said with a grin.

Hitching himself up on the counter, Stan took a sip of his coffee and regarded Kara somberly. His charcoal hair was rumpled and his long lank frame moved with natural grace. He was a police officer who didn't frighten kids. Stan Manning could inspire trust with his gentle understanding, as well as win cooperation with his playful humor. His longer-than-regulation mustache made him appear more like a trustworthy friend than a cop, and he and Kara had instantly made friends.

"Now tell me what's been bothering you all morning," he urged as she sank down onto a hardbacked lunchroom chair.

Kara's tailored suit skillfully camouflaged her feminine contours, but it couldn't hide her sagging spirit.

"It's Craig Taylor, the case I was assigned two days ago," she admitted. "He's fourteen and he won't go home at night or attend school during the day. His parents can't control him anymore." She didn't add that there were other shadows haunting her. It was best to stick to the relevant facts.

"Since when does a new case ever get you down? You're usually brimming with enthusiasm to steer another lost soul onto a lawful path."

Kara smiled weakly. "You're teasing me. I can't really look that much like a missionary."

"Maybe I'm exaggerating a bit to make my point," Stan conceded, "but I don't know another cop who lives this job twenty-four hours a day. After a full day of patrolling the streets, appearing in court, preparing paperwork and interviewing witnesses, I like to take a break. You relax by inspecting group homes. I like to go home and forget about the whole thing for a while."

"No wonder!" Kara protested. "You have someone to go home to. Sandy and your two boys are more important than what goes on here. I just have a few plants I say hello to each evening."

"I don't know, Kara," Stan said slowly, shaking his head. "Somehow I get the feeling this place means more to you than anyone else could. I hope not, because that's a lonely existence."

Kara squirmed silently in her chair. She trusted Stan more than she trusted anyone. He was one of the few friends she let come close enough to see her softer, more emotional side. But there was still a private core she protected from everyone. Her attachment to her work was more than she'd wanted him to see.

"Anyway, I'm going to let you off the hook for now and change the subject," Stan said kindly, noticing her discomfort. "What's so different about Craig that he could demoralize the Guelph Police Department's star performer?"

"It's not Craig himself who is so different," she explained, feeling a little more energetic now that she was back in familiar territory. "It's the situation and who I have to work with. No one can control Craig, but he hasn't done anything really wrong yet, although he did steal money from his father's wallet before he left. But his father won't press charges, so it doesn't qualify as a crime."

"Those kids are tricky to handle," Stan agreed.

Kara nodded. "I had him in for one of our little chats. I gave him my spiel about how lucky he was to have parents who cared about him, and how much less sympathetic we'd be if we caught him doing something illegal. But I realized very quickly that it would be a serious mistake to send him back home just now.

"He despises his parents," she explained. "I get the feeling he isn't interested in committing any real criminal act, but for some unknown reason he's made their lives miserable. They don't want him home, either. Their lives have been peaceful since he's been out of the house. I've seen his act. He can be a truly miserable kid when he puts his mind to it."

"I see why you're looking at group homes. He sounds like a perfect candidate."

"I think it would help him put his home life into perspective."

"So where is he now?" Stan asked as he got up and reached for the coffeepot. He raised his eyebrows as he lifted the pot, and Kara pushed her cup along the table toward him.

"Right now I have him with Children's Aid," she explained, watching as Stan filled her cup. "But he can't stay there past Monday. And the Hanson group home is full. They were about to discharge a sixteen-year-old girl, but the plans fell through. They had to keep her even though they'd already accepted her replacement. She had nowhere else to go."

"I'm sure I don't need to remind you, Kara, that it's not your job to worry about what group home this kid gets placed in. The responsibility for that belongs to Children's Aid.''

"I know," Kara acknowledged defensively. "But I've built a close working relationship with the Children's Aid workers. They know I tend to go above and beyond the call of duty, and they like to place my kids in a home I'm comfortable with. I don't see where that's a problem, Stan. I do most of that work on my own time."

"Oh, it's no problem as far as the police department is concerned," Stan clarified. "I'm sure they'd love to clone you. But, okay, you want to be happy with the group home. There's still more than one group home in Guelph, and if you're desperate you might even place him in a home in Toronto."

"I knew you'd say that," she replied, setting her cup down on the table. "The two other homes downtown can't promise anything for a week and that one about ten miles out of town is only for drug patients. Craig is unmanageable, but I don't think he's graduated to drugs—yet. As for Toronto, it would be terrible to place him so far from home, and Toronto homes are almost always full anyway. Besides, I trust the Hansons. They run a good clean place. They handle the kids the way I would. They understand that being too easy on kids makes life harder for them in the long run. A group home needs to be strict, yet even-handed, and the Hansons do the job well. They've never let me down."

Stan stroked his mustache thoughtfully, determined to be helpful. "Maybe it's an opportunity in disguise. Sometimes problems make you discover things you wouldn't have discovered ordinarily. What about that new place down by the river?"

"Aiken House? It's not new anymore. It's been around for five years."

"Have you tried there?"

"Yes. And he has a bed open."

"Aha," Stan pronounced triumphantly. "You knew all along you had a bed if you wanted it. You must have some grudge against the place. Now what might it be—the program or Peter Aiken himself?"

Kara winced. Stan didn't take long to flush out his answers. "Both," she admitted.

He looked at her with a playful grin on his face. "You know, I've sent a couple of kids to him and they didn't come out any more delinquent than they were when I sent them in."

Kara couldn't resist a smile. Stan's down-to-earth sense of humor had jollied her out of more than a few discouraging situations.

"This kind of optimism is the last thing I wanted to hear."

"Don't I know it," Stan replied with a laugh. "But let me at least tell you what I've heard about the place. The year before Aiken bought it, it was nearly condemned, and he renovated it all himself. He's stubborn. You'd like that at least."

"Just because you can renovate a house for a group home doesn't mean you know what to do with the kids once you get them inside the place."

"But a lot of people think he does know what to do. You know old man Bernard, who runs the general store down there? He's Aiken's biggest supporter.

Back before you joined the force there was a rash of break-ins at his store, and the cops could never catch the kids red-handed. Bernard was so fed up he even put his store up for sale. Seems Aiken came into the store one day and heard about the problem. He got his kids to join forces with the owner and they staked out the store one weekend. Sure enough, they caught the roughnecks who were doing all the damage. Bernard was doubly impressed because Aiken's kids held on to the offenders until the cops got there.''

"But that's been a quiet neighborhood for the three years I've been here," Kara said. Aiken House was located along a very pretty stretch of the Speed River Valley. The area was especially popular with Guelph University students for its old houses and casual atmosphere. "Stan, surely you're not trying to tell me that Peter Aiken single-handedly cleaned up a crime-infested neighborhood, are you? I would find that very hard to believe."

"It's not nearly as dramatic as that," Stan insisted. "Very simply, the kids caught the two ringleaders. Once they were rounded up, all the trouble stopped. But the incident backfired on Aiken. The neighbors decided that juvenile delinquency was a problem. They campaigned to get the group home out of the neighborhood, and they nearly succeeded."

"Didn't they know it was so-called juvenile delinquents who solved the problem?" Kara asked. She tried not to sound as interested as she was, but she caught a look in Stan's eyes.

"Yes, but the neighbors still saw them as delinquents. They might have saved the day once, but they could be the vandals the next time. We knew that was unlikely, and Aiken knew it, but the neighbors wouldn't listen. Finally Bernard trooped down to a meeting at city hall to tell his story to the politicians. He must have been persuasive because the whole idea of closing Aiken House was dropped like a hot potato."

Kara felt a grudging admiration for Aiken and his kids. Most young offenders would die before helping the police. But there were other things about this group-home operator that stopped her admiration short of support.

"I still don't want to send Craig to Aiken House, Stan."

"Why? What's your beef against him?"

"It's…everything," Kara answered, at a loss to list every facet of Aiken's philosophy that flew directly in the face of her own ideas. "It's the way he *sees* these kids that's so wrong. After reading that interview with him in the paper a few weeks ago, I don't need a tour of Aiken House to tell me how dangerous he is to the kids in his care."

She felt a little guilty, knowing it was more than a newspaper article that made her feel so strongly. But she didn't feel obliged to explain any more to Stan.

Stan sat and looked quietly at Kara for a moment before answering. "I've always figured it's important for a cop to trust his instincts. But a decision needs to be based on more than simple narrow-mindedness. Aiken's got a good record, Kara. Maybe it's only a few years to look back on, but his kids don't tend to repeat their offenses. That in itself deserves some attention."

"Maybe he's just been lucky," Kara insisted. "I can't accept that we should simply leave young offenders alone to do as they please until they decide for themselves to obey the rules. I can't imagine that approach turning out anything but happier criminals, Stan."

"All I'm saying is that it isn't like you to dismiss something before you investigate it for yourself. Why don't you go down there and take a look, or at least call and ask more about the program. How could that be a waste of time?"

Kara shifted her position in the hard chair. Even though she'd never met Peter Aiken face to face, she felt he represented a threat to everything she believed in. Craig Taylor needed order and discipline, not a free hand.

Stan drained his coffee cup. "Anyway, I've got to excuse myself," he concluded as he slid off the counter and rinsed his cup. "Right now a gymnasium full of eight-year-olds is waiting for me to tell them everything I know about bicycle safety. I don't know how this police force would survive without me."

"Absolutely. You're a cop who can keep kids on the straight and narrow—from bicycles to motorcycle gangs."

"Just till they're eighteen," Stan tossed back at her.

Kara returned his good-natured smile. But she couldn't let their conversation end with him feeling disappointed in her.

"Hey, Stan?"

He paused at the door, then turned to face her. She looked at him for a moment, wondering what she'd ever do without his friendship.

"Thanks. I can always depend on you to be honest with me, whether I like it or not. I'll probably call and check out the stupid place."

Stan's smile deepened to an approving grin. "I've got a lot of faith in you, kid. By the way, Sandy and I are still expecting you for that barbecue at six. The boys have been talking about it all week."

"You know I wouldn't miss it for the world," she said, giving him a wave as he left the lunchroom.

An instant later he popped his head back through the door. "I almost forgot. I need to ask you a favor on one of my cases. Remind me to tell you about it."

"Sounds intriguing."

"Not really. I'm just looking for a new way to look at the same old story."

"I'll do my best," she assured him. "See you tonight."

Kara returned to her desk, where she continued stewing over Craig's placement until early afternoon. No alternatives to Aiken House presented themselves, and finally she gave up. Grabbing her coat and purse, Kara headed downstairs toward the exit. First she'd visit Craig to see how he was doing, she decided. Then she'd call the woman she'd spoken to yesterday at Aiken House and ask a few questions. If she could tell Stan that she'd checked their program and still found it unacceptable, she'd feel vindicated. She'd be sure to make a list of all her reasons, too.

As she opened the door leading to the parking lot, a flood of early-autumn sunshine cascaded over her. "Umm, delicious," she murmured to herself. The Canadian autumn was her favorite time of year. She found it impossible to be downcast when the world was bursting with beauty. As she drove through Guelph's downtown streets, she marveled at how much she loved this city, with it's shady, tree-lined streets and large stone houses.

Despite her improved mood, however, something still disturbed her. Her thoughts drifted back to Peter Aiken. She hadn't told Stan that although she'd never actually met Aiken, she knew only too well who he was. It would have been too long and involved a story to tell, she rationalized. Besides, it had all happened long ago.

She'd tried to erase his name and face from her memory many times over the years. But it was a small city, and inevitably something would remind her of him sooner or later. Then her old memories would be stirred up all over again—as they had been two weeks ago when she'd seen the article about him in the paper. The paper had run a photograph, too. Peter Aiken was an arrestingly good-looking man in his late thirties or early forties. But what Kara had found most familiar about him was the distrust in his eyes.

What could motivate such a man to run a group home? You didn't go into social work for money or glory. Perhaps, she thought, he was motivated by a misplaced need for importance. If he couldn't succeed elsewhere, then at least he could be the center of the universe for a bunch of troubled teenagers. If so, she felt even more pity for the kids in his care. Juveniles didn't need someone who had to surround himself with problem kids because he couldn't be important anywhere else. These kids needed leadership.

The way Joey had.

The sudden thought of her brother surprised her. It had seemed to pop out of nowhere. But the analogy was accurate. Her impressionable brother Joey had once needed someone strong more desperately than he'd needed food or water. But Kara had been too young then to know what strength was. She'd been devoted to him, but she hadn't known how to help him. If he'd needed her today, she'd know what to do. Joey was the reason she was a Youth Bureau cop.

When she'd first discovered that Joey was stealing from the corner variety store, she'd told him she was afraid he'd be caught. But because he was older, she'd believed his assurances that he wasn't doing anything wrong. "Everybody does it," he'd said.

Now, she wished he had been caught. At least he would have had restrictions placed on him which might have prevented him from getting worse. Instead, he'd become more involved with a group of kids who were taking greater and greater risks. Finally he'd been convicted for breaking-and-entering and possession of marijuana. He'd been sentenced to training school. Through her tears, Kara had watched him being led from the courtroom. He'd looked betrayed. The world had let him get away with so much for so long. Then, without warning, he'd had to pay for it all.

She'd never forgive herself for having accepted her parents' way of supporting Joey. "He's a good boy," her mother had always said when Kara had confided her fears about her brother. "You just have to believe in the goodness you know is there," her mother would say. "He's going through a hard time and has to know his family supports him. Don't worry, dear, bad things don't happen to good kids. He's our Joey, same as he always was. He'll grow out of it."

Kara had wished a million times since then that she'd done something to knock down their blind support so that her parents would have finally had to confront the person Joey had become. That way he might have gotten what he needed. She should have gone to the police, or she should have threatened to turn him in. At least, she should have told him she was angry with him for what he was doing. But she'd acquiesced to her parents and made herself trust a boy who was headed for disaster.

Kara blinked back the tears that always welled up when she thought of Joey. These memories never seemed to lose their awful power to upset her, despite the passing years. They lurked behind her reserved facade, ready to ambush her on even the sunniest of days.

*You'll make quite an impression as an authority figure,* she chided herself. Even when they weren't all puffy, her big brown eyes tended to undermine her image as a tough cop.

This predicament with Craig had unsettled her, she realized. She'd worked with hundreds of young people like him but had always had the Hanson group home at her disposal. She couldn't help but feel that to leave Craig in the irresponsible clutches of Peter Aiken was to betray him. The boy couldn't possibly receive proper guidance from someone with Peter Aiken's ideas.

With his dirty blond hair hanging over his eyes, his permanently pursed lips and his arms always folded across his chest, Craig Taylor dared the world to let him down. Kara promised herself she wouldn't be the one to oblige him. She wheeled into the driveway of the suburban Children's Aid shelter, resolved to place Craig only where it would do him some good.

Inside, Kara found Craig in the shelter's simply furnished living room. He was slouched on the sofa, watching television.

"Hope you don't mind the interruption," she said, pausing by the set. "Mind if I turn it off?"

Craig shrugged. "Not if you tell me when you're going to get me out of this hole."

"That's *one* of the things I've come to talk to you about, Craig," she said quietly. She turned off the T.V. and sat in an easy chair across from him. "I've also come to talk to you about a police matter."

"What police matter?" he asked, doing his best to sound outraged. But the fear Kara detected in his voice was a dead giveaway.

"The matter of a hundred and seventy dollars that was stolen from your father's wallet the day you left home."

"What are you talking about?" he demanded unconvincingly.

"Don't play games, Craig. You know what I'm talking about. I want that money returned."

"I don't know what you're talking—"

"Craig, you don't need any more trouble than you've already got. I want you to return that money—now."

"What are you going to do, officer, arrest me?"

"First I'll have you back home with your parents so fast your head will spin."

"What will that prove?"

"Then we'll just wait until you really mess up." Kara continued, as if Craig hadn't said a word. "And make no mistake, you're headed down that road, pulling stunts like stealing from your parents. Sooner or later you'll do something serious and find yourself slapped in training school, where we can really keep an eye on you. Now give me your father's money."

Craig jumped to his feet and angrily shoved his hands into his pants pockets. "Go ahead," he spat. "You don't trust me, so take everything I have." He pulled crumpled bills out of his pockets and dropped them in front of her on the coffee table. "This is all the money I have in the world. I've saved it up over my entire life, but what do you care about that? Go ahead and take it if it gets you off my back."

Kara counted the money. "There's only sixty-three dollars here, Craig. What happened to the rest of it? Spent already?"

Craig didn't answer.

"I hope this is enough," she said doubtfully as she spread out the bills one by one and folded them up. "Your father said he was willing to forget pressing charges, but only if the money was returned. I hope sixty-three dollars is enough to keep him in such a generous mood."

"Oh, yeah, he's generous city, all right," Craig retorted sarcastically.

"Understand something, Craig," she said in her best matter-of-fact tone. "If I were your father, I might have had you charged even if you returned every last cent. Stealing is stealing in my books."

Craig refolded his arms over his chest. But his tough exterior was transparent to Kara. She could see through it to the boy who was too afraid even to admit his fears, and was searching for someone strong and confidant to rely on. His sulkiness, she knew, was a defense.

"Now, we've got another problem. The group home I normally use is full."

"What difference does that make to you?" he retorted, extra-sensitive now that he'd been exposed for stealing. "What you really mean is *I've* got the problem. I'm sure you've got a place to stay."

"No, Craig, that's where you're wrong," she countered, her voice a shade softer. "As long as I'm responsible for you, I have the problem, too." At times like this, Craig reminded her most strongly of Joey. It wasn't that they looked at all alike. Craig was about the same age as Joey had been when he'd first got in trouble, but beyond that the physical similarities ended. Joey's face had always looked innocent, framed by the same brown curls Kara had. Craig always wore a mask of blatant rebellion, his resentful eyes always hooded by his lank blond hair. What the two had in common wasn't visible: they were both at the mercy of decisions adults made for them.

But at least one thing was going to be different with Craig—the treatment he'd receive. She wouldn't repeat the mistakes her parents had made with Joey. There would be no excuses for the things Craig did. He would be dealt with straight, without an ounce of sugar-coating. He would know that he had to take responsibility for his own actions and that Kara Ridgeway would be there to make sure he did.

"I have one more place to check," she continued in a calm voice. "It's called Aiken House. I know they have an opening there, but I want to check them out first."

"If it gets me out of here it's good enough for me. I'm just looking for a bed that's close to downtown. This place is a dive."

"I think you need more than a bed," she returned steadily. "I think you need to be with someone strong enough to set limits for you."

Craig objected with a joyless laugh. "Are you for real? Why don't you just come out and say what you mean? You want to put me under someone who will keep me in line. Someone who'll bully me into whatever you want me to do."

"No, Craig. I want someone strong enough for you to respect, someone you can't manipulate."

Craig sighed with frustration. "Look, it really doesn't matter where I go. They're all the same, these places."

"Listen to me, Craig," Kara said firmly, leaning forward in her seat. A boy like Craig needed to recognize when someone truly cared and when they were merely taking the path of least resistance. He needed to realize that it took more love to be strict. "First of all, I care," she said. "Second, where you go does make a difference. As long as you are in my care, I am going to make sure you get what I think you need. You can't stay here much longer, but if I can possibly help it, I'm not going to shuffle you off someplace just because it's convenient."

Craig sat up on the couch and unfolded his arms. "You're a pretty strange lady for a cop," he said, regarding her suspiciously.

"You think so?"

"Yeah. Cops are supposed to catch you for breaking the law. They aren't supposed to care. But you're sitting there telling me how much you care. There's something about you that's not right. You sound like you're on some kind of crusade."

Kara swallowed hard. He'd hit the bull's-eye. "Cops are people too, Craig. They have their reasons for what they do, just like anyone else," she said quietly, hoping Craig would accept what she said and leave the subject alone.

"So what are your reasons?" Craig asked.

"Well," Kara hedged, "I knew someone very much like you."

"Who?"

"My brother, Joey. But that was a long time ago. You remind me of him when he was your age."

"Did he get in trouble, too?"

"Yes. He was your age exactly when he was convicted."

"What did he get busted for?"

Kara pulled her purse onto her lap and looked at her watch to indicate she was ready to go. She'd already told Craig more than she'd wanted to. He was brighter and bolder than most of her juveniles.

"Drugs, and breaking-and-entering," she finally answered.

Craig hesitated for a second before he slouched back to his former position on the sofa. "Anybody who'd bust a kid for drugs is the real criminal in my books," he pronounced.

Kara tensed involuntarily. Craig didn't know enough about the world to recognize its dangers. On his own, with his naive insolence, he was doomed to failure.

"Well, Craig," Kara said, strengthened in her resolve to find the proper group home. "It looks like you'll be here for the weekend, but I'm sure I'll have something by Monday. It may not be convenient, but it'll be right."

Craig stood up and shoved his hands in his pants pockets. Somehow he appeared more vulnerable standing up, perhaps because he only came up to her shoulders.

"So what happened to him?" he asked. "How'd your brother turn out?"

"He didn't make it to his sixteenth birthday. He died of a drug overdose while in a group home," she replied coldly, wondering if Craig would have pushed so hard for the truth had he known the answer that lay in wait.

Valiantly he recovered enough to answer sarcastically. "And I suppose you think I'm headed for the same thing."

"No, that doesn't have to happen to you. That's why I want to make sure I get you in the right home."

"I can hardly wait," Craig replied, rolling his eyes. But he didn't press the point.

Kara left him, sensing she'd won a measure of grudging respect for the strength of her convictions. She also thought she detected more than a little relief that he'd found someone he could rely on, someone to help him swim to shore.

As she drove home to her flat in a large red brick house on the Speed River, Kara felt exhausted but gratified. As a youngster watching her brother slowly self-destruct, she'd felt a terrible helplessness. At least now she could do something constructive to help, she reflected as she parked and let herself into the house.

The moment she opened the door to her apartment and drew in a long deep breath of the serene atmosphere, Kara could feel her neck muscles begin to relax. Often after she returned from a taxing day at work, she'd simply sit quietly and let the tranquil colors she'd chosen for her apartment do their work. The cream-colored walls and the earth tones in her Indian carpets were as soothing as a massage. Only her bedroom was done in a more fanciful fresh green and white.

Kara stepped out of her shoes and sank into the couch, but stopped herself from swinging her feet up onto the armrest. She couldn't make herself too comfortable, not with the unpleasant chore that still awaited.

Kara reached over to her telephone table and picked up a notepad and pen. Quickly she jotted down several questions about Aiken House and its program. Once she got this over with, she could go out for a relaxing evening at Stan's. Kara marshaled her willpower to sit up, dial the number and wait for an answer.

It rang three times before a male voice said, "Aiken House. Peter Aiken here."

Kara stifled a groan. She'd expected the phone to be answered by the woman she'd spoken to the day before. "Constable Ridgeway here," she responded rather stiffly. "I'd like to ask a few questions about your program."

"Well, hello, Constable Ridgeway." She sensed a silent chuckle behind Peter Aiken's good humor. "Is it very important that I call you by your full name and title, or do you have a first name?"

"Kara," she answered, too surprised to respond otherwise. He was more relaxed and friendly than she'd expected.

"Kara," he repeated approvingly. "You must be calling about your juvenile. I noticed a note in our logbook that you called yesterday."

There was a very comfortable feel about him, but she knew it would be a mistake to let her guard down. "I have a few questions to ask, Mr. Aiken, but—"

"Peter, please."

"All right, Peter. But I'm going to be honest with you."

Unexpectedly Peter laughed. "I'm sorry," he explained. "We have a joke around the house about the line 'I'm going to be honest with you.' It usually means the next comment is going to be negative."

Kara smiled despite herself. "You're right again."

"Our answer is just to say 'Uh-oh' and listen. So, go ahead."

"Mr. Aiken—Peter—it's hard to be serious in the face of an 'uh-oh.' This *is* serious, though. I have a juvenile I need to place, but I don't want to send him to Aiken House. I don't think your home is right for him."

Peter exhaled with mock relief. "That wasn't so hard to take. We can't expect to be the right place for everyone."

His somewhat flippant manner irritated her, but she had to admit she admired him, too. There weren't many people who could operate for so many years, with such an independent attitude.

"Perhaps I should be more specific then," she suggested carefully. "I'm not convinced Aiken House is right for anyone. I've been with the Youth Bureau for three years and I've purposely avoided using your home. I've always used the Hanson place."

"I know Marg and Hank. They run a good home. Why haven't you used them this time?"

"They're full."

"I'm beginning to get the picture here," Peter said slowly, his voice at last revealing a more serious side. "Circumstances have forced you to be open-minded and make this call to ask a few questions. If I don't reverse all your lifelong beliefs about how to raise young offenders in three minutes or less, you go away smug and self-satisfied that you were right about this place all along.''

Kara sucked in a deep breath and waited several long silent moments before she answered. "You can have a bit longer than three minutes."

"Your generosity knows no bounds," Peter said, laughing again. "But I've found that minds aren't so easily changed. It's no secret that I have my own philosophy about dealing with kids, and I make no apology for it. Kids do make their own decisions, and by the time a young offender sees me, he's already made some choices in his life and faced some consequences. In that way he's a bit older than kids his age who haven't been in trouble."

"But the choices have been inappropriate, or he wouldn't be in trouble."

"True," Peter conceded. "And in that way he's younger than other kids his age. For a variety of reasons, he's chosen behavior that will make his life harder rather than easier. I think, though, that if kids realize that they are making choices—and that no one can stop them from making them—they'll have less need to rebel. If they're willing to accept a life spent in and out of jail, they're free to choose it. But I still want them to see they really can choose the kind of life they want. If they realize they have choices, I can help them channel their energies into things that will help them get where they want to go," he explained. "But I doubt I can convince you of anything you don't already believe. I am interested, though, in why you're so dead set against my approach when we've never discussed it before.''

"I read the interview with you in the *Times* a couple of weeks ago,'' she replied. It wouldn't do to remind him of Joey's trial.

"Uh-oh. You saw the picture that makes me look like a murderer on the verge of a rampage, and it offended your police sensibilities.''

This time Kara laughed easily. "The picture was pretty scary.''

"I swear it's not a true likeness. I'm actually a very pleasant fellow. My kids like me. Even my dog likes me.''

"If it were just the picture, I'd have no problem,'' Kara confessed. "You sound much friendlier than you looked. It's what you say about young offenders that alarms me. I can't accept that leaving troubled kids to their own devices is going to help anyone. We owe them some form of guidance, or we're shirking our responsibility to them. Surely they need limits placed on them.''

"Have you ever been down here, Kara? Even just driven by and taken a look?''

"No,'' she admitted, slightly disconcerted by his change in direction.

"It's a perfect place for kids,'' Peter continued. "It's like a summer camp or a farm in the middle of the city. There are two and a half acres of land right on the Speed River. The house is a huge old place, the kind of home that's stuffed with character. No two rooms are the same shape, but every window has a huge maple in plain view. Out here the kids don't have to rebel against their parents or the law or me. Apart from a few basic house rules, they have the room to make decisions for themselves. They can decide who to trust, who to be friends with and what they want to talk about. What they do here is grow up, and that's something no one else can do for them. You need to meet them to see how this program works. You need to get a feel for what it's like to live here to see why these kids are so unlikely to meet up with the police again.''

''You sound very sure of what you're doing,'' Kara said slowly.

''I believe in it.''

''Unfortunately I'd need to believe in it too, before I'd bring a juvenile to you. And I'm still a very long way from being convinced.''

Even over the phone she could sense Peter's mood change. He was puzzling over something, searching deeper for answers. ''You know, it's a funny thing,'' he said thoughtfully. ''By now I would have told anyone else to take a hike and find another group home if they didn't like the sound of this one. But something stops me with you. I get the feeling you really do want to make the right decision. You seem to have some strange ideas about raising kids, but I think you're sincere.''

''I wouldn't say I'm the one with the strange ideas!''

''Well, let's test it out, then,'' Peter challenged suddenly. ''This Friday night the kids are going to cook something we've never tried before. They've decided it will be pasta night. I can't guarantee the food will turn out, but I can promise you'll get a good feel for the program. If you don't like what you see, then you've proved your intuition was right in the first place. But at least you'll know you gave it a chance."

Kara secretly balked at the idea, knowing that her views on raising juveniles were unlikely to change with even a month's observation. Yet Stan's words haunted her. He'd never let her live it down if she didn't give Aiken House a chance.

"I can't think of a good enough reason to say no," she answered honestly.

"Good. I don't mind if you do the right thing for the wrong reason. What's important is that you're coming. Be here at five o'clock and come prepared to work. I'll have an apron for you."

"Do you put all your guests to work?" she asked, trying to picture Stan wearing an apron for the sake of an open mind.

"Just the special ones," Peter answered. "I'm looking forward to meeting you, Kara. There's something very familiar about you." He paused, and for a moment Kara feared he might recognize her name. "Is there any chance I might have met you before?" he asked.

"No, I'm sure we haven't met," Kara answered with carefully chosen words. "Maybe I remind you of someone," she offered, hoping to detract him.

"Maybe," he echoed doubtfully, then seemed to dismiss a vague memory. "More likely it's just that I'd like to meet you. Most people don't question, they just agree or disagree. You've got the integrity to take another look at something you disagree with. I like that."

A minute later, Kara had copied down his directions and they'd said their goodbyes. As she hung up the phone, she wondered fleetingly if he could be very different from her earlier impressions of him. She frowned a moment, then quickly dismissed such an unlikely idea from her mind.

# CHAPTER TWO

STAN'S BOYS, Robbie and Evan, were standing at the fence waiting for her as Kara drove up. She always parked on the side street that ran alongside their back yard, and the boys eagerly anticipated performing their well-practiced ritual. Kara could smell delicious barbecue smoke from behind them in the yard.

"Stay there," Kara warned as she closed her car door. Immediately the two began to laugh.

"I mean it." She smiled as she crossed the sidewalk and walked slowly toward them. Robbie, five years old and the taller of the pair, gently pushed Evan who squealed with delight.

"Okay," she called and instantly the boys ran full steam toward her. Laughing, she crouched down in time to catch one boy in each arm, then stood to swing them as she spun around and around in a circle.

Their happy shrieks made Kara yearn for children of her own.

"One day you guys are going to be too big for me to do this," she laughed, breathless, as she hugged them and set them down. Each of the boys took one of her hands and led her into the back yard.

Stan's wife, Sandy, was flipping hamburgers on the barbecue. Kara noticed once more how her short blond hair and energetic face made her a perfect match for Stan's youthful appearance.

"They've been waiting at that fence for half an hour," Sandy said, giving Kara a hug. "I don't know why they can't be that patient all the time. Want a drink?"

"I'd love a cold soda pop," Kara said, prompting the boys to race to the house, each wanting to be the first to fill her order.

Sandy looked at her thoughtfully. "You know, Kara, it would be a real waste if you didn't have kids. Only Stan and I are more special to those kids than you. There's something unique about the way you communicate with them."

"Yeah, well, it's easy when they're that age," Kara said with a shrug, privately pleased with the compliment all the same.

"From what Stan tells me, you have the same knack with kids right up until they're eighteen."

"I don't know about that," Kara replied with a laugh. "But I appreciate the vote of confidence. It means a lot coming from people like you and Stan."

Stan came out of the house with Robbie and Evan behind him. Each carried a can of pop—obviously a compromise to avoid an argument. They followed Stan to the picnic table, where he set down his tray of glasses and ice.

"All right, boys," he said. "Now I'll put the pop in a glass for Kara. Thank you for your help."

The boys dutifully handed over their cans to their father.

Kara giggled. "That's quite a trick, Stan."

Stan quickly poured the contents of one can into a glass and handed it to her. "It's the only way you'd get away with drinking one at a time. Did you call your friend Aiken?"

"I have a dinner invitation at the group home tomorrow night."

"Good work," he said with a wink.

As they all devoured hamburgers and potato salad, Kara chatted comfortably with Stan and Sandy. She felt welcome enough to be part of the family, but over the past few months she'd been leaving Stan's with a feeling of loneliness. When she visited, she felt like a favorite aunt, a symbol of fun and a cause for celebration. But no one really needed her. Not even her juveniles needed her in any personal way. She made decisions that affected their lives, and until recently that had been enough.

After supper Sandy took the boys off for their baths, leaving Kara and Stan to clean up the aftermath of the barbecue.

"So what's this case you wanted to talk to me about?" Kara asked, trailing Stan into the kitchen with a tray of dirty dishes. The pleasant smell of dying charcoal embers wafted through the open kitchen window.

"James E. Chalmers," Stan answered as he filled the sink with soap suds. "He's a boy who's in a lot of trouble but doesn't realize it. He's seventeen years old and in training school for assault."

"That is serious," Kara agreed, recapping the mustard and relish jars.

"He roughed up another guy at the gas station where he worked," Stan went on. "It seems his co-worker didn't want to buy any alcohol for James, and James wasn't about to take no for an answer. This is his third time in training school for assault."

"Whew." Kara shook her head as she picked up a dish towel. "Where do you go from there at seventeen?"

"You go from bad to worse. When we were called to the scene, we searched his car and found two rifles in the trunk. Of course they weren't registered, and we want to know where a seventeen-year-old in this town can get guns. We could charge him with possession, but we want to nail whoever sold them to him."

"I can imagine how fruitful those conversations have been."

Stan laughed. "I'm sure you could recite them word for word. This kid obviously needs help. I have to charge him on the weapon if it looks like he's going to protect the real criminal. I'm stumped. I can't think of anything else to try."

Kara considered the problem as she dried the few plates and glasses in the dish rack. "He might be too far gone to help," she said thoughtfully. "Does he have anyone else who's close to him? A friend, or girlfriend? Maybe you could get someone else to convince him to turn things around and talk."

"Apparently the guy he beat up was as close a friend as he's got. Kara, I thought you might be able to help. I know you've worked with kids who were up in that training school. You know how hard it is for them. I thought you might try talking to him. Maybe you could see some weak spot I've missed."

"I can't imagine you missing anything, Stan, but I'd be happy to do what I can."

"Thanks," he said and, finishing the last of the dishes, pulled the plug with a flourish. "Sandy must be done with the baths by now. Come and kiss the boys good-night or they'll never go to sleep."

Soon Kara had said her good-nights and goodbyes and was steering her car homeward. She felt again the feeling of emptiness that had haunted her lately. Maybe she was getting soft in her old age, but she found she longed for a pair of tiny arms to hug her around the neck and not let go.

Her chances were narrowing, she reminded herself. At twenty-eight, she'd never even come close to having a relationship that would be strong enough for children. Perhaps she'd just have to accept that her relationships would be with other people's kids. And even at that, her job would be to correct other people's mistakes.

IN FRIDAY NIGHT'S TWILIGHT, the long, tree-lined driveway of Aiken House resembled the entrance to an enchanted forest. Kara stopped the car at the end of the drive in front of a massive country house that seemed to rise magically out of the rustic landscape. Its pale stone facade was adorned with a long gray veranda. Bay windows and spired towers hinted that inside lived special people who concocted magic potions, fought duels and slew dragons.

The dim light among the maples muted the autumn leaves to deep shades of olive and pumpkin. But through the trees lining the river bank, Kara could still spot fading sunlight dancing over the water. If the house wasn't enchanted, she thought it must have at least contained spirits from past generations. It was so easy to picture men in breeches hauling cartloads of local harvest—squash, tomatoes, apples, peppers—to be canned and stored for winter.

Kara drew a deep breath, relishing the smell of burning wood that hung in the air. Aiken House was stuffed with character; there was no disputing Peter Aiken on that count. But it didn't prove his theories about problem kids, she reminded herself as she shuffled through a drift of fallen leaves on her way toward the house.

*This isn't a social call,* she reminded herself, trying to suppress the lightheartedness the scene inspired. Her clothing, though, was definitely casual. Earlier, while dressing, it had seemed ridiculous to wear her conservative work clothes, much less a police uniform, to make pasta with a houseful of juveniles on a Friday night. She was more comfortable in a plaid shirt and a pair of well-washed jeans, and the kids would be more comfortable with her, too.

Even if this were a social call, Kara didn't suppose she would act any differently. She hadn't really made a distinction between work and play in a long time. A voice in the back of her mind told her it wasn't right to be on duty twenty-four hours a day, but in the past few years socializing had become a burden. She'd felt more involved with a kid in need than with a pleasant date who wouldn't relate to what she found important. Still, when she thought of Robbie and Evan and the joy they brought to Stan and Sandy, she suspected that her solitary ways could cost her dearly in the long run.

Arriving at the front door of Aiken House, Kara clanked the huge brass knocker several times on the heavy oak door, pleased that it made such an authoritative sound. But her composure evaporated instantly when the door was pulled open. She hardly noticed the tanned face that smiled back at her or the man's thick honey-colored hair. Her attention was arrested by his clear azure eyes.

"Constable Ridgeway, I presume?" Peter Aiken asked, giving Kara a smile as he extended his right hand. He wore a white baker's apron tied around his slim, jean-clad hips, and his navy polo shirt was sprinkled with flour dust. "I'm glad you came."

"Mr. Aiken," she returned and slipped her hand into his. The handshake should have been a simple and uneventful ritual, almost unnoticed against the chatter of greeting. But the way Peter took her hand seemed somehow intimate, and Kara was too unnerved to speak again until after he'd invited her into a majestic, high-ceilinged front hallway.

As he slowly released Kara's hand and gestured for her to enter the house, Peter fought the smile within him. She was right out of a dream. He'd expected a scowling, middle-aged woman, a battle-ax with a heart buried so deep that it hadn't been seen in years. But soft auburn hair and doe-brown eyes immediately gave away Kara's sensitivity.

"This is an impressive-looking house," she said, as she paused, pretending to admire her new surroundings and privately struggling to regain her lost equilibrium. "Everything is just as you said. I almost felt as if I'd seen it before as I turned down your driveway. I don't know if I got my images out of my imagination or a story book from when I was a child."

Peter's laugh was a magical sound, one that could become addictive. "I'm glad you see its attractions," he said, taking her coat and hanging it up. "But obviously anyone who can so accurately picture something beforehand has a creative imagination. I think it means you're a good listener. That's rare. Take me, for example. I must be a terrible listener because you're not at all how I pictured you."

Under Peter's intense gaze, Kara suddenly craved the protection afforded by her regular conservative outfits. She craved protection even more as Peter continued to look at her as if he'd seen something in her face that fascinated him but that he couldn't explain.

Suddenly, he snapped himself to attention. "But listen to me. A police officer like yourself doesn't want to hear such drivel. You came here for an inspection and that's exactly what I'm going to be sure you get. Please, step this way and we'll start the royal Aiken House tour."

Curious, Kara followed him down a hallway. What had he expected her to look like? Had he deliberately left his comment unexplained to gauge its effect on her? Apparently fourteen years had made enough of a difference that he didn't recognize her. Then again maybe he'd never really taken notice of her in the first place—or maybe a dim memory was what caused him to look at her so probingly. As for Peter, he looked much the same as he had back then. A little older, maybe, more mature. It would be harder for him to recognize her. The last time he saw her she was only fourteen.

The hallway opened into a spacious living room with a polished pine floor, partly covered by a mocha and cream Indian carpet. The TV was on, and several teenagers lounged on a pair of russet-colored couches, watching a hockey game. An arm raised from the couch to wave, and Peter waved back.

"This is my pièce de résistance," Peter said leaning casually against the archway. "I suppose I really should have ended my tour with this room as the grand finale, but I'm anxious to make a good first impression."

Kara smiled almost shyly and saw his eyes dance with humor. "It takes more than a beautiful house to make a good group home," she said.

"True," he agreed heartily. His eyes lingered on her thoughtfully before he turned back to the room. "But a room sets a mood and conveys a message about a home the way clothing does a person. I wanted the mood in here to be welcoming and comfortable, yet with a touch of excitement."

He steered her away, guiding her over to the vestibule of a side entrance. A bright mosaic of yellow, blue and red coats hung from pegs on the walls, and a staircase led from there to the second floor.

Peter paused, and leaned back against a ledge holding an assortment of mitts. "I love sunlight, and the rooms were all big enough and open enough to be updated with some large windows," he told her. "I worked on the floors, the walls and the ceilings, and on things you can't see—plumbing and electrical work. Improvements like these pegs for the coats were the easiest to make."

Kara turned to look out the small window in the side door and caught a glimpse of the river. "But there's still a strong sense that we're in an old house. Who built it in the first place?"

Peter smiled at her question. People usually just nodded politely as he gave them this tour. But the genuine enthusiasm he detected in her voice told him she wasn't interested in small talk. "I had to do some digging for that story," he replied, "because the house has changed hands quite a few times. There was a string of landlords who bought it cheaply and let it run down by renting to desperate university students. But the original owner was an industrialist from Toronto who wanted to try his hand at farming and country-estate living. According to old newspaper articles, he and his family considered this to be very rustic living."

The way Peter spoke about his research breathed life into the house for Kara. She pictured everything he described. Just as Peter obviously was, Kara was fascinated by the people of past generations who'd left their imprint on the buildings they'd lived and worked in.

"It's hard to believe anyone would think this rustic even by today's standards," she marveled.

"It got much more rustic as the years wore on. The family fell on hard times during the Depression. Bit by bit they had to sell most of the farmland they'd accumulated. There was no money for maintenance, and they had to sell to speculators. When I bought it, it was a step away from being condemned by the city. You can see it's far too big for one family to handle anymore."

"Or even one group home," Kara added.

"It could have been," he agreed, and turned to lead her up the stairs. "But by the time I bought the house, it was worth much less than its original cost, even with inflation taken into account. And, of course, I did the renovations myself. Come and I'll show you the upstairs."

Kara followed him up the staircase and along a hallway where she inspected room after carefully tended room. Each one was slightly different from the last. Peter had found a way to make himself felt everywhere. Every little detail illustrated how important this place was to its creator.

At the end of the hall Kara was greeted by a young boy who couldn't have been older than ten. His smaller-than-average size made him appear much younger. His eyes were huge and trusting.

"I'm Stevie. Would you like to see my turtle?"

Kara crouched down to his level and admired the turtle nestled in his outstretched hand, waiting patiently until the little creature ventured to stick its head out of its shell. Stevie, apparently pleased with her attention, invited her into his room to meet his two goldfish. Then Kara had to look out the bedroom window at "his" river. She chatted easily with the boy about all the animals that lived within a stone's throw of the house: squirrels, tadpoles, worms, ants, birds, fish—the list seemed endless.

She listened and watched with interest as Peter demonstrated the finer points of the bedroom furniture. He'd built convenient drawers under the bunk beds. He showed her how the collapsible desktops he'd mounted on the wall could be folded back when not in use.

As he showed his creations, Kara noticed his sinewy forearms. From their well-defined muscles, she guessed that he was always using them for these kinds of projects. His arms also looked capable of providing a mountain of comfort—to the kids, of course.

She didn't realize how far her mind had wandered until Stevie asked her a question and snapped her back to attention.

"Are you coming for supper?" he asked as he gently fingered his pet's shell.

"Why, yes. Are you going to be there with your turtle?"

His face dropped to a look of stern disapproval. "Peter won't let me bring my turtle to the table."

"Oh, well," she sympathized and grimaced at Peter apologetically. "I suppose the turtle likes eating his supper in his own room anyway."

Stevie's young face perked up. "Do you think so?"

"If you were a turtle, would you want to eat with a bunch of people?" Kara returned, trying to sound as nonchalant and confident as she could. The subject was obviously close to the boy's heart.

Stevie looked doubtful. "I guess he probably does like eating in his room," Stevie finally agreed.

Over the boy's shoulder, Kara saw Peter wipe his hand across his forehead in exaggerated relief.

She smiled. "Well, Stevie, I'll look forward to seeing you at supper."

"Okay," Stevie agreed as Peter led Kara out into the hallway.

"You have quite a knack with kids," Peter said quietly. "There's something natural there."

"Thank you," she said blushing self-consciously. "I don't usually get a chance to meet them so young."

"Stevie is a bit young to be in this kind of a group home," Peter explained once they were safely out of earshot. "I hesitated about taking him. His mother is in the hospital, and the doctors aren't sure if she'll ever be well enough to come out. His parents were divorced shortly after his younger sister was born and no one can locate the father. His sister is eight and developmentally handicapped, so she's in another group home for children with special needs. She's with kids her own age, but it was hard to find an appropriate place for Stevie, since he's more of a housing crisis than anything. It was Stevie himself who convinced me to take him in. He told me he'd be a great help to me because all older kids needed a younger brother like him. I believed him."

As he talked, Peter had led Kara down a back staircase into a narrow breathtakingly peaceful room. Rows of books covered one long wall and rows of windows covered the opposite wall. The room invited its visitor to sink into one of the two plush upholstered chairs or merely curl up on the cushions strewn over a thick carpet.

Peter sat on the corner of an oak desk and folded his arms loosely. Kara intrigued him. During their tour she'd seemed interested in every detail. Yet she still held herself at a disapproving distance. Her disapproval bothered him, which was odd. Disapproval was usually the last thing in the world that would ever bother him. Still, he thought Kara was someone who could really appreciate what he was doing at Aiken House. "You didn't really want to come here today, did you?" he asked.

Kara paused in the act of lowering herself into a chair. His question was asked with genuine concern, but she still wished he hadn't asked it. There was only one place this subject could lead, and that was to conflict.

"I think it's easier for people with similar views to work together," she said tactfully. "I've seen years of good intentions go down the drain because a kid was getting mixed signals. That's the tragedy. I think it's best for everyone if the care-givers at least are consistent with each other."

"You think we'd undo each other's efforts?"

"I think it's possible," she said mildly. Her calm professionalism was a well-practiced mask. Only with someone she trusted, like Stan, could she reveal her emotional commitment to these ideas. Even Stan didn't know how strongly Joey's death had affected her.

"I'm interested," he ventured carefully, "in what situations you feel we would handle so differently."

"It's not even so much what's done in a situation. It's the message the child gets. It's all the little issues that come up every day, like doing homework and household chores, when to come home or go to bed. Those situations all present opportunities to teach the kids what you and the world expect of them."

"And you think that you and I would have such drastically different expectations?"

"I think we look at the world very differently," she allowed diplomatically. "I feel that young people—especially ones who have been in trouble—need to know in no uncertain terms that they have responsibilities to those around them, to the people who love them. Kids who have got in trouble can't expect to be treated with trust until they prove themselves trustworthy. They need to be watched and tested and monitored to make sure they have straightened themselves out. I don't get the impression that this is your philosophy."

Peter rubbed his hand over his chin and regarded her pensively. "Maybe you just put it in different terms. We both want to produce well-adjusted, law-abiding adults. I generally make it seem fun to be straight. And I want to teach the kids that they are responsible for their own lives, so I let them make a lot of their own decisions."

"That doesn't sound like a smart thing to do with kids who have already made bad decisions," Kara said. "Maybe they need you to make the decisions until they learn more responsible ways of behaving."

Peter shook his head slowly. "That's missing the whole point. The fact is they do make decisions for themselves whether you think they should or not. You might make a decision they decide not to obey, and you might never find out they disobeyed. They have to want to be honest with you. I'm here to challenge their decisions and point out the consequences of them. Let's not kid ourselves. These kids can decide to be whatever they want, despite anything we try to force on them."

Kara smiled and sighed at the same time. "You see?" she said, lifting her palms in a show of resignation. "We're in trouble already. With Craig in your home, he'd be getting your message, and you'd be contradicting what I've been trying to get him to understand. The important thing is to establish a set of guidelines to drill into these young and forgetful minds. Young kids like these have absolutely no notion of what's expected of them. That's why they make bad decisions, and that's why they need help from responsible adults."

"You're an interesting person, Kara," Peter said, letting his eyes roam for a moment over her gentle curves. "Your words contain a harsh message, but everything else about you is so soft."

"Is that what you meant when you said I was different from how you imagined?"

"Ah-ha! So that finally got to you, did it? Good, I was right, you really are human. I wondered if you might never ask because you had so much police discipline in you."

"I shall confess to only a mild curiosity," she said lightly. "That's all."

"You definitely look softer than I imagined you," he confirmed, and Kara felt the pull of his tropical blue eyes. "I pictured you as more the sergeant-major type with poker-straight black hair. Yet I heard something in your voice that I liked."

"That's quite an impression," Kara complained.

"It's why I wore this navy polo shirt," he said, pulling at his collar. "I thought I should hide my wardrobe of corduroy jeans and sweatshirts and try to look conservative."

Kara laughed heartily at his remark. "Sorry, Peter, even with the polo shirt, the flour on your apron gave you away. You're just not the military type."

"All that planning and I blew it!" Peter threw up his hands and rolled his eyes to the ceiling as they laughed together. Then he looked at her more seriously, his voice growing soft. "But here you are, fresh and natural, with gentle curls and soft brown eyes. How do you manage to seem so harsh sometimes?"

"Maybe I am the sergeant-major type," she suggested half-kidding, hoping to shrug off his question. But something inside her rebelled at leaving him with that impression of her, and she heard herself add, "Or maybe I'm a creampuff under this tough cop exterior."

He smiled. "I think so."

Kara could feel her color beginning to rise as Peter roused himself from his lingering gaze. "Anyway," he said with sudden energy, "I'm about to put you to work in the kitchen. Today's kitchen crew has three girls and two boys from ages twelve to seventeen."

"Oh? That's unusual," Kara said. "Most homes don't accept both boys and girls. And their ages are usually closer together, aren't they? You have Stevie at ten and young adults of seventeen."

"Make no mistake," Peter said with a smile, "I pride myself on Aiken House being unusual. Most homes are for either boys or girls because the programming is easier. I won't settle for 'easier.' I'm always aiming for 'better.' I want to approximate a regular family, where both sexes and a wide age range are normal. I don't want my kids to feel like they're in an institution. For the time they're here, this is their family. There are other homes that function the same way. Not many, but together we form a stable minority."

Kara considered his answer and decided she liked the idea of approximating a regular family, but wondered how it really worked out. "This pasta night you're having," she asked, "I presume it's just your regular macaroni and cheese that most group homes serve?"

"I don't think so," he said, smiling. "The kids can make whatever they want—within reason—and I think they have a taste for something more exotic than macaroni and cheese."

"But mightn't that be a bit expensive for a group home?"

"Probably not," Peter answered. "Most pasta dishes, no matter how exotic, are usually inexpensive to make. I don't expect tonight's dinner will cost much more than macaroni and cheese.''

"But surely if it was that easy and cheap, every group home would be serving exotic food.''

"I didn't say it was easy. It's very time consuming. But we make pasta night a special occasion that the kids can look forward to. They'll spend three or four hours fussing with homemade noodles because it's fun, not because it's easy. Which reminds me—it's time I put you to work, constable.''

Peter led her to a kitchen of pine cupboards, well-placed track lighting and a red tile floor. The half-dozen teenagers in the room appeared powered by the steady beat of rock and roll music sounding from a large tape recorder.

Peter placed a hand on her shoulder and called out his introductions. "That's Joan and Kate at the counter kneading the pasta.'' The girls looked older, maybe fifteen or sixteen. They nodded to her pleasantly. "That's Phil fussing with the table.'' Phil was younger, around twelve, and he was placing an extra leaf in a long rectangular table in an adjoining sunroom.

"Phil's in charge of decoration and atmosphere. As you can see from the look of great concentration on his face, he's taking his job very seriously.''

At first Phil looked embarrassed. Kara imagined he was asking himself how to erase his look of concentration. But she gave him a heartfelt smile, which seemed to put him at ease.

"And Randy, Kyle and Sharon are just getting in the way,'' Peter accused good-naturedly.

Sharon, a pretty brown-eyed girl protested, "Gee, how can we help it? We're on kitchen duty but no one's given us a job yet."

"Yeah," Randy and Kyle agreed in chorus. "We don't have a job yet."

"The problem is we can't decide what to do with the pasta," Kate explained. She had several large cookbooks scattered over the counter, and she flipped the pages in exasperation.

"What about spaghetti?" Peter suggested as he strode across the room and opened a large cupboard stacked neatly with kitchen supplies. He plucked a white apron from the top of a pile as the room reverberated with groans and protests.

"There's nothing exotic about spaghetti," Kate said. "Everybody's had that before. We should try something special, like cannelloni or something."

"Fine with me," Peter agreed as he reached Kara with the apron. "Looks like you're going to have to wait awhile for your job, constable, but at least you'll be wearing the proper uniform when the need arises," Peter said, looping the apron over her head.

He noticed she seemed a bit shy in front of the kids and was doing his best to put her at ease—a job he found strangely pleasurable.

"This is the problem with group democracy, of course," he explained as he finished tying the apron strings. "Confusion will reign supreme until a decision is made. But once they finally decide, they're usually pretty happy."

"Thank you," Kara said hesitantly as Peter continued to fuss with the apron. He stood close enough to

Kara for her to detect the subtle fragrance of his after-shave. She was concerned she might be allowing him too much familiarity until she realized his actions weren't out of place here. The kids seemed to take no notice. His affectionate nature was likely an integral part of the man. Meanwhile, the discussion about what sort of pasta to cook was becoming passionate. Randy and Kyle were arguing that cannelloni would be too hard to make with their homemade pasta, and suggested ravioli.

"Naw," Phil disagreed, looking up from his job of spreading a red-checkered tablecloth over the large table. "I used to get ravioli for lunch at my old school. It's no good."

"Hey, what about lasagna!" Joan exclaimed.

"That's not exotic," Phil said, and laughed. "Who hasn't had lasagna before?"

"What's so wrong with having it again?" Joan said heatedly, her feelings slightly bruised.

"Well, maybe we could make it exotic with a salad," Kate suggested in a show of support for Joan.

"Yeah," Joan said, perking up. "We've got all kinds of lettuce and olives and croutons. Maybe a Greek or a Caesar salad. I know I had one of them once, but I forget which it was."

The idea of a salad gained overall acceptance, and Kyle and Sharon embarked upon a fact-finding tour through a cookbook to find out which ingredients went into which salad. But the problem of what pasta to serve with the salad still remained.

Peter leaned over a spare counter and contented himself with listening to the proceedings. Kara felt again the oddly enjoyable sensation of being gently touched by the perceptive blue eyes at her back. What troubled her, though, was that rather than wanting to hang back to observe and judge what happened here, she felt an urge to participate. She wrestled with whether or not she should voice the idea that had been formulating in her mind. It wasn't her place to offer a suggestion. It might even go against Peter's non-interference credo.

"I have a tortellini recipe that's not too hard to make," she heard herself say to the crowd.

"What's tortellini?" Kate asked, and the others turned interested faces toward her.

"It's a sort of ravioli," she explained, trying to think of ways to describe the dish. "But the pasta can be stuffed with a cheese or meat mixture and served in a cream or tomato sauce. When I make it I usually serve it with a vegetable called finocchio that tastes a little like licorice. But if you have the ingredients for a Caesar salad, that would do nicely in its place." She turned to Peter impulsively and smiled. "And it won't be much more expensive than macaroni and cheese."

Sharon had found a recipe for Caesar salad, and was now the self-appointed expert of the group. "We'll have to leave some of the stinky stuff like garlic out of the salad for the younger kids," she advised. "They hate anything you can taste."

"I'll go for tortellini and salad," Joan said.

"Do we have everything we need?" Randy asked, and began lifting bottles out of the spice rack. "What spices does your recipe call for, Kara?"

"Let's see," she said, smoothing her hands over the white cotton apron. "We'll need some pepper and basil and, oh yes, some chives."

"Check on the pepper and basil," Randy called out, holding up each of the spice bottles in turn as he located them. "But no chives."

"We can substitute green onion."

"No problem," Kyle announced triumphantly as he produced a bunch from the refrigerator.

"And fresh garlic and ricotta cheese. Do you have any of that?"

"No ricotta," Kyle said from his post behind the fridge door. "But I can go downtown for it."

"Okay. We don't need meat if you can get the cheese. For the sauce we'll need very finely chopped tomatoes, carrots and onions."

Kyle threw on his coat and trooped out to his bicycle. The room bustled with activity, and Kara was caught up in the excitement. She was familiar with the satisfaction that came from making good food and serving it to appreciative guests. But the feeling that came from sharing the preparation with a group of kids came as a surprise. She felt a part of a large family. Kara realized she'd never seen this phenomenon at the Hanson group home, where Mrs. Hanson made all the meals herself.

Kara felt Peter's presence and when she raised her eyes to take in his openly approving face, she was relieved to see that she'd done the right thing.

"Are you going to give me a job?" he asked.

"It depends. How good are you at following instructions?"

The smile lines around his eyes creased. "It's my forte," he assured her. "It's what I'm known for."

"A team effort doesn't need some hotshot who thinks he knows everything, you know," she said with playful significance. "This is my tortellini recipe and I don't need any bright ideas on how to change it."

"I wouldn't dream of changing a thing," he said warmly. "I've always maintained that if something works, stick with it."

"And how do you know this will work out?"

"I've got a feeling about it." His gaze lingered on her face.

"You can lead the assembly line," she directed, retreating hurriedly from their banter. "Roll the pasta out like this," she said, demonstrating as she spoke. "Then cut out a circle about three inches or so in diameter like this."

As Peter rolled and cut the pasta, concentrating on performing his task exactly right, Kara stole glances at him and unsuccessfully attempted to stifle a grin. He was extremely appealing sitting on a high kitchen stool pulled up to the counter. He was in his element, and the relaxation on his face proved it. She tore her attention away from Peter and moved on to supervise the making of the cheese stuffing, first tasting, then advising changes. Randy had chopped enough tomatoes and carrots to feed an army. Tears ran down Kyle's cheeks as he diced the onions.

"Okay, the vegetables can be added to the pot and heated to start the sauce," Kara instructed. "The cheese is ready for stuffing. I need some volunteers."

She returned to her post at Peter's side and picked up one of the pasta circles he'd made. She placed a spoonful of stuffing in the center and folded the corners, then showed the group of absorbed faces how to seal the little pasta envelope with a fork.

"You seal it like you would the crust of a pie," she explained as her fingers worked.

"I always wondered how that was done!" Kate exclaimed.

"You can take over here, Kate," Kara offered. "Start a production line."

"Can you check the sauce here please, Kara?" Randy called. "I'm not sure if it's cooked enough."

Kara inspected Randy's progress with the sauce, then helped Joan with the finishing touches to her Caesar salad. The kids were eager to learn, and Kara was impressed by the initiative they took with her instructions. *Peter has truly achieved something special here,* she admitted to herself. He had made this home environment a place where the children expected to learn. This was not a typical institution.

Her ironclad opinions had begun to weaken in the face of Peter's warmth and charm. But, she reminded herself gruffly, the successful rehabilitation of young offenders took more than personal warmth and charm. She would accept the prevailing attitudes for the sake of a pleasant visit, but she couldn't afford to forget why she was here.

Eventually the tortellini was ready. Kara gave the signal. The lights went out and the kitchen was magically transformed into an Italian bistro. Phil's red-and-white checked table was illuminated by red candles and laden with dinnerware and napkins. The rock and roll was even changed to an Italian folk song.

Anxious to sit down and eat, Kara fumbled with the apron ties behind her. But she stopped the moment she felt her fingers entangle with Peter's.

"Let me help," he whispered softly in her ear.

When the apron hung loose around her neck, he turned her at the waist to face him.

"Thank you," he said. He was a dark silhouette in front of her. "Thank you from me. Thank you from the kids. You've made this special."

*Take control, Kara,* she implored herself as she shakily found her seat. He was different. There was no disputing that. But there was no excuse for this kind of adolescent reaction. Perhaps she was more vulnerable than she'd realized. He seemed to easily see past her police role to her well-protected femininity, and she found it unnerving to be recognized as a woman by that particular pair of electric blue eyes.

As the kids jostled for prized seats at the table, Kara noticed one of the older boys shove a younger one out of his chair. She watched with interest as Peter placed his hand on the older boy's shoulder, then stooped to say something to him privately. Peter's voice was just a low murmur to Kara, but whatever he said it motivated the older boy to switch back to the original arrangement. There was no doubt, she realized, that Peter was in full control here.

Kara tasted the tortellini and returned the approving nods of the other chefs. It was delicious—tender and zesty.

"Even my turtle would like this!" Stevie announced.

"That's a compliment of the highest order," Peter said, laughing and nodding to Kara. He felt a special lift as he watched her face light up with pleasure. "The likes and dislikes of Stevie's turtle bear a remarkable resemblance to Stevie's own finicky tastes. You've managed to please the two pickiest eaters of the house."

Stevie nodded in hearty agreement and everyone laughed. To Stevie, the "remarkable resemblance" was pure coincidence.

A warm blanket of contentment settled over the room as they ate, and Kara found each of her stolen glances at Peter intercepted by one of his own. Confusion seeped into her. How could she find this group home so attractive when she disagreed with so much of the philosophy it was built on? More to the point, how could she find Peter so attractive?

## CHAPTER THREE

THE DISHES WERE CLEARED but everyone was still seated at the table—laughing and talking, telling jokes and planning the next Italian feast. Then the discordant sound of a loud knock at the kitchen door shattered the serenity of the home. The door swung open to reveal a rotund middle-aged man. Several hushed "uh-ohs" echoed around the table, and the mood of the room stiffened.

"Brice," Peter said, welcoming the newcomer with ill-disguised reluctance. He motioned the man to step inside but clearly felt no obligation to extend a heartfelt welcome. The two had obviously gone through these motions before. "How can I help you tonight?" Peter asked tensely.

The older man's face was permanently set with deep furrows and a down-turned mouth. "We both expected this, Mr. Aiken. I know I did. There has been another assault on my property by the members of this so-called home. This time it's your delinquent dog. There is a gaping hole that leads from your yard, under my new fence and into my flowerbeds."

"That hardly sounds like a major catastrophe, Mr. Brice."

A couple of kids giggled, and Kara fought down a chuckle, too. Peter really should have shown a more mature reaction. He was a role model, after all.

"I expected your reaction to be one of indifference, at best," Brice went on with a melodramatic sigh. "And that is why I wanted to deliver my message in the presence of these children. If that dog is not kept chained up or in this house at all hours, day and night, I'll have the Humane Society collect the animal and dispose of it."

Brice's threat brought a wail from Stevie. "You'll never catch him! You'll never catch Ketchup!"

"That's all right, Stevie," Kara whispered reassuringly. "No one is going to do anything to your dog. Where is he?"

She leaned over and Stevie cupped a conspiratorial hand around his mouth to convey his secret. "I hid him under my bed. And I shut the door."

"He's safe, then. Don't worry. Tell me, how did he get a funny name like Ketchup?" she asked in an attempt to distract him from the argument raging at the kitchen door. "Did you give it to him?"

"No, I wasn't here then." His eyes suddenly twinkled. "Peter says another boy just like me named him. He was almost the same age as me and everything. Well, anyways, not too much older than me. Peter told him to pick his favorite thing in the world—except for the puppy—and that would be his name."

"So he said Ketchup because he loved ketchup?" Kara asked with a giggle.

Stevie nodded, his eyes earnest. "He put it on everything, even ice cream! I would have said peanut butter, but that's a dumber name than Ketchup, so it's a good thing I wasn't here yet. But now it's my job to name my turtle."

"You'll want to choose a good name for him," Kara said, smiling. Satisfied Stevie was well distracted, she turned her attention to the doorway, where Peter had become furious.

"I've had enough of your attempts to upset these kids, Brice. You've got no business barging in here at dinnertime with your ridiculous threats. You've got nothing better to do than stir up trouble with your trivial and meaningless complaints."

"Me? Me?" the man repeated loudly, as though he couldn't believe his ears. "You make it sound as if I'm the one out there on my hands and knees digging a hole under *your* fence!"

"You can't even see the fence from your house," Peter countered. "You have to go looking for it. Don't you have anything better to do than a daily fence inspection?"

"No wonder the neighbors around here still want to run you out," Brice growled. "You people are all the same. You don't care a scrap for anyone around you. These kids don't care. They're going to go through their lives ruining good neighborhoods."

Kara could not stand another moment of the argument. Kids, especially kids already labeled as juvenile delinquents, did not need to hear that they were the scourge of the earth. Even more, they needed an example of how they should be settling differences. Her disgust with the childishness of both men propelled her across the room.

"Mr. Brice, I'm Kara Ridgeway, Youth Bureau police officer."

Brice took her outstretched hand and shook it, disarmed by her unexpected intervention.

"What Mr. Aiken means is that the children are sorry about the hole, and they'll fill it back in tomorrow. Dogs will be dogs just as kids will be kids and I'm sure you understand these accidents happen."

"It's no accident." Brice's protest sounded close to a whine. "They've done this before."

"I know it must be annoying, but I'm sure it's just a phase the dog is going through. And I'm sure you want the children to know you don't want to see any harm done to the dog. You just want him to stop digging."

"I suppose you're right," Brice agreed. His head drooped a bit sheepishly.

"Now," Kara concluded, "I hope the next time you have a complaint to lodge against Aiken House you will use your discretion and telephone Mr. Aiken. I think this kind of disagreement can be handled most effectively by a private conversation between two adults in the absence of impressionable kids."

The man ventured a thin smile before he shook her hand again and retreated out the door, back into the darkness.

When the door clicked closed, Peter faced the kids, barely controlling himself. "Well, let's get on with it. Kitchen crew can start the cleanup." His hands were rolled into tight fists, making his arm muscles tense. He said nothing to Kara as he strode from the room, but his body language all but screamed at her.

As kids went to work washing the dishes or drifted over to the television set, Kara felt increasingly isolated and forgotten. A couple of girls congratulated her and thanked her for a lovely dinner idea, but their words provided no comfort. At last she followed Peter's path to the quiet room he called his office.

He had his back to her. His shoulders were hunched; his hands thrust into his pockets.

"I hope you don't mind my saying something," she said to his back.

When he turned to face her, his eyes were icy blue. He leaned closer to her, his expression cold and his stance taut.

"I've been asking myself just who you must think you are, Constable Kara Ridgeway," he said, his voice just above a whisper. "First you decide my program isn't good enough for your lofty ideals. Then you get off your high horse long enough to come out here and stick your nose in business that is none of your concern."

"I thought I could help."

"Your kind of help I don't need," Peter charged. "Believe it or not, I've managed to run this place just fine for the past five years. You might get a charge out of your self-appointed salvation mission, but I'd appreciate your taking it somewhere it might be more welcome."

Kara stared at him. This was the same man who, only an hour ago, had treated her with unbelievable tenderness.

"I don't think you've been doing as well as you think," she choked, "if that's the best you can do to get along with people. I came here to learn about your program. I can now tell you that your program suffers from the inexcusable ego that controls it."

She hardly remembered leaving Peter and stumbling through her goodbyes to the kids. She didn't want to burden them with a second conflict tonight. The important thing was to leave quickly before her feelings registered on her face. Stan had warned her many times that she flashed her emotions like a neon sign.

Stevie came to introduce Ketchup. The tiny black dog, undersized even in little Stevie's arms, didn't look in the least ashamed of the crime he'd committed. Kara gave both boy and dog a pat before waving goodbye for the last time.

Once Kara had left the house and got into her car, though, her hands started to shake in delayed reaction. A dark and depressing thought seeped into her mind. Peter had revealed his true temperament.

She'd known he was trouble from when she'd first seen him more than a decade ago, yet, when she'd met him tonight, she'd wanted to see the good in him. Why? Because she'd begun to see a sensitive and understanding side to him. While everything was going smoothly, he had almost sold the "warm home" idea to her. But it had all fallen apart at the first disruption.

Kara imagined Stan's shock when she told him she'd been driven away from the group home by an angry Peter Aiken. He was probably expecting to hear that she'd stormed out early after a heated discussion on the merits of discipline in child rearing. Anyway, there was no need now to ask herself if Craig would fit in better at Aiken House or another group home. Peter had made that decision for her. Now if only she could find another group home that would take him....

ON MONDAY MORNING, Kara's spirits were bleak, and not just because of the light drizzle and fog. She waited in the driveway of the Children's Aid shelter for Craig to pack his bag and join her. He had finally worn out his welcome there, and the weekend had turned up no alternative shelter. She had no choice but to place Craig in Aiken House.

Her phone call to the home had been tense. Both she and Peter had been careful to stay well within their roles as counsellor and police officer. If they relaxed and allowed their true selves to emerge, they knew conflict awaited them. Kara had listened attentively to his tone of voice for signs of smugness or triumph over her change of mind with Craig. To his credit, she couldn't detect a trace. Perhaps, though, her usual perceptiveness was dulled by her state of mind.

"It will take about an hour to admit Craig," Peter had advised her. "I could meet with you before lunch, say eleven-thirty?"

Kara had paused before confirming, wondering if ordinarily he would have tacked on an invitation for her to stay for lunch. In any case, she was thankful to be spared the ordeal of gracefully declining such a suggestion.

"Eleven-thirty will be fine," she agreed. She knew her voice betrayed her discomfort at having to meet with him at all.

"I don't get the feeling you're very happy with your decision to bring Craig," he offered.

"I wouldn't call it a decision," she returned in a clipped tone. "I was left with no choice. The other homes in town are still booked. I look at the arrangement with Aiken House as only temporary."

"I see," he'd said quietly, then added professionally, "Well, I'm pleased we can at least be of help in an emergency. I'll look forward to meeting your Craig at eleven-thirty."

Kara glanced up and spotted Craig in his red sweatshirt as he emerged from the front door of Children's Aid. The bright color he wore contradicted the mood of such a gray day, and he seemed unnecessarily buoyant about leaving. Kara watched as he pitched his gym bag into the back of her car, then opened the front door to flop into the seat beside her.

"What's the matter with you?" he asked bluntly, seeing her grim expression. His eyes showed concern.

"Haven't you ever seen a depressed person before?" she answered as she placed the car in reverse and backed down the driveway onto the street.

"What are you depressed for?" he asked. "Things are working out great."

"That's what you think," she grumbled as she steered toward downtown.

"I'm sure not depressed anymore," he announced as he arranged his seat belt. "Anything's got to be better than that prison camp."

Kara eyed him curiously. He seemed very relaxed and companionable with her, as if he regarded her more as a big sister than a cop. She didn't know if that was a good sign or a bad one.

"I made you a promise last week," she reminded him, "that I wouldn't place you somewhere just because it was convenient. I didn't think the issue of convenience would be replaced by desperation."

"Don't worry," Craig said. "I forgive you."

Kara laughed despite herself. "Your forgiveness I need like a hole in the head."

PETER SAT BEHIND his office desk, trying to remember how he usually acted when admitting a new kid to Aiken House. Ordinarily it was such a natural process he didn't have to think about what he was doing, nor feel nervous. Yet, with Kara sitting in one of his visitors' chairs—glaring at him—he felt as if Craig were his first admission. He found himself already apprehensive about the boy's future. Usually he was far more philosophical about such situations.

He'd thought Kara had been guarded and distant on the phone, but the frostiness he'd heard in her voice was no match for the disapproval evident on her face now. On Friday, her quick intelligent eyes had brimmed with laughter, and she'd seemed to recognize something in him when her gaze had connected with his. He thought it almost seemed like a familiarity, as if she'd known him at some other time. Perhaps she'd realized they shared a kindred spirit despite their differences. But today her chestnut eyes had darkened to muddy chocolate. Her approving smile had hardened to a look of hostile disappointment.

Her outrage of the other night had upset him more than he could have predicted. Interference from anyone older than voting age had always been intolerable to him. But she'd had no way of knowing that. He could see how she must have felt ambushed when he'd blown up at her. Before now he'd never felt guilty for telling an adult to mind his own business. But as he led Kara and the young boy with the dirty blond hair into his study, he definitely felt like a heel.

For some reason her approval was important to him, and more importantly, he worried that he'd hurt her. She'd shown him a side of herself he suspected other people didn't get to see. He knew now there was a creampuff under that tough exterior, but he had severely breached the trust she'd shown in him.

Kara sat in one easy chair, her back poker straight, while Craig sprawled contentedly over the other. Peter opened a file that lay waiting on the desk. "Craig, why don't you sit up here by the desk," Peter suggested, and indicated a far less comfortable-looking wooden chair. "I'll be needing you to fill out a couple of forms for me."

Kara struggled with her threatening smile when she saw the look of relaxation fall from Craig's face. He had clearly thought he was on easy street now, and Kara felt more than a little responsible for having given him that impression. She noticed that Peter acted in a more businesslike fashion than she'd expected. Was this a side of him she hadn't noticed? Or was he making some concession to her because of what happened the last time they were together in this room?

Craig answered Peter's questions about his parents, about why he needed a group home and what he thought about the school he used to attend. Peter gave him a sheet of paper that listed everything expected of him while he was at Aiken House, and Craig dutifully signed the bottom of it to show he understood and agreed to the terms. Craig also filled out an inventory of the belongings he was bringing in with him.

"I want to make sure you understand something, Craig," Peter said when they had completed all the paperwork. "You're as welcome here as any family member would be. But while you're here I expect you to accomplish one thing—and you won't have me or any other staff member telling you how to do it each step of the way. By the time you leave Aiken House, I want to be convinced you won't get into trouble again. Do we understand each other?"

"Yes, sir," Craig answered quietly. Clearly Aiken House was not what he had expected, and Kara could see he didn't know quite what to make of it.

"Good," Peter said smiling as he stood up. "If you'll excuse me for a minute, I'm going to see if one of the boys is home from school so he can show you around."

Kara lowered her eyes as Peter strode by her. As long as she could be the fly on the wall and not be directly involved with Peter, the situation was halfway tolerable. But when she could feel his attention shift from the adolescent in the room to rest on her, every muscle in her body tensed. Peter appeared a touch edgy, too, but he at least seemed pleased that Craig was here.

Kara wasn't pleased. She felt as though she were watching herself in a dream. She wanted to drag Craig out of Aiken House with her, but knew she had to stick it through the admission procedure. She wanted to turn her back on Peter Aiken because of his unforgivable treatment of her on Friday night, but had to remain seated, feeling beholden to him for taking Craig. Oddly enough she also felt she wanted to sit and talk pleasantly with Peter, as they had before his temper had flared. But that was ridiculous.

Craig twisted around in his seat to face her. "I don't know why you were so worried," he said. "This guy's no pushover. I mean, I can tell pretty quick if I can walk all over somebody, and I can tell you I wouldn't want to try it with him. He seems nice enough, but he's not stupid."

"You just make sure you keep your nose clean," Kara warned him. She was heartened, though, by his candid assessment of the director of Aiken House. She just hoped he was right. "I'm going to be keeping a close watch on you, and if things aren't working out I'll have you out of here the minute a space opens up somewhere else."

"Sheesh," Craig complained, rolling his eyes. "It's sure nice to be trusted."

"I told you before, Craig, I care enough to be hard on you. In the long run I'll do you more good by making sure you're on the right track than I would by just trusting you."

Kara dropped the subject when she heard Peter's voice drawing closer to the room. He seemed to be explaining something. She turned to see Peter with Randy in tow.

"Hi, Kara!" Randy called, genuinely excited to see her.

"Hello, Randy," she smiled. "Nice to see you."

"Everybody's still talking about your tortellini. That was a real professional meal."

"You guys did a great job putting it together," Kara said.

"Sharon was saying she hoped if you had any more special dishes like that if you'd consider giving us the recipes."

"I'd be happy to," Kara replied, feeling very pleased. Randy was just too friendly for her to remain subdued. "I promise I'll look through my recipe box."

"Thanks. That'd be great."

"Randy," Peter said, "this is Craig. Craig, Randy. You two will be sharing a room, Craig, so Randy is going to show you around. He'll give you a good idea of the routine here. You can have lunch, and later I'll take you over to the school to get registered."

Craig nodded, picked up his gym bag and turned to follow Randy. Kara noticed that Craig made no protest about enrolling in school. Yet he wouldn't go to school at all while he lived with his parents. Had she got through to him or was it Peter?

Abruptly Craig stopped and turned back to Peter. "Thanks, sir," he said, and stretched his hand out to shake. As Craig turned to leave again, he gave Kara a salute. "Don't lose touch, chief," he said with a warm smile, then disappeared out the door behind Randy.

Kara found herself suddenly left alone with Peter. The silence seemed overwhelming. They looked at each other, and for a moment their eyes spoke only about their concern and appreciation for a boy who had so much life in him and a world of opportunity before him—if only he didn't get in more trouble. But Kara quickly recovered and directed her eyes to the floor.

"Well, I'd better be going," she said, and stood to leave, hoping he wouldn't say anything, because when he did, she found herself wanting to listen. But she knew how deceptive his apparent sensitivity was. Lurking in the shadows lay a harshness she thought it wise not to forget.

"I get the feeling that Craig wants very much to please you," he commented. "It's unusual for a kid to get at all close to a police officer. I think it's a feat that should be commended."

"Thank you," she said as naturally as she could while carefully avoiding his eyes. "He said he liked you, too."

"Maybe he just likes everybody," Peter suggested with a chuckle. "Maybe he's such an accepting kid that it doesn't matter who he comes in contact with."

"He's not so accepting of his parents," Kara pointed out. "And I think it does matter who he comes in contact with."

"You're right," Peter agreed, sobering. "As a matter of fact, I'd planned on calling his parents this afternoon. I want to keep them informed of his progress. Have you met them?"

"Not in person, but I've spoken with them on the phone. They seem like very concerned, responsible people," Kara said, wishing Peter wouldn't stand so near to her. Kara could almost forget what had happened between them. His face still seemed to light up when he looked at her, and his smile was still quick to flicker across his lips. She still felt tempted to slip her arms around his waist to rest her head on his shoulder, sure of the soothing warmth she would feel from him. Soothing—but deceptive—warmth.

She was aware of him studying her, as if there was something important he wanted to say. "Kara, I'm glad you brought him—"

"Yes, well," she interrupted him nervously, "I hope I am too."

She turned abruptly to leave, and Peter followed her out to the kitchen, where the kids were sitting down for lunch. A pleasant, attractive redhead in her early twenties was setting out plates of sandwiches and filling glasses with milk. Peter introduced her to Kara as Andrea, one of his relief staff. Several of the kids said "Hi" and waved to Kara as she walked through to the front hallway.

Peter opened the door for her—reluctantly, she thought—and she stepped out onto the front porch.

"Will I see you around again soon?" he asked. He leaned against the frame with the door wide open. He didn't look happy.

It was an odd question to ask her, she thought. First he'd as good as told her to keep her nose the hell out of his business. Now he was practically inviting her to stick her nose back in. Was it possible he was confused about what he did want? "I plan to keep a close eye on Craig," she answered at last.

"It would be nice to see you for more than just that."

"Yeah, well, thanks for taking him," she stammered, and hurried down the steps to her car. As she wheeled the car around to face back down the driveway, she allowed herself one quick glance back at the porch. The door to Aiken House was closed.

AN UNSEASONABLY WARM autumn sun streamed into Kara's room when she opened her eyes at six-thirty Saturday morning. Despite its being one of her days off, she threw off the covers. Wakefulness was a welcome escape from her restless sleep. Besides, this was going to be a workday until she'd checked to see if any spaces had come available at other group homes.

First though, a few drops of peppermint oil under the flow of her bathwater transported Kara to an imaginary luxurious Swiss spa. Saturday might be a self-proclaimed working day, but she couldn't deny herself her weekend ritual of a long, completely relaxed and self-indulgent bath. When she had dried herself and slipped on her rose knit sweater and her favorite pair of jeans, she brewed a pot of mocha coffee and carried her breakfast tray to the patio. The sunrise had already chased away any trace of frost. She loved to eat outside and had braved much cooler weather than this to enjoy her early mornings. Once she was quite settled, she allowed thoughts of Aiken House to surface.

Peter was a mystery. He'd managed to open her mind to the positive environment he'd created. Then, just as she'd been about to grant him no small measure of her respect, he'd pulled the rug out with his high-handed treatment of his neighbor and then of her.

Why would he do that? She had been drawn to him and thought he'd been interested in her.

Kara gazed out over the brilliant forest below, as if seeking answers within the dense thickets of trees lining the river. But none appeared.

"A hopeless case of ego," she said aloud, and raised her cup, as if toasting her conclusion. "It has to be."

As she sipped her coffee and watched the steam rise from the mug, her thoughts turned to Craig. She'd check the group homes in neighboring towns in today's round of phone calls. She wondered how he had fared over the past few days at Aiken House.

By ten o'clock, after a peaceful early morning, Kara felt ready to call a few group homes. If luck was with her, some last minute change might leave room for Craig. Just then her tranquility was shattered by the shrill ring of the telephone.

"Kara?" a man asked as she picked up the receiver.

"Speaking."

"I need to talk to you. It's Peter Aiken."

"Peter?" she repeated.

"I don't have a good excuse to call, Kara, except that I really need to see you right away."

Her surprise at hearing from him suddenly rose to alarm. "Is everything all right with Craig?"

"Craig is fine," he assured her. "I don't expect this to mean much to you after last weekend, but I'm the one who has the problem. Kara, may I please come over?"

"When, right now?"

"It'll take me ten minutes to get there. I've got your address from the phone book."

Kara wavered. She should probably say no. Already he'd caused her more emotional disruption than she'd felt in a long time. She didn't need it. Yet she wanted to hear what he had to say. "Well, if it's that important."

"I'm leaving now," he answered immediately. "And Kara? Thanks. I mean it."

Ten minutes later there was a knock at her door, and Kara checked her watch in disbelief. She'd have thought the route from Aiken House would have taken at least twenty minutes at the speed limit. She opened the door to a man who was even more attractive than she remembered. The powder blue shirt under Peter's jean jacket set off his deep blue eyes. Today, though, she noticed his eyes seemed cloudy. Last weekend's easy charm had deepened to a more compelling vulnerability.

"I have some fresh coffee on the stove," she offered reluctantly as she motioned him in.

Peter shook his head. "I've been drinking coffee all morning. But thanks."

With no task before her, Kara floundered. They suffered a strained silence until Peter spoke.

"I was worried you'd give me a cold military shoulder," he admitted quietly. "I thought you might even hang up on me."

Kara tried to shrug off his observation. She looked away. "I didn't expect you to call. You caught me before I had a chance to get my guard up," she answered, feeling awkward. She had a sudden impulse to run outside and gulp a mouthful of cool, steadying air.

Obviously Peter felt the same way, because he quickly suggested a walk. She accepted as quickly as he'd offered, glad to have something to do other than look into his eyes. Kara led him outside, across the street and down to the river.

"Aiken House isn't really that far from here," Peter said, trying to avoid the inevitable. "The river almost makes us neighbors."

"I guess." She could feel the weak smile on her face betray her discomfort. "I don't really think of the river much. I guess it's because I don't really have anything to do with it."

Peter nodded his understanding. They both stared at the river as if there was something new about it to study.

Kara turned back to face the parking lot. "Which car is yours?"

Kara followed his pointing finger to the pale yellow Mercedes. She was no expert on cars, but this one looked like a true vintage model—at least thirty-five years old and in pristine condition.

"How did you get here inside of ten minutes in a car that old?"

"It's not the original motor. I put in a new one."

"You renovate cars as well as houses, do you?"

"This car is special. My parents bought it at an auction and always intended to fix it up. I worked on it all through high school. Would you like a ride?"

"No, no thanks," she answered quickly.

"Look, Kara, we could drive out to Elora," he persisted, "and drop into the mill for a hot chocolate."

This time she allowed herself to look at him. "I have a few things I want to do today, so I can't be gone for long."

"I'll get you back in plenty of time."

Kara looked at her feet, then nodded and walked toward the car.

In a few minutes Peter was driving them north along Highway 6. The last housing subdivision ended abruptly and the glorious countryside exploded around them. They sped by crimsons and yellows that could appear so richly painted only when kissed by autumn sunshine. Kara sank comfortably into her seat, content to sit silently and absorb the restorative effects of the drive. She noticed Peter, too, was very quiet. She had the feeling he was wrestling with something. She wondered what she was doing in this car with this man she'd only just met.

When he spoke, the force of his personality made his words as intense as last week's anger. "You know something interesting? Until today, I don't think I've ever apologized to anyone for anything. Well, maybe for the little things, like when I've bumped into someone on the sidewalk. But never for the big things. I was unfair to you last weekend, Kara. And I want you to know I'm truly sorry."

She glanced over at his tired face, noting the laugh lines etched around his eyes and the worry that now creased his forehead. His forthright admission impressed her.

"What changed your mind?" she asked curiously. "You were still angry when I left last Friday night and you haven't mentioned it since. What happened between then and now?"

"I've been doing some thinking, and I've realized a few things about myself. I want to tell you about them, if you've got the slightest little bit of interest in listening."

Kara took a moment to consider his words. As she stared absently at the dashboard in front of her, she noticed there wasn't a speck of dirt or dust anywhere on it. She liked people who were organized and took care of things. And in truth, she just plain liked Peter.

"I think I'd like to hear about your realizations," she said softly.

"I was hoping you would," Peter said, and smiled broadly for the first time that morning.

# CHAPTER FOUR

EVIDENCE OF THE DAY'S coming excitement was already apparent as Peter and Kara drove down the main street of Elora. Shopkeepers were busy preparing their stores for the flood of visitors who would soon triple the population of the picturesque village. A tiny smile spread across Kara's lips as she imagined the eager shoppers bustling from shop to shop in search of the handiwork of the artisans who made the village famous. She'd heard Elora was a craftsman's dream, and here it was about to come true for another Saturday. Peter detoured down a side street and parked outside the imposing gray wall of the mill.

The Elora Mill, after decades of use as a gristmill, had in recent years been renovated into a small resort hotel. Visitors from miles away came for Elora's special blend of country charm and its view of the famous natural land formation, the Elora Gorge. The Grand River rushed by the windows of the mill's dining room and hurtled over a high rocky cliff.

Inside, Kara followed the waiter to a table by a huge picture window, savoring the mixed aromas of a wood fire and scrumptious food.

"I've never been here before," Kara confessed after the waiter had left with their orders for hot chocolate. The short trip to this romantic hamlet had been at the back of her mind for ages, but work had always filled up her free time. Now, thrilled by the sight of the water thundering into the gorge, she had to concentrate to avoid staring in wide-eyed, open-mouthed wonder like a child.

She leaned over the table for a closer look at the rushing water that had at one time turned the wheels of the old gristmill. The grinding stone had long since been removed. Now the water generated electricity for the hotel—and enthusiasm among tourists and hikers who made pilgrimages here all year round.

"I've wanted to come back here at this time of year for a long time," Peter said thoughtfully as he, too, leaned over for a better view.

"That's what they call the Tooth of Time," he said, nodding to the tiny island just above the falls. "It's been here as long as the river has, and over time, the water has worn it into the shape of a molar."

"I see you've been here before."

"I used to come here every Saturday as a kid. The mill wasn't renovated back then."

Kara straightened to focus on his ruggedly handsome face. "Did you grow up around here?"

"My parents worked a farm a few miles north."

Kara tried to imagine him as a young boy, carefree and happy. "For some reason I can't picture you as ever being a kid," she confessed. "You just seem too serious to have ever had a childhood." Too serious and much too sensual, she thought.

The waiter reappeared and Kara sat back to give him room to set down two wide-mouthed mugs of steaming hot chocolate slathered with whipped cream and garnished with a cinnamon stick.

When the waiter retreated, Peter leaned closer to her. "You're a very perceptive woman," he began. "I don't often meet people who notice as much at a casual glance as you do. Maybe that's why I was so hard on you. You got close too fast, and it made me uncomfortable. You must have thought I was a completely unreasonable boor by the time you left last week."

"I must admit the thought did cross my mind," she agreed with a shadow of a smile.

"You may not know it, Kara, but last weekend you turned the tables on me. And that doesn't happen to me very often. As a matter of fact, I can't remember the last time it did."

His unrelenting seriousness robbed her of a response. She had to clear her throat to force the words out. "How did I manage that?"

"To explain, I have to tell you something about myself, and that's never an easy thing for me to do," he admitted taking a sip of his hot chocolate. "I've always been a loner. It doesn't appear that way because of the work I do. But I know how badly these kids need someone to talk to only because I don't have anyone myself and never have."

"I noticed you're quite protective of your territory," Kara said.

"That's an understatement," he acknowledged with a chuckle. "I'm used to defending my borders from everyone, friend or foe. As a boy I decided that one day I was going to have my own group home. But I didn't tell a soul about it. It became my driving force, the idea that motivated everything I did, but no one else knew about it until the day I applied for my license to operate a home.''

"It was your private mission,'' Kara concluded, and thought of her brother, Joey. What had happened to him had been her motivating force and still was. But he was the hardest thing in the world for her to talk about.

"My mission,'' he agreed. "And I've hugged it to myself and hid inside my shell like Stevie's turtle.''

Kara thought about how she would feel if a stranger broke into a conversation she was having with Craig and contradicted everything she said. That must have been how Peter perceived her attempt to help. "Peter, I really didn't set out to change anything,'' she assured him. "Aiken House is your business, not mine. I may not agree with everything you do, but I never intended to interfere.''

"That's not what I meant,'' Peter said, reaching across the table to take her hand loosely in his. "I know you weren't trying to change anything. What happened is very simple. I didn't handle the situation at all well.''

Kara looked down at his strong, yet smooth and sensitive fingers. She liked the feel of them wrapped around her own. "You're right,'' she conceded generously, trying to maintain a serious face.

Peter laughed outright. "That's one of my favorite things about you, Constable Ridgeway. You don't get carried away with the romance of the moment. Your practical feet are always rooted firmly in the ground.''

If only Peter knew how shaky the ground felt under her right now! she thought.

"For your information," Peter continued, "I never do handle that kind of situation very well. My way of dealing with the Brices of the world is to steamroll over their complaints. I'm a natural with kids, Kara, but with adults I'm unforgivably impatient."

Kara leaned forward. "Why? What's wrong with adults?"

Peter's eyes narrowed slightly as he searched for the words to explain this feeling that had apparently shaped so many of his convictions. "Adults should know it's their job to do the giving. But everywhere I look, they're giving less than the kids. In order to develop, kids need love and support from the people closest to them. But adults are worried about the stupid kinds of things that Brice worries about."

"Like fences?" Kara offered.

"And property values and what the neighbors will think and how many votes it will cost and so on."

"But treating Brice as an enemy only makes him worse," Kara pointed out.

"That's never bothered me before. And the only reason it bothers me now is because of you. When I saw that look of disappointment on your face, I couldn't stand it."

Her capacity for a quick comeback failed her. "I'm a little surprised," she managed to say.

"Kara, I can't dismiss you as another adult who doesn't care. Last week you were putting the kids first when you were trying to set things right with Brice. I let my ego get in the way—as you observed. But this morning I asked myself whose attitude showed more consideration for the kids, yours or mine. There was only one answer I could honestly give and that rattled me. I've never been shown up in my own territory before, and I'm not going to let my impatience get the better of me like that again.''

Kara couldn't recall ever being paid so high a compliment. Self-consciously she picked up her mug, and hot chocolate spilled over the brim. "Oh, no," she groaned as she quickly dabbed at the spill with her napkin. "I'm making quite a mess here," she apologized, flustered.

"I've grown rather attached to messes in recent years," he reassured her. "But if you're finished with your cocoa, would you like me to show you a side of the gorge most people don't see?"

"Why, do you have a special hideout?" she asked, laughing, thankful for the diversion from her clumsiness.

"You may laugh, but that's exactly what it was. I used to explore around here with my father while my mother did the shopping. We were convinced he and I were the only ones in the world who ever knew this hideout existed. Do you feel like a bit of a hike?"

Kara loved the idea of a hike.

They paid the bill, and Peter took her hand, then led her out of the mill and up the cobblestone street to the bridge over the Grand River. Here, the water was calm, unaware of the violence the gorge would awaken in it. With the warm sun on their backs they crossed the bridge, then doubled back toward the gorge. Peter led the way over the uneven ground. She smiled as she imagined the happiness he must have felt as a young boy picking his way carefully over such adventurous terrain.

Kara knew they'd reached a lookout spot when a thunderous rush of water appeared almost directly below their feet. She stepped back quickly and Peter's arms closed protectively around her.

They stood for a moment, peering first into the mist that rose from the gorge, then down to the churning foam below.

"Why does the measly little gorge frighten a big tough cop like you?" Peter whispered into her ear.

"I'm not afraid of the gorge. It just came as a surprise."

"You don't like surprises?"

Kara stared at the violent flood as it dropped out of control, over the limestone cliff. "No, I don't." They retreated from the edge of the gorge, but Peter's arm remained around her shoulder as he steered her into a small clearing.

Through the loose web of leaves and branches, Kara could see the mill on the opposite bank. But no one from the mill would be able to make out their two figures through the brush.

Being able to see the mill made it seem close, but it stood across a thundering natural divide. It might just as well have been a million miles away. That was how she felt about Peter, too. It seemed impossible that they stood on the same side. And yet here they stood, autumn air lapping gently against their cheeks. They both ached to bridge the chasm between them.

"This is the hideout, isn't it?"

"This is it. You're the only one I've brought here besides my father."

"I'm flattered," she said, looking up at him. His eyes were the color of a tropical sky, and Kara felt drawn to them, the way a person who can't swim feels pulled down by the slippery shore of a pond. She knew the danger but felt helpless to do anything about it.

Cautiously Peter touched her face to brush back a curl the breeze had blown over her eyes. His fingers felt so gentle against her skin, so disarmingly intimate and affectionate that Kara was transfixed.

He bent toward her, and his lips settled feather light against her own. When she didn't pull away, but returned his tentative kiss, he raised his free hand to cradle her cheeks in his palms and pulled her closer. They tasted each other hungrily, finding themselves unable to drink in enough to quench their thirst.

Kara wound her arms around his neck, wishing that just for this one happy moment she could be free of the little voice that dogged her every second she was with Peter. The voice knew how much she wanted to lower her guard completely and revel in the feelings he was able to produce in her. The voice seemed to take an almost perverse pleasure in denying her what she craved. She tried to ignore it, to push it to the back of her mind, to let it be drowned out by the roar of the gorge, and as Peter coiled his arms around her, for a fleeting moment Kara felt sure they would melt together without regard for the boundaries of flesh and bone.

Peter drew his head back to look at her. She'd never seen his face so soft.

"I want you to know something," he said. "Before I met you I didn't think I needed anyone. I was so consumed by my kids, I thought I didn't have needs myself. I was wrong," he said, caressing her continually as if trying to confirm she was real. His fingers traced the outline of her face and neck, then combed through her hair. He kissed her again, and Kara understood perfectly the wordless language he spoke.

She kept her eyes open ever so slightly, stamping Peter's image into her memory. But she knew she could not enjoy his touch for long. All she could do was capture this moment to keep alive inside her.

The voice in her head rose above her thundering pulse. *Remember Joey,* it said, and she tore herself from Peter's coaxing lips.

"I'm sorry, Peter," she choked, her gaze falling to the ground.

"What is it?" he asked. He lifted her chin and scrutinized her face. "You're fighting something. What is it you're afraid of?"

She couldn't tell him. She couldn't tell him flat out that she blamed him for what had happened to her brother. She couldn't admit she was afraid something as bad might happen to Craig.

But she had to tell him something. "I need time to get to know Peter Aiken," she ventured. "I need time to trust what you're doing with kids like Craig." She knew her explanation was vague, but felt it was the best she could do right now.

Peter nodded slowly, his eyes pinched. He allowed his hands to slide down her arms, to hang loosely by his sides. He wondered if their different attitudes toward caring for juveniles could really be all that stood in their way. It sure didn't interfere with his attraction to her. He noticed a nearby log and, deep in thought, strode over to it and sat down.

"You're angry," she said, following closely behind him.

Peter threw her a reassuring smile as he sat. "Not angry. Disappointed and puzzled, yes. Angry, no."

Kara smiled significantly and raised her eyebrows. "I guess that makes us even then."

"Oh? Then you feel the same way toward me as I feel toward you?"

"Uh, let's just say I'm not angry."

"So how are you going to get to know me better?" he asked. "I thought we were doing just fine."

Kara relaxed, relieved to feel the tension between them evaporate. "Well, why don't you start by telling me what you were like as the little boy who roamed the woods along the Elora Gorge? What did you want a group home for, why didn't you tell anyone, and—"

"Whoa! Let me take these one at a time," he pleaded. "Let's see. I'd say that before I was eight I was a fairly regular kid. A bit on the shy side of Stevie and not anywhere as rebellious as your Craig."

"What happened when you were eight?"

"My parents went to a county fair one Sunday afternoon. I was in bed sick, and a neighbor was looking after me. That evening we got a visit from the police. My parents had been killed in a head-on collision on their way home."

Kara gasped with shock. What child could cope with such tragedy? "Did you have brothers or sisters?"

"No, I was an only child, and so were both my parents, so I had no uncles or aunts."

"You were left with no family?"

"Just a carton of pictures."

"I can't imagine how terrible that must have been. What happened to you?"

"I was placed with foster parents," Peter answered. "They were an older couple. He'd been in the army, and they'd never had kids of their own. They tried as best they could, but the house always felt like a military camp to me. Everything ran on schedule. My physical needs were met, but I desperately missed being loved. They were kind people and meant well. They were just caretakers, though."

Kara's stomach knotted with pain as she imagined how terrible it would be to be left all alone. Peter leaned forward, his elbows on his knees and looked at his hands thoughtfully. Kara studied his firmly set features, knowing he was reliving painful memories.

"How long did you live with your foster parents?" she asked softly.

"A couple of years, on and off."

"You must have been very lonely."

"I was, but I had an odd way of coping with it. I'd run away to some friend's house after school. I'd convince him to hide me under his bed or in his toy chest." Peter laughed painfully. "I was never away long—my foster parents figured out my pattern early on. Soon my friend's parents would come clattering around his room in search of the stowaway. Eventually I ran away so many times that I was offered the option of a group home if I promised to stay put."

"Was that when you decided you wanted to run a group home of your own one day?"

Peter nodded. "I was lucky. I was placed in a home that was so well run that I felt I belonged to a family again. That's where I learned kids need help to grow into the shoes they've picked for themselves.

"Group-home kids, like most kids, are immature. And group-home kids are often less mature for their ages—because they've already had so much bad luck in their lives. But they're fighting hard for their own identities. That's usually what gets them into trouble in the first place. I can give kids like Craig and Stevie independence with training wheels, and be there to catch them when they fall."

Kara sat back thoughtfully. "No wonder you're such a loner," she mused.

"I was a loner until last weekend, Kara," Peter qualified quietly.

Kara's pulse quickened, disarmed by his honesty. "How old were you when you left the group home?" she prodded, casually avoiding the new direction the conversation had just taken.

"Enough, my sweet investigating officer, enough!" he pleaded. "I made a promise that I wouldn't keep you out too long, remember? And I don't want you to get the idea I'm a man who doesn't keep his promises."

"But you've left your story half-told," Kara complained, "and if there's one thing I can't stand it's suspense."

"I suppose for a cop that comes with the territory?"

"It sure does."

Peter stood up and helped her to her feet. But when she stood before him, he held onto her hands and raised them to his lips. Then he gently wrapped her arms around his waist, and rested his arms around her shoulders. He brushed a leaf from her hair.

"There's not much left to tell," he said as his touch started to play havoc with Kara's senses again. "I left home after high school and went to university. I got my masters degree in social work, then worked my way up to supervising several group homes. When I thought I knew enough to handle one of my own, I bought Aiken House. There, now you know at least as much about me as anyone else in the world."

"So why do I have a whole pile of questions left to ask?"

Peter's eyes sparkled. "Because you are a person who needs to completely understand every little detail about everything that's important to you. I think it has to do with being a cop."

"Hmm," she responded. A warm glow was slowly igniting within her. "That sounds like you think you're important to me."

"I fully intend to be."

Kara swayed toward him, drawn by the strength of his confidence. He kissed her gently and hugged her close. Suddenly she realized just how starved for affection she'd been for so many years.

"We'd better get going," Peter murmured. "Or my idle hands are going to find something to get them into trouble again."

She battled her own reluctance and took his extended hand to return along the steep bank. The sun had risen to its highest point in the sky and cast a rich sheen over the mottled trees.

"You haven't been quite fair in all of this, constable," Peter admonished over his shoulder.

"Oh?" she queried. A cool breeze blew through her hair as they emerged from the wooded area, but she still felt flushed with warmth. "How's that?"

"I don't know a single thing about you. You're a woman with strong opinions yourself, and I don't know any of the whys or wherefores. Fair is fair."

"It's too late now," she teased. "You should have asked your questions earlier."

"Wait a minute," he protested, pulling her close. Her long legs kept pace with his as they walked. "I think the least you can do is come to my place for dinner tomorrow night and explain yourself."

"I was just at your place for dinner."

Peter turned to her, his face shadowed with fleeting confusion. "I don't live at the group home."

"I thought you did."

"I'm committed to my work, but I still manage a few outside interests. I always have relief staff available so I can come and go as I please."

They came to the bridge near the river and crossed into Elora, which was already crowded with sightseers. Peter's attentive face was noticeably brighter than when he had appeared at her door. Although tired, he generated an energy that excited Kara. Now that she understood what had happened in his life to force his emotions underground, she found his resilience and courage admirable.

"Where do you live, then?" she asked as they walked down the cobblestone street.

"Down by the river. Down *in* the river really. My place is on the same property as the group home and was a boat house back when the big house was first built."

"It must be very soothing, falling asleep to the sound of lapping water. Sounds very romantic," Kara said dreamily as they reached Peter's old Mercedes.

Peter started to open the car door for her, then paused. "Are you a romantic, Kara?"

"Well, I've never thought of myself as one. I always figured I was too realistic to be a romantic." But maybe Stan had been right all those times he'd told her there was a part of herself she was afraid to let out of its cage, she thought.

"I have a true test of whether you can be romantic and realistic at the same time. Meet me tomorrow at four o'clock down by the bridge behind your place."

"At the bridge—what on earth for?"

"I'm going to pick you up in my canoe for dinner."

"You have to be kidding," Kara said laughing. She had a sudden image of Stan's shocked face as he watched her float down the Speed River with Peter

Aiken. "It must be a long way from my place to yours!"

"It won't even take an hour. Besides, it's downstream. The current will practically do my paddling for me. I'll put a foam pad and a blanket in the bow, and you'll be more than comfortable."

"Sounds like the North American answer to a Venetian gondola," Kara said laughing again.

"Sure it is. And if you like the ride, I'll officially brand you a romantic realist. Or is it a realistic romantic?"

"It's ridiculous, that's what it is, but it sounds like fun."

Peter smiled and opened the door fully for Kara to get in. Once they were in motion with the autumn trees behind them accelerating into streams of color, Peter said, "Then you will come? It's settled, right?"

"Turn your eyes back to the road, Mr. Aiken, or you'll have us floating down the river in a rather unseaworthy old Mercedes."

"But you'll come?" he insisted.

Kara sighed, happily trapped. "You win." He grinned, then quickly turned back to face the road. "I certainly do."

He seemed so different now, she thought, after Peter had dropped her off in front of her apartment. Why did she wish she were still with him? she thought as the pale yellow car disappeared around the corner. Grinning, she headed into the house. Tomorrow was only hours away.

## CHAPTER FIVE

PETER GUIDED HIS CANOE around the last bend and spotted Kara standing on the bridge in the distance. She hadn't seen him yet. She stood at one end of the bridge, looking back toward downtown, as if expecting someone to show up on foot or in a car instead of a canoe. When she turned to glance down the river, he tipped his paddle in greeting. She didn't wave, but immediately left the bridge and slid down the hill to the bank to wait for him.

He guided the canoe toward her. She wore white jeans and a billowy white blouse that darkened her fair complexion. She carried an oversized denim jacket slung over her arm, though it was warm enough today to pass for late August. A delicate pink glow lit her face. She looked pretty and feminine standing there waiting for him. But she also looked restless.

Kara crouched to grab the gunwale of the canoe and brought its slow forward motion to a stop. She climbed in quickly, and they shoved off again.

"Been waiting long?" he asked.

"Not more than ten minutes, but it felt like ten hours."

"Why?" he asked, paddling quickly. Somehow he felt he should be hurrying.

Kara looked back at the bridge once more, as if to satisfy herself of something, then settled back on the seat of cushions he'd made for her.

"Do you have any idea," she said as she draped her jacket around her shoulders, "how embarrassing it would be for me to have a fellow police officer see me in this position?"

"No," he said smiling. "Tell me."

Her face deepened to a rose pink when she realized he was teasing her.

"It may be all right for a social worker to climb into a canoe and commune with nature up the Speed River. Cops would see that as a quite normal thing for..." She faltered.

Peter finished the sentence for her. "For freaks, flakes and other assorted oddballs?"

She looked instantly guilty. "I didn't mean to sound so critical."

He laughed. "Don't worry. I don't stay up nights worrying about what cops think of social workers. I like floating up the Speed River communing with nature."

"So do I," she said, then laughed. "Maybe I'm a flaky social worker at heart, too. But police officers don't commune. They do something practical, like hunt or fish. If another cop saw me like this, everyone at the station would know about it instantly. I'd walk into work on Monday and someone would say, 'Looking for boating offenses these days, constable?'"

Peter laughed aloud.

She picked up a twig from the bottom of the canoe and drew it through the water. "Then," she added, pointing the dripping twig at him, "I'd have to suffer about four million references to boats over the next month. A toy canoe would mysteriously appear on my desk. Every cop who went out for lunch would ask me if he could bring me back a float. The shortwave radio would be the stage for a running comedy act, and I'd have to listen to it. And, if anyone knew I was in this canoe with you—well, that would be the end of it."

"I'm not that bad!"

Kara's look of alarm was so attractive that he wished he could throw her off balance that way with every sentence.

"No, I didn't mean you were. It's just that everyone at the station knows how I feel about how young offenders should be treated. And your views are well known, too. So for the two of us to be together in this canoe...it's ridiculous."

"It doesn't feel ridiculous to me."

Kara threw the twig back into the water. "I give up. I'm sorry, Peter. Every time I open my mouth, I just shove my foot in deeper."

Peter smiled. "It's okay, Kara."

The canoe sliced gracefully through the water, adding no sound to disturb their comfortable silence. In the distance they could hear faint city noises—buses and cars, the occasional blast of a horn.

To Peter, the river seemed a ribbon of serenity winding through the city. "I never went in for this stuff much when I was a kid, you know," Peter said thoughtfully.

Curious, Kara looked up at him. "What stuff?"

"Nature," he said, gesturing at the trees and the overhanging branches. "I went in more for reading. I was a fanatic about mystery books—the Hardy Boys and that sort of stuff. I liked to imagine myself chasing bad guys. It's a wonder I didn't turn out to be a cop."

Kara laughed. "That is ironic. I liked the adventure stories. I remember there was a series of books I just lived for. The books had titles like *Mountain of Adventure*, *Sea of Adventure* and *Island of Adventure*. The stories were about a few kids pitted against the elements. There were bad guys too, of course, but it was the adventure I loved. I've looked for those books recently because I'd like to read them again, but I can't find them anywhere."

They continued to chat easily about stories they remembered as kids. But after a while, as they neared his boat house, Kara grew quiet and pensive, and he wondered why.

Peter's boat house stood over the river on stilts buried deep in the riverbed. The doors on the water stood open. As Peter steered their silent craft into the boat house, they were greeted by the scent of sun-warmed wood. Light reflected off the minute ripples on the water's surface and danced over the maple walls and ceiling.

As Kara helped Peter lift the canoe out of the water and onto the deck, she stole a long look at him. He seemed so strong and happy—comforting really—that she felt an overwhelming desire to reach out and touch him.

Turning, he caught her glance. "Are you ready for another tour?" he asked.

"I'm waiting with bated breath." As he guided her up the wooden staircase with his hand on her back, she wished she didn't like him so much. It made it harder to do what she'd come here to do.

When she stepped through the door into his living quarters, Kara had the feeling she'd entered a sanctuary. The gray barn-board walls and the watercolor-blue couch and chair somehow conveyed the serene impression of a captain's cabin in an ancient sailing ship. The space was small, but it had been cared for by reverent hands.

"Grab a seat anywhere you like," Peter invited. "I have a few things to finish up in the kitchen." He served her a glass of white wine, then retreated to his post at the kitchen counter, where he could see her out of the corner of his eye. He'd built the kitchen walls to a height of only four feet so as to preserve an open feeling in the small house.

She'd become very quiet. He watched her standing at the window, taking in the impressive view upstream. Her slender frame looked strong and athletic, yet there was a fragility about her that aroused deep feelings of protectiveness in him. He could see, too, that something was troubling her. He wished he could hear her private thoughts as she stood at the window.

Kara returned to sit on the carpet and leaned her back comfortably against the couch. "This is a very special place," she said. "You've obviously put a lot of work into it."

"Had to," he agreed. "Boat houses aren't considered the safest structures for living quarters. People are allowed to repair old boat houses, but I wouldn't be allowed to build one from scratch now. Once this place falls down, it'll have to stay down."

"That would be a real shame," Kara murmured, half to herself. It was tempting to ask him more questions about his boat house, to get sidetracked into enjoyable conversation. But she knew she had to get on with what she'd come to say.

"I have a confession to make," she said.

"Good," Peter said pleasantly. "That's what you're here for."

"So that's why you invited me here. I knew you had an ulterior motive." *Quit stalling,* she told herself.

"Of course," Peter agreed, matter-of-factly. "You lured me out to a wilderness paradise yesterday, made me delirious with sunshine and coaxed out all my little secrets. Then, just as I regained my senses and thought of some questions to ask you, the day was declared over. You owe me a lot of confessions. Just a minute before you start, though," he said.

Kara watched him as he clattered about the kitchen. His tanned face bore a healthy glow. His hair was sun-bleached with streaks of lighter blond, and he wore a royal blue T-shirt that revealed his tightly muscular chest. To Kara, he looked like a man without a care in the world. He showed none of the strain one would expect in a man who had the responsibility for a bunch of delinquent kids.

The oven door banged shut, and he rounded the half-wall that separated the kitchen from the living room. "There," he announced, "the quiche is in. I'm all yours."

"I thought real men weren't supposed to eat quiche," she teased.

"I'll let you be the judge of that," he said as he folded himself cross-legged in front of her.

"Of what, the quiche or whether you're a real man?"

"Both, I hope." He held her gaze, sensing she was struggling with something important despite her attempt at light banter. He could see Kara was fighting her feelings for him and hoped it was just what she'd said, that she needed time to trust what he was doing with kids like Craig. But he didn't believe it.

"Okay, officer," he said quietly, "shoot. Not literally, of course."

Kara heaved a deep steadying sigh. "Okay," she agreed, nodding. "I already know you."

Peter looked confused. "I thought we'd never met."

"I did say that. It's true. We never have met, but I still know you."

Peter couldn't resist a grin. He dropped his voice to a whisper. "Do you mean you know me in some cosmic way? Have our souls encountered each other in another life? Or do you mean you know me in a more intimate way? I can't imagine something that important escaping my memory."

Kara closed her eyes, and Peter was struck by how beautiful she looked. "You're making this difficult," she sighed.

"Terribly sorry. I will now conduct myself with appropriate somberness."

"Thank you," she replied indulgently. "To answer your question, I know you from this earth and in this dimension. It was about fourteen years ago."

Suddenly pensive, Peter stared absently out the window. "Fourteen years," he repeated. "That was long before Aiken House. I was working at another group home."

"Maple Glen Boys' Home," Kara supplied.

"That's right," he answered, turning his gaze back to rest on her well-controlled features. "I was the director there for four years."

"And you were often called in as an expert witness in juvenile cases. You gave your expert opinions for sentencing purposes."

Peter's thoughts turned inward as he searched his memory for what had happened fourteen years ago that could be of significance to her. "Yes, and I still do that now. I review pre-sentence reports and tell the court how a particular child might respond in particular settings."

"And you make rebellious kids look more attractive and manageable than the rest of the world sees them."

"I can't help that," Peter answered testily. He knew she was leading somewhere, but he wasn't yet sure where. "I sincerely find rebellious kids more attractive than the rest of the world does."

"I know," she concluded. She felt more depressed than triumphant at her knowledge of his point of view. "Sometimes you accepted kids into your home who had just been released from training school. And sometimes the court would place a juvenile in your home to serve his sentence so that he didn't have to go to training school."

"Kara, I feel I'm getting the third degree here for some reason. What is it? Let's get it out in the open where we can deal with it."

Kara felt a wave of anger surge through her veins, but she maintained a tight rein on her expression. Thoughts of Joey always touched her so deeply that she had to exercise all her self-control to maintain a level head. "I knew one of those rebellious boys you accepted into your home and gave a good prognosis for," Kara informed him quietly. "He was my brother, Joey Ridgeway."

"I knew it," Peter exhaled. "I knew I recognized that name. I guess over the years I've stifled the memory."

"Joey was convicted on a drug charge and for breaking-and-entering," Kara answered. "You convinced the judge to let him serve his sentence in your group home. The judge allowed it. Joey died there two weeks later of a drug overdose."

The memory flooded back into Peter's mind as Kara spoke. Joey Ridgeway had been an unremarkable case. His notoriety had come later, after his death. No one knew if his overdose had been accidental or deliberate. It was never even discovered where he'd got the drugs or how long he'd been hoarding them. For a long time after that, Peter had struggled with himself, certain he should have noticed something was wrong. He should have been able to help the boy, he'd told himself, and he'd never really accepted that there was nothing he could have done.

"His death must have been agonizing for you," Peter finally said.

He himself was reeling under the impact of memories he had long tried to suppress. He remembered Joey well. A lot better than he wished he did. He was responsible for Joey's death, he told himself. Joey had been in his care.

He was not surprised by the return of Joey Ridgeway's ghost into his life. The ghost had never truly disappeared.

He became aware that Kara was speaking. "Nothing else in my life has affected me so deeply," she was saying. "It's the whole reason I'm a Youth Bureau cop. My whole life has been fashioned by the loss of my brother.

"Oddly enough," Kara said, "before Joey's death I'd decided on a career very much like yours. I wanted to be a counsellor. It was quite popular back then to believe that you could make a difference in a person's life by listening to his problems and encouraging him to strive for something better."

"There's a lot of bitterness in your voice, Kara," Peter said. "I take it your bitterness is directed toward me."

"Counsellors and social workers didn't help Joey. A firm hand would have done him more good."

Yes, she held Peter responsible. But she relented for a moment when she saw how downcast he looked. "Maybe it would have been better if I hadn't come today to explain myself," she said.

Peter had always known he would have to answer some day for Joey Ridgeway's death. But he had no explanations. An apology would fall pitifully short of the mark. "It's always better when people understand each other," he said finally, because he owed her some kind of response. "Even if it doesn't help, it's still better to know."

Kara said nothing. Evening shadows darkened the room from pale to deep blue. Peter started to say a hundred things, but no words came out.

"Tell me," he managed at last. "How did your parents handle all this? You haven't mentioned them."

Kara stiffened. She didn't like to talk about her parents. "They were very distressed, of course, but they didn't seem to realize that Joey's being arrested had anything to do with their lax control over him."

"Did you ever mention your disagreement with how they were handling him?"

Kara suddenly felt very tired. What was the use of talking?

"I discussed it with my mother several times," she said wearily. "I remember saying that I didn't think Joey was as innocent as he claimed. Maybe the world was against him, but I'd seen things he'd done to turn the world against him. I remember one day when I was about eleven—so Joey would have been thirteen—he sneaked into my room and stole money from my dresser. I knew he'd done it, and I knew Joey's favorite hiding places, so when he was having his bath, I searched his room and found my money.

"I confronted both my mother and Joey with what I'd found. Joey apologized and tried to look contrite, but I knew he didn't feel truly sorry. Maybe he was already into drugs by then—I don't know. Anyway, my mother told me that no harm had been done because what was mine had been returned. After all, she pointed out, Joey had said he was sorry. The fact that Joey had stolen something was hardly noticed. My mother seemed sure Joey wouldn't steal anymore. I wasn't, but I kept quiet. I shouldn't have."

Kara felt suddenly self-conscious. She'd exposed herself more than she'd intended. Peter had a way of eliciting her deepest and most personal thoughts. What was it? His attentive listening? His poignant questions? Or was it her secret wish for him to truly understand who she was?

"Kara, what makes you think that I handle kids the same way your parents did?"

Kara shook her head, and Peter wasn't sure she'd heard his question. "I had so much faith in you back then," she whispered hoarsely. "I remember how you looked that day you took the stand during his trial. I saw you as the cavalry riding in at the last minute to save the day. We already knew that the verdict was guilty. What sentence he would receive was the all-important question on our minds. You were young and dynamic, with a fire in your belly about helping kids like Joey. You made it sound so simple, as if Joey really could straighten his life out, even after all that had happened. When the judge said he could go to Maple Glen I thought we were home free. That was the silly hope of a young girl.

"The reality of life is that you eventually pay your dues. Joey's dues were a long time in coming, but he paid them all at once. People like you and my parents perpetuate the illusion that somehow it won't happen. You have too much hope. If kids knew they would undoubtedly pay for their actions, they'd be a lot more responsible.''

Kara set her wineglass safely down on the carpet, and Peter noticed her hands were shaking and her brown eyes were muddied with quiet tears. He ached to take her in his arms and soothe her. Now that he understood the hurt that Kara was hiding, Peter found that all her rough edges melted before his eyes. He could see through to a warm compassionate soul trying to cope with tragedy the best she could. But to Peter, the real tragedy was that she seemed to carry the full burden of responsibility for a death she couldn't have prevented.

"Do you have a picture of him?" Peter asked. "Your brother," he prompted when she didn't respond, "do you carry a picture of him?"

Obediently Kara reached for her purse and flipped through her wallet until she found the dog-eared photo of Joey that she'd studied and cried over a thousand times. She couldn't remember when she'd let anyone else see Joey's photo and felt strange about letting Peter see it now.

Peter shuffled closer beside her to look over her shoulder at Joey's beaming face. She could feel the warmth of his body close to hers and feel his breath gently kiss her cheek as he spoke. "Those curls are quite a family trait, aren't they?"

Joey was fourteen, and sitting on his bike. He'd been in trouble even then, but nobody had known it yet. Kara sat on a nearby step—an adoring twelve-year-old watching her big brother, who was obviously in the midst of showing off for her, or for the camera. His face revealed none of the trouble he was in, and her own face revealed no worry. Their apparent innocence was why she liked the picture.

Peter's words blew gently against her cheek. "Your instincts are worth trusting, Kara. I think you've had them buried too long. I've always blamed myself as much as you blame me, Kara. But it's possible no one is to blame, that even if we had all given him what he needed, the same fate could have awaited him."

Kara sucked in her breath. She'd never considered that possibility. She'd never doubted the right help would have worked.

"I think you blame yourself too much," Peter went on, "and that you buried your instincts because you don't trust yourself."

"I'm following my instincts as a cop."

"Are you?"

"Of course I am. Just what makes you think I'm not?"

"I watched you with Craig. He's a kid who needs more than just someone to make sure he's not breaking the law. He needs a friend, a parent, a confidante, a devil's advocate. Can you be all those things to him?"

"Of course not. I'm a police officer. It wouldn't be appropriate."

"Exactly. On the one hand you like to think you care so much and go beyond the call of duty because you check out group homes on your own initiative.

But you only go so far. Your role as a cop tells you what's right and wrong, and that shields you from having to operate on your gut instincts. As a cop, you can't show all the sides, all the strengths and sensitivities of Kara Ridgeway.''

"One job can't allow you to show all sides of yourself.''

"This one would.''

Kara blinked. "What? Your job?''

"Yes, my job. If you had stuck with your original decision to go into counselling, the career choice you made on gut instinct, you wouldn't have restricted yourself. I saw the gift you have for this kind of work the day I met you.''

"Thank you very much, Mr. Aiken. I'm sure your job is terribly important to the world. But I think even I manage to make some small contribution as a police officer.''

"I mean what I say as a compliment, not an insult, Kara. You do your police work well. I just think you're capable of doing more.''

Kara's mouth dropped open, but as she was about to give him a piece of her mind, their attention was abruptly distracted by the boat house shifting beneath them. Muffled laughter drifted up from beneath the floorboards.

"Looks like we've got company,'' Peter whispered.

"Were you expecting anyone?'' Kara returned, wide-eyed.

"I'll bet your police buddies have picked up via E.S.P. that I was trying to lure away their prized performer. Now they're knocking the stilts out from under my boat house to shut me up. You cops are a ruthless lot.''

Kara spontaneously returned his smile, amused by his carefree silliness. She followed him out the door and down the wooden staircase.

Dusk had stretched long shadows over the river, but Kara could still make out the small wooden rowboat lodged inside the boat house. The three dark figures on board were laughing and paddling furiously, trying to escape into the free flowing river.

"Mr. Aiken," a young male voice exclaimed as Peter switched on the overhead light.

"Richard," Peter returned with a chuckle. "What an odd time for you to be dropping in."

Three good-looking twenty-year-old faces stared with silent open mouths. Their faces bore the flush of afternoon partying.

"Actually, sir, we're sort of here by accident," Richard explained valiantly as his two companions shook with the kind of laughter that erupts in situations where one shouldn't laugh at all.

Peter didn't miss a beat. "Well, it's quite marvelous that you happened along at this particular time. Constable Ridgeway and I were just discussing her latest crusade against alcohol consumption. You might have seen her on television. She's famous around these parts for the number of busts she makes. I'll tell you she's got a nose for it—that's the only way to describe it. If there's a party going on in the city, Officer Ridgeway is inevitably parked just down the road—or down the river—waiting for festivities to break up.

Impaired driving is, of course, a boating offense as well as a motoring offense."

Three concerned faces scrutinized Kara as they rocked gently in their boat. They couldn't remember seeing her on television and didn't know if rowing under the influence was an offense, but who could be sure?

Peter continued relentlessly. "Anyway, Officer Ridgeway was just demonstrating her new breathalyzer machine. She's come to ask for permission to set up her spot checks here on my property. She's a cagey one all right. She figures she can nab people who drive vehicles on the water, as well as those who drive along the road to the house. Don't you think that's an excellent idea, considering the irresponsible way some people treat alcohol?"

The three heads nodded at his insistent pause.

"By the way, officer," Peter said, swinging around to face her. "I forgot to tell you that Richard is a university student who does volunteer work for Aiken House." Peter turned back to the group and lowered his voice to a conspiratorial tone. "The good officer is very concerned about the moral fiber of people who have any contact with young offenders. She feels that everyone who has an influence on troubled youth should have impeccable moral character. After all, she has to bust the kids when they're doing something wrong. She'd feel very depressed if she sent them here and we turned them back out on the street with more problems than they had when they came in."

"I'm no bleeding heart social worker," Kara said, getting into the spirit of Peter's charade. "And I feel no obligation to 'touch base' or 'know where you're coming from' or wear corduroy jeans, for that matter.''

"You see?" Peter shrugged with resignation. "It's also her belief that being easy on kids virtually produces criminals."

"That's why," Kara continued, "I'm concerned about Aiken House. I think the place needs a more military atmosphere."

"I've assured the officer that the staff and volunteers at Aiken House are too responsible to produce drunks and drug abusers," Peter went on. "But she's pretty thick-skinned about the subject, a real hard-nosed type. Richard, can you think of anything I've missed that might help convince her?"

Richard cleared his throat before addressing himself seriously to the matter. "I think it's important to remember," he noted professorially, "that any kid can get into a little trouble and still be quite normal."

"Thank you, Richard," Peter said solemnly, and Kara had to step back into the shadows to control her threatening laughter. "But you see, Richard," Peter continued, "I think Constable Ridgeway is one of those rare specimens who never did anything wrong while she was growing up. I think we'll need to convince her about Aiken House in another way. I have an idea. Let's get the breathalyzer machine out and you can give us a breath sample to show Constable Ridgeway what kind of moral fiber Aiken House volunteers have. If you do us proud on such an impromptu occasion, I'm sure she'd be impressed."

"That would be pretty impressive," Kara agreed, nodding. "I'll get the machine," she added, then disappeared upstairs to get her purse and turn off the quiche. When she returned to the dock, the boat had been tied up, and the three culprits looked ready to walk the plank.

"I'm afraid we've got some bad news, constable," Peter informed her before she could speak. His sentence caught her by surprise because it was the same one she'd been planning to use to claim the breathalyzer wasn't functioning properly. "Oh?" she said. "What's that?"

"Richard here has a touch of bronchitis, and therefore he won't be able to give a proper breath sample. And his two friends are economic majors who claim to have absolutely no intention of ever having anything to do with group homes or young offenders."

Richard was quick, Kara thought, smiling to herself. University students would be more likely than younger kids to know the loopholes of the breathalyzer machine.

"Richard is absolutely correct," Kara agreed, although if he'd been a motorist she'd pulled over in a legitimate circumstance, she would have tested him anyway. "But in that case, it's important that we get him out of this night air as soon as possible. You should be in bed with bronchitis, Richard."

"Yes, ma'am," Richard agreed, visibly relieved.

As they all walked to the car, Peter established that the party the trio had come from was being given by one of Richard's roommates. A ride home entailed leading the police back to the party, but without running lights, no one could insist on taking the boat now that dusk had fallen.

It was just a short ride to Richard's house. There they found the driveway crowded with parked cars. Music blared out of the open windows.

"This would be a perfect place to set up your spot check," Peter enthused, turning to Kara. "We could just wait here until people start to leave."

Kara finally decided the joke had gone far enough. "Mr. Aiken," she said with authority, "do you know what I just realized?"

"What's that, officer?"

"I didn't turn down the oven. If we stay here any longer, your beautiful quiche will burn to a crisp."

"I completely forgot about the quiche," Peter said, and banged his hand on the steering wheel for emphasis. "I wanted to test some of our other student volunteers. A few of them are friends of yours, aren't they, Richard? They're probably here tonight."

"Yes," Richard agreed, "and I'm sure they'll be disappointed they couldn't have pitched in and done something for the cause of Aiken House. We're very devoted volunteers, Miss Ridgeway, and Aiken House is a very responsible group home. Say, maybe we'll get a chance to do this again sometime!" he added, certain now that he was in the clear.

Peter and Kara laughed once the three young people had scrambled out of the car.

"That was close," Peter commented with a chuckle as the Mercedes shifted into reverse and they backed out of the driveway.

"I have a confession to make," Kara announced.

"Another one? I don't know if I can handle any more."

"I did turn off the quiche."

"I hoped you would," Peter said, and winked. "But tell me, constable," he continued, "what if you'd had a spare breathalyzer in your purse? Would you have done anything differently?"

"You'll never know, will you? Besides, university students are hardly in the age group I think needs protection."

"Still," Peter smiled and looked at her. "I saw a little glimpse of Kara Ridgeway without her cop persona on. It's very attractive."

"My purpose in being a cop is not to look attractive."

"I know that. I just realize all the more that you've got so much more to give than you can give as a cop."

When they arrived back at the boat house, they found the delicate aroma of Peter's quiche had permeated every corner. After taking the dish out of the oven, Peter carefully lifted out a perfectly baked slice and slid it onto her plate, then put one on his.

"I'm really glad you had to bring Craig to the home," he said seriously.

"You like to see me miserable, right?"

"No, for two quite different reasons."

He left Kara to sit in mild suspense as he topped up her wine and served the salad. "To Craig and his future," he toasted as he sat down.

"Can't argue with that," Kara said, flushing under his warm gaze. The dim lighting in the boat house darkened his hair and softened his features, and she felt a strong urge to run her hands along the tops of his ample shoulders and down his well-tanned arms. Clearing her throat, Kara asked, "So, what's your first reason?"

"Well, to start with, I can tell you don't trust me and that you blame me for Joey's death. What's more, you presume our differences will lead to conflict. But I don't think we're at such odds as you think we are. Of course, Joey was your brother, not mine, but I deeply share your sorrow. I think, also, that we actually respect each other's motivations. We both recognize we're genuinely concerned about helping the kids in our care. You just figure I'm misguided. Am I right about that part?"

"Couldn't be righter," she agreed as she tasted another delicious mouthful of quiche. "But don't you think I'm misguided?"

"Not in the same way. When you stick to your instincts, I think you're absolutely on track. It's your head that gets you in trouble."

"So what has this got to do with Craig being at Aiken House?"

"I get the chance to prove something to you," Peter answered with simple confidence. "You blame yourself for things beyond your control. You blame me for things beyond my control. I figure that by the time Craig leaves Aiken House you'll trust both of us much more—not to mention Craig."

Kara was relieved when they eventually walked out into the cool night for Peter to drive her home. The longer she spent in his company, the harder it was for her to remember why her principles were so important, or even which convictions were actually her own. It was hard to maintain her certainty that Peter was responsible for her brother's death.

"I just want to check in at the house," Peter said, as they reached the driveway. "I was expecting a phone call tonight and I want to check the logbook."

Kara opted to wait in the car as he took the porch stairs two at a time. Moments later he returned.

"Did you get your phone call?" Kara asked as he swept into the car with the smell of early autumn around him.

"Yup," he answered as the car came to life. "It was from Craig's parents. They want to come for counselling."

Kara tensed. "They're not the ones who need to be placed in a group home."

"True," Peter agreed with a laugh, seemingly oblivious to her change of mood. "And by the way, while I was in there, I realized that I forgot to tell you the second reason I'm glad you had to bring Craig to me."

"The first was that you'd get a chance to prove yourself."

"And the second is that you'll be around to see it happen."

"Peter, I wouldn't sound so hopeful if I were you. I'm dead set against parent counselling."

# CHAPTER SIX

DELLCREST TRAINING SCHOOL looked to Kara like a high school with bars on the windows. In the three years she'd been with the Youth Bureau, she'd never felt at ease coming here. Yet places like these were a necessary evil, she believed. Inside the front entrance she nodded pleasantly to the guard behind the Plexiglas.

"Who is it today, constable?" The man's voice sounded very distant, coming through the small hole in the glass.

"James Chalmers. He's supposed to be in Unit D."

The guard passed her through the main door, and she nodded her thanks. She passed through several more locked doors, nodding to the guards as they let her through, before she reached the visiting area. When that door was opened, she found a boy of about seventeen, with black hair combed straight back.

"James Chalmers?" she ventured to the kid at the table.

"You must be a cop," he returned with an insincere smile. "Only cops call me James. The name's Jimmy."

Kara pulled out the nearest chair and sat down. "All right, Jimmy. I'm Constable Ridgeway."

"Oh, yeah," he recalled as he leaned his chair back on two legs. "Stan the Man told me you'd be coming." He paused as he studied her. "I hear that lady cops are the meanest cops around because they're out to prove they can hack it. You figure that's true?"

Kara noticed several small amateurish tattoos on his fingers. Jimmy was no stranger to training school. "I figure there's a grain of truth to it," she returned pleasantly. "I don't have much sympathy for punks who are going nowhere. You tell me. Are you one of those kids?"

"Sure thing," he agreed, laughing obnoxiously. "You ought to know that. All Dellcrest kids are going nowhere."

Kara looked around the sterile institutional room. It seemed more imposing than usual. "How long have you been in here?"

"Eight months, why?"

"You must be turning eighteen soon if you were seventeen when the offense occurred."

Jimmy cocked his head suspiciously. "Next month. So?"

Kara crossed her legs and leaned back, emphasizing her nonchalance. She'd come here to test the boy. "There's a possibility your weapons charge could be tried in adult court. It's a serious enough charge to warrant it. Do you know what adult court means?"

"Sure. Correctional center. Adult court, adult jail."

"Doesn't that bother you?"

Jimmy shifted uneasily. "Why should it?"

Kara looked at him curiously. "Don't you have higher hopes for your future, Jimmy? Isn't there something you'd like to work toward? You must know how employers feel about hiring people with records."

"Guys with records get jobs," he returned defensively.

"I know they do, but is pumping gas enough for you? You still have a chance to avoid a record if you cooperate on the weapons charge. At least without a record you'd have the same chance as everyone else to make a good life for yourself. We don't want to get you. A young fellow like you deserves a chance to make it."

Jimmy looked at her with narrowed eyes. "Who are you trying to kid?" he challenged bitterly. "I've never had the same chance as everyone else. My parents busted up when I was three. My mother had to bring up four kids with no help. Other kids had parents and homes and went to school. I'm seventeen and I haven't seen the inside of a classroom for two years."

Kara looked up at the fluorescent lights stretched across the ceiling as she listened to him. Training school really was a depressing place.

"You know," she said, "there's a man in town who runs a group home called Aiken House. You may have heard of him. His name is Peter Aiken."

Jimmy shook his head.

"Both his parents died in a car accident when he was eight. He had no other relatives, not even a sister or brother to hold on to. So he was bounced around from foster home to group home until he grew up. Now there's a guy who had every excuse to do exactly what you're doing. Yet he went to school and devoted his life to helping kids in trouble. I don't get it, Jimmy.

Explain to me why Peter Aiken had all the same strikes against him you do, and still he was able to do something productive with his life.''

Kara felt like a bit of a hypocrite, trotting Peter out as a shining example of success when she disagreed so strenuously with what he did in his group home. But she supposed she could still respect him for what he'd done with his own life without necessarily agreeing with what he did in his job.

Jimmy's lips were taut, his mouth firmly set. His retort smacked of sarcasm. "I don't know, maybe this guy's Superman. I thought you came here to bug me about that weapons charge."

"I came to see if there was any hope of avoiding a record," she corrected him. "Stan has given up. I'm afraid I'm going to have to agree with him if you don't change your mind pretty quickly. If you work with us, maybe we could get you into a group home and back into school. But you have to help yourself, Jimmy, before we can help you. You have to show us you learned what you were sent here to learn."

Jimmy let the front legs of his chair down with a sudden loud scrape. "I don't know what planet you come from, lady. You don't seem to realize what training school does to a person. I learned exactly what I was sent here to learn. I learned that nobody cares. I learned how to commit better crimes. People are thrown in jail to rot, not to learn anything."

Kara sat quietly. She could hear his quick heaving breaths in the silence. "Well," she said at length. "I guess that's that. I won't keep you any longer. It sounds like you have some rotting to do."

Jimmy's laugh was so unexpected that Kara stood motionless somewhere between sitting and breezing out the door.

"You're a hard one to stay mad at," he explained with a smile. "The cops I've met know better than to try so hard. They threaten to stay on my case, but they never come to see me because they're worried about my future. I want to shake your hand, officer."

Kara was startled. She watched him reach for her hand, and she shook with him automatically.

"Listen," Jimmy said, "it was nice of you to think of me, but it's too late. I gave up on myself the first time I came into this place."

Kara blinked. "Surely it's never too late."

"Oh, yes, officer," Jimmy returned, "yes it is."

Kara reminded him that her offer would only stand for a short while longer, then extricated herself from the visiting area as quickly and smoothly as she could.

She tried to imagine Craig in Jimmy's shoes, then quickly chased away the image.

It was crazy, but Kara suddenly felt like talking to Peter. He should have been the last person she'd think of. But she needed to be consoled or reassured that she was helping Craig, because suddenly nowhere seemed safe for him. She started the car quickly and drove the three blocks to a telephone booth. She dialed and listened to the phone ring, battling her impulse to hang up while she still had the chance.

"Aiken House."

She wished his voice didn't sound quite so welcome. "Hi, it's me."

"Kara. You sound upset. You okay?"

"Oh, yeah, I'm fine. I just wanted to see how Craig was doing."

She felt slightly guilty about using Craig as an excuse. She did want to see how Craig was, but to be honest, mostly she just wanted to talk to Peter.

"I guess you haven't received the message I left for you at the station yet," Peter was saying. "I called to tell you that Craig's parents are coming for counselling this afternoon. They'll be here at three-thirty."

Kara groaned. "Thanks. You just made my day."

"It gets better."

"I can't imagine."

"I want you to come, too."

Kara laughed in spite of herself. "You're kidding me, right?"

"Not at all."

Kara leaned back against the glass of the phone booth. Oddly enough, she felt happier.

"Well, Mr. Aiken, I must admit you've got nerve. You don't seem to be at all disturbed by the fact that I don't like parent counselling."

"I don't think you've given it a chance."

"And you always know best, I suppose," she said sarcastically.

"No, Kara. You of all people know I don't always know best. I'm not just asking you to do this for me. It's important to Craig, too. He's asked me specifically to make sure you come."

"It's not fair to bring Craig into this," she said, recognizing the trap he'd set, but fighting to stave off defeat. "You're trying to manipulate me. I'm not going to get involved with this counselling just to make you feel better about it. If something goes wrong because of your decision, you take the responsibility. It's on your head, not mine."

"Kara, I'll make you a deal," he proposed, his voice soft but earnest. "Come to Aiken House now so we can have some time together before Craig's parents arrive. Tell me all the reasons you disapprove of this counselling business. Debate with me, argue with me, then sit in on this afternoon's session—just as an observer. If, after all that, you still vehemently disagree with the process, I'll call the whole thing off."

Kara was astonished. "You'd do that?"

"I wouldn't like it, but, yes, I'd do it. If I'm going to ask you to put yourself on the line and risk something, then I have to be prepared to do the same. I am, of course, banking on your seeing that I'm right once you give the thing a chance."

"But if I don't see the light the way you expect me to?"

"I'll honor my commitment and cancel any further sessions."

Kara's meditative mood deepened. "I don't get it. If you're convinced that counselling is the right way to go, why would you let me influence you?"

"I guess it's because I think there's always more than one way to accomplish something. You're very important to Craig. For all my ideals, I'm a pragmatic man, Kara. I'm willing to barter the counselling to keep you involved with Craig. To be perfectly honest, I want to keep you involved with Aiken House for myself, too."

Did he mean he wanted her involved with him as the owner of a group home or as a man who was attracted to her? She couldn't ask. She wasn't sure which answer would rattle her most.

"I still don't like it," she said. "But I don't see how I can turn down your offer. I'll leave right away."

As Kara drove to Aiken House, she shook her head, wondering at herself. She wouldn't have thought anything could make her go willingly to a counselling session with parents—not that she'd always been so categorically opposed to parent counselling. When she'd first become a cop, she'd encouraged counselling sessions between parents and kids. But she'd found that young offenders blamed everyone but themselves for what they'd done—just as Jimmy up in Dellcrest did. It was his parents' fault. It was the system. He was the victim of circumstances. When you counselled their parents, kids figured you agreed it was the parents' fault. It was the parents who needed counselling, not the kid who'd got himself in trouble.

Yet here she was on her way, and strangely enough it didn't feel as outrageous as she'd thought it would. Both she and Peter held such strong beliefs, so maybe it was natural to allow each other to have some effects on their actions.

As Kara turned the car into the long Aiken House driveway, she realized she had more trouble on her hands than a counselling session. The way Craig was slouched on the porch steps, with his arms folded defiantly, spelled trouble even from this distance. As Kara parked, got out of her car and walked toward him, Craig scrutinized her every step.

"You didn't want to come," he said accusingly. The pain in his voice surprised and disarmed her.

"Are you sitting out here waiting for me?" she asked gently.

"That's right," he retorted with barely concealed outrage. "You weren't even going to come, were you?"

"Well, I considered not coming."

"Why?" he demanded in a voice that sounded more like an anguished wail.

"Because, Craig, I don't approve of counselling sessions with parents. This is something Peter and I disagree on. If I don't think the counselling is going to be good for you, I can hardly come and participate with a clear conscience, now can I?"

Craig stared at the ground as he digested her logic. Kara noticed that he was more dressed up than she'd ever seen him. He'd taken care to smooth his hair and tuck the sides back behind his ears. His shirt was clean and freshly ironed. For the first time, it struck her just how important this session must have been to him.

"You're here, though," he finally noted. "Why'd you change your mind?"

"I'm not sure I have changed my mind, but Peter convinced me to come for one session to see how things went. I still don't like the whole idea. Remember back when I was worried about bringing you to Aiken House? Well things haven't changed much."

Privately, though, now that she'd seen how offended Craig would have been if she'd stayed away, Kara was relieved she hadn't disappointed him.

"It would have been wrong if you hadn't come," Craig was saying. "I've never talked with my parents before—I mean *really* talked. They've been on my back about things, but they never knew how I felt ... I guess I never told them. Anyway, I want to tell them now."

Kara drew in a deep breath. This earnest and serious young man was a side of Craig Taylor she hadn't seen before. Until now she'd never seen anything really matter to him. Just then the front door opened and Peter stepped out onto the porch. "Good to see you," he said. His mauve knit sweater looked rich and warm in the strong light. The color reflected an especially relaxed healthy glow over his face. "Has Craig managed to make you feel guilty yet?"

"He's working on it," Kara said smiling, then lied, "but so far I've been holding my own."

"Good. I figured an experienced cop could protect herself from the emotional onslaught of a fourteen-year-old."

"However," Kara conceded, "he has made some headway. He had the element of surprise on his side. I didn't expect his shirt to be ironed."

Craig laughed and years melted from his face, making him look like the child he really was.

"I thought we could walk down to the boat house and sit on the dock for our discussion," Peter suggested. "I don't suppose there will be many more days warm enough to do that."

Kara nodded her agreement. It was best that they argue things out in private.

On cue, Craig rose and took a few steps toward the house. "You're still going to come this afternoon, though, right?" he said to Kara.

Peter answered for her. "Yes, Craig," he said patiently. "She said she would. Now give her a break. You've got your work to do, and we're going to do ours. No more worrying for now, kiddo. You've got enough on your plate."

Craig accepted an affectionate clap on the back before he disappeared into the house.

Peter trotted down the stairs to her side. "I'm glad you're here," he said intimately, almost breathlessly. Kara picked up his stride as they walked toward the boat house, and Peter dropped a friendly arm over her shoulder. It felt strangely reassuring. "Thanks for coming. It means a lot to Craig and to me, too."

"To tell you the truth," she admitted, "I'm a little mystified as to why it does mean so much to Craig whether or not I'm here. I never would have predicted he'd care so much."

Peter's answer was matter-of-fact. "I imagine Craig's reasons for caring are similar to mine. There's something special about you. You care enough to struggle for the answers that may be hard to see at first. That kind of emotional strength and sincerity attracts people and makes them want you to be involved in their lives."

His words made her blush with pleasure and she had an urge to slip her arm around his waist, but she had to be wary of him.

"If it's true I mean so much to Craig," she ventured, "it makes me feel a bit guilty for not wanting to be here. Thank you for pushing me. I didn't like it at the time, but I appreciate it now.''

"I won't say it was a pleasure," Peter teased. "But you could make it worthwhile by keeping your appreciation in mind as you give me your reasons for not wanting Craig's parents in counselling.''

"I'll try," Kara said with a smirk as they reached the end of the dock. She sat with her feet dangling over the shimmering water and pulled her red and black plaid car coat around her as a block against the cool breeze.

"I'm going to challenge you, you know," he warned.

"I don't doubt that."

"I'm not going to let you make your pronouncements without having to defend them," he said with mock severity.

"I'd have a heart attack from shock if you did anything else."

"Okay, then, I think we're ready."

"Okay, then," Kara agreed, laughing. "Let's say we have this perfectly obedient, perfectly acceptable teenager," she said.

"I hate him already," Peter replied, smiling at her and noting how the sun highlighted the auburn in her brown curls and the delicate spray of freckles across her cheeks. He hadn't noticed the freckles before.

"This is serious."

"I know. So am I. Teenagers shouldn't be that perfectly acceptable."

"You know what I mean," Kara said. "He doesn't break rules as a matter of course at home or school or at the shopping center after school. Even though he's so good, he still has to live in a world that demands adjustments. There will be things he doesn't like, doesn't think are fair, but he adapts. I think the reason the kid is so well adjusted is because he understands one thing. He doesn't have a license to break rules just because the world isn't perfect. But kids who get into trouble don't understand this. They want to blame someone else for their own misfortune, and counselling parents supports that illusion."

"Okay, that's a possibility," Peter conceded. "I can see that some kids might use the parent counselling as an excuse—especially if the idea came from anyone but the kid himself. But it's different with Craig. He wanted the session. It was his idea from the start."

"Even so, Craig might want a session with his parents for the wrong reasons, and the mere fact that the parents are there in the room implies they carry some blame."

Peter lifted his eyes from the water. "Let's take your perfectly normal obedient kid. He probably feels isolated and alienated because that's a part of growing up. It's easy for him to assume no one else knows how he's feeling or that no one else ever felt this way. Now let's take the kid who gets into trouble. He feels this alienation even more because other people *aren't* going through the same thing and he knows it. But the more connected he feels, the more normal he can afford to be. If he can feel his parents understand—even if they don't approve—it can help. And let's face it, the reality here is probably that the parents are partly to blame. That usually is the reality."

"Says who!" Kara protested, letting her frustration show. "Dammit, why can't you just accept what I say?"

Peter snapped his head up, then relaxed and smiled. "I could ask you the same question."

"It drives me crazy," she continued, punctuating her words with animated gestures. "Every time I give you a perfectly good, perfectly logical explanation, you argue with it."

Peter chuckled, and looked at her as if he'd just now seen a side of her he'd never seen before. "And I give you a perfectly logical argument."

"That's what makes you so annoying! I'd love to write you off as a lunatic social worker. But you keep making just enough sense to make it difficult." It was more than that, she knew. She felt good around him, happier and more carefree. She noticed how light reflecting off the river danced softly over his face.

"I'm glad you hang in and struggle with me, Kara. I feel I've got something to prove to you." But Kara was only half listening. She could hear the distinctive gurgling sounds of the river beneath her and the distant chirping of birds. She could feel the light breeze gently tug at her loose curls. She realized that sitting there, arguing with Peter, she felt strangely, deliciously alive, and a little chill rang up her spine.

Peter noticed her shiver. "I didn't mean to wear you down with physical discomfort," he said, standing and offering her his hand. "Come on, we'll head back. You can judge for yourself if the counselling has any redeeming qualities."

"You're still planning to hold to your bargain, are you?"

"Of course. I don't go back on my promises."

"I don't know why I let you get to me," she said, taking his hand.

"It's because you are such a superlative judge of character," he offered as he pulled her to her feet. "Come on, constable. Craig's parents ought to be here any minute. It's time to face the music."

In fact, Craig's parents were waiting in their car. As soon as Peter spotted them, he strode quickly over and extended an invitation for them to look around and feel at home.

To Kara, the Taylors looked remarkably normal and well adjusted despite their inevitable nervousness. Mrs. Taylor looked as if she could be a high-school teacher. Her face was youthful and friendly, yet she carried an air of authority. She'd obviously taken great care to appear respectable, adorning her gray tailored suit with a carefully arranged rose scarf. It suddenly occurred to Kara that it had taken some courage for Mrs. Taylor to come to see her son in a group home, and Kara realized how distressed the woman must be behind her calm facade.

Except for his receding hairline, Mr. Taylor looked very much like an older version of his son. He seemed very shy and uncomfortable. Kara had forgotten what an ordeal counselling sessions were for parents. It comforted her to think she had the power to spare these poor people from further sessions.

Craig was waiting for them in the living room. He hugged his mother and shook hands somberly with his father. Meanwhile, Peter stoked a fire that already burned in the grate. The dancing flames seemed to chase both physical and emotional chill from the room, and Kara wondered fleetingly how much a homey fire might account for any positive outcome from this kind of meeting.

"I think we're ready now," Peter announced as he got up from his crouched position in front of the fire and brushed off his jeans. He pulled in a chair to complete their circle of seats and added, "As ready as we'll ever be anyway."

Kara chuckled with the rest, but noticed how Peter's comment had somehow helped to dissipate the tension.

"I expect," Peter continued, "that as the kids begin to arrive home from school we might get a few interruptions. The kids know that when the door is closed, the room is being used for something more important than watching T.V. But Stevie, our ten-year-old, likes to see for himself what's so interesting. And he's likely to bring in Ketchup, our dog, who needs to extend a personal hello to everyone in the room. Then there are the older kids who get halfway across the room before they clue in to the fact that the door is closed and the T.V. isn't on.

"Now, I figure the best way to start is for each of us to say what we'd like to accomplish today. Craig, since you asked for this meeting, I think we should start with you."

At least Peter was placing the responsibility for this meeting squarely in Craig's lap, Kara thought.

"I think the most important thing for me," Craig said haltingly, "the thing I want more than anything, is to be trusted. Since I've been here at Aiken House, I've figured out that much. What I want to find out today is why my parents never did trust me."

Kara was a bit taken aback. She hadn't expected quite so mature or serious an answer.

Peter managed to smooth the awkwardness that greeted Craig's reply by asking Mr. Taylor what his hopes were for today.

The older man readjusted his tie nervously. "Maybe we've been too strict," he allowed quietly, "but that was only because we cared so much. I'm here today to get my son back. That's all that matters."

From the look of surprise on Craig's face, Kara could tell that Mr. Taylor had spoken more emotionally than was normal for him. Mrs. Taylor's cheeks betrayed the beginning of some quiet tears, and Kara found herself leaning forward in her seat. She wanted to jump in and reassure Mr. Taylor that things could have been much worse. At least a young person knew his parents cared when they were strict. But she noticed Peter's eyes on her. His eyebrows were slightly arched, as if asking her a silent question or making a silent statement.

Kara felt suddenly angered. Peter looked self-satisfied. But Mr. Taylor was feeling unnecessarily guilty, and this was exactly her beef with parent counselling. She wasn't going to give him the satisfaction of disrupting his session, but, as far as she was concerned, she already had her rationale for calling off any more parent counselling. Calmly, she leaned back until she could feel her shoulder blades touch the back of the couch. She answered his quizzical stare by crossing her eyes.

Peter squelched a smile. "Mrs. Taylor," he invited. "Do you have anything to add?" Mrs. Taylor had quickly regained her air of authority, and the tears were gone.

"Yes, Mr. Aiken, I do want to add something. I would like to explain a little bit about what Craig was like as a little boy and why we became so strict. It's not answering your question directly, I suppose, but I still think it might help."

"Sounds good to me," Peter said, nodding for her to continue.

"Craig has become a very private boy in the past few years," Mrs. Taylor said. "Perhaps that's perfectly normal—you would know better than us, Mr. Aiken—but it frightened us. We never knew where he was going, and he wouldn't tell us when we asked.

"You see, when Craig was five or six, I knew everything he thought, even everything he dreamed. At that age he wanted me to know. But over the years he began to keep things from me, little insignificant things, but I still felt concerned that he didn't want me to know. I'd find out from teachers or other parents that he had a new friend or what his favorite stories were. I thought it was a secretive phase he'd grow out of, but he never did."

"I always thought you were suspicious about me doing things I wasn't doing," Craig interjected. "I had the feeling you expected me to be doing something terribly wrong."

"We didn't want to mistrust you, Craig," Mrs. Taylor said. "And maybe we made a big mistake by trying to keep such close tabs on you. Perhaps we let our fears get the better of us."

When Mrs. Taylor's voice wavered, her husband jumped in to help. "There's more to it than that," he said gravely. "We were suspicious, son, but it didn't have anything directly to do with you. It had more to do with me. When I was your age, I wanted very much to fit in with a group of older boys at my school. The price a kid had to pay to stay in that group, however, was steep. You had to constantly prove your loyalty. I proved myself a few times by doing things I'm too ashamed to admit. The crunch came when several of us got into stealing cars. I was the only one in the group who was so naive that I confessed when the police questioned me. I spent a year in reform school for it. We didn't call them training schools back then."

"Reform school!" Craig repeated, dumbstruck. "You?"

Mr. Taylor answered slowly. "Yes, Craig, and I would never want my son to live what I had to go through during that year. It makes you grow up too fast. So, we watched you closely—maybe too closely, like your mother said. We wanted to be able to help at the first sign of your getting into trouble and let you know that kids who dare you to do things you shouldn't do aren't interested in your friendship."

Kara could sense a thousand questions forming in Craig's mind. Suddenly a whole new side of his father had sprung to life, a side he'd never so much as glimpsed before. But for now all he could do was sit silently in stunned amazement.

She, too, felt stunned. Craig and his family didn't fit the mold of the families she usually worked with. They hadn't been too easy on Craig, yet Craig had still got into trouble. Ordinarily she could have dismissed the implications by chalking up the Taylor family as an exception. But there was more to it than that. If she hadn't become involved with Peter, she never would have recognized the Taylors as exceptions. How many other families over the years had been "exceptions"? An uncomfortable feeling enveloped her.

Kara only half listened to the ensuing discussion. Craig and his parents were excited, hopeful that their new perspective would help them out of their problems. They had avoided talking for so long, and now, as if by magic, they suddenly wanted to learn everything there was to know about each other.

Peter called back everyone's attention. "Craig, you seem very relieved. Even happy. Tell us why."

Craig clasped one hand in the other, and let them hang between his knees as he collected his thoughts. "I dunno," he answered characteristically. "I guess I feel like I kind of understand what went wrong now."

Peter's face was serious. "Maybe you realize that a lot of what happened wasn't your fault," he suggested.

*What!* thought Kara. She wanted to throttle Peter! He couldn't have planted his foot more squarely into his mouth.

"No, Peter. That's not right at all," Craig protested. "Maybe I'm even more to blame than I thought. There was a reason my parents were so worried. But I never bothered to even try to find out what it was. I never even thought that there might be a decent reason.''

"Good point," Peter said easily, accepting the correction. Then as they all heard the front door banging closed, he added, "I can hear the thunder of big and little feet arriving home already. I think it would be best to call it quits for today before it gets called for us. Is it safe to say that we all accomplished what we wanted to today?"

To Kara, the murmurs of agreement felt like accusations. She hadn't wanted this session, but if it hadn't happened, how many more years would have gone by before Craig and his parents had understood each other? This wasn't what was supposed to have happened. She had thought it would be other people's ideas that would be shaken, not hers.

Even before Peter had escorted the Taylors to the end of the hallway, Kara felt Craig's perceptive eyes on her.

"So?" he said hoarsely, then cleared his throat.

"So what?" she returned, thinking what a coward she was, but the last thing she wanted was to be pressed for her opinion. She wasn't sure what she thought anymore.

"So what do you think?" he insisted.

Kara finally met his intent stare, and took in a face that looked younger and more trusting than before.

"You tell me how you feel first. I think that's more important."

"Well, it's weird," he replied thoughtfully. "I always figured my parents didn't trust me because there was something wrong with me. I even went and did a lot of things they accused me of just because they'd suspected me. The way I figured it, I had nothing to lose if everybody thought I'd done these things already."

She supposed that was a reasonable reaction. "So what now?" she asked gently.

"I guess I have some decisions to make."

"Like what?"

"I dunno, like what I want my life to be, I guess. Up until today I had good excuses for doing what I was doing. But those are gone. From now on, whatever I do will just be because I want to do it."

Kara's mouth felt parched. She craved a glass of water.

"So what about you?" Craig asked. "Was this the big waste of time you thought it would be?"

"I wouldn't call it a waste of time, no."

"Then where to from here?"

Kara smiled. "I guess I also have some decisions to make, Craig. My excuses seem to be disappearing on me, too."

"You mean your brother, don't you?" he guessed intuitively.

"Yeah," she said quietly, nodding. She could hear Peter's footsteps down the hall. "I've got some thinking to do about my brother."

## · *CHAPTER SEVEN*

KARA HAD HOPED the familiar bustle of the police station would help her regain her bearings. Maybe parent counselling sessions weren't always "the big waste of time" she'd thought they were, but that revelation wasn't the end of the world, of her world—or was it?

All the activity in the station was familiar to her, yet suddenly she felt as if she was an intruder, as if she was out of place. What on earth was happening to her?

She spotted Stan hunched over his desk, deep in concentration, and sighed with relief. She needed a friend right now. Kara flopped herself down in her chair and watched him for a few moments. Finally she caught his attention, and he glanced up from his paperwork.

"Hi," he said with an absent smile, still partially distracted by his work.

"Hi," she returned. "Have you had your afternoon coffee yet?"

"Yeah," he answered adding a final line to his report. "Kara, remember that kid who broke into the grocery store at three in the morning last year?"

"The one who said he did it because he got the munchies?"

"That's the one. You did a 'failing to appear' on him last week when he didn't show up for court."

"He'd be hard to forget. He was a real card, destined for big trouble, I'm sure."

"Well the provincial police caught him. He was trying to hitchhike to the West Coast and got as far as Wabigoon, a small town just outside of Dryden on the Trans-Canada Highway. He broke into a gas station there and was eating his fourth bag of potato chips when the owners arrived. They phoned the provincial police, who checked and found out we had a warrant out on him. They're shipping him back tomorrow."

Kara laughed. Sometimes you had to have a sense of humor in this job, she thought. Then she said, "I met your Jimmy Chalmers today."

Stan set down his pen and looked up with interest. "Great. Thanks for going so soon. What did you think?"

Kara twirled a pencil absently on the desk in front of her. "I don't think you missed anything, if that's what you're worried about. He's a hard nut to crack, all right."

Stan looked disappointed. "So you don't think his chances for cooperating are very good."

"Pretty slim. If he doesn't change his mind by the next time you talk to him, I'd say go ahead and charge him."

"It's too bad," Stan sighed. "I thought he might have enough smarts to see he was being a hero for nothing. Anyway, thanks for trying. You're right. I'll start getting the paperwork together."

Kara felt lost when Stan put his head back down and poured over his report. "Stan," she blurted suddenly. "Can I buy you a beer after work?"

Instantly his face registered understanding, and his oversized mustache couldn't conceal the concern that lined his features.

"I'll just call Sandy and tell her I'll be late."

Kara nodded and quickly fished out an unfinished "breach of probation" report from her desk. Stan's unquestioning agreement touched her to the point that her eyes started manufacturing those damnable tears.

*Smarten up, Constable Ridgeway,* she ordered herself.

MULRONEY'S WAS A LOCAL BAR owned by Michael Mulroney, an ex-cop. Located two blocks from the police station, it was the undisputed hangout of the police crowd. Pine furniture and green walls decorated with pictures of famous crooks gave the place a casual, humorous atmosphere. The music was loud enough to allow a private conversation at each table.

When she and Stan arrived, Kara ordered hot chicken wings and nachos slathered with jalapeno peppers and cheddar cheese. She promised Stan that the finger food would hold him over until suppertime. As they munched their food and sipped frothy beer from their mugs, they enjoyed the surroundings much as they usually would. There were other fellow officers in for an after work brew who inevitably nodded a greeting or stopped by for a chat. There was much laughter and shoptalk.

It wasn't until they'd got well settled that Kara realized her conversation with Stan had begun to wane. The silence quickly grew oppressive. Suddenly Kara realized she didn't know what she wanted to say. She needed some kind of reassurance but wasn't quite sure about what. The counselling session at Aiken House had bothered her, she knew. She hadn't counted on having to change ideas she'd had for such a long time and supposed she needed Stan to reassure her those ideas weren't wrong.

She wasn't certain of exactly what had got to her. It could have been Peter or Craig or her attachment to Aiken House. Her emotions were too jumbled to sort out. She tottered on the brink of telling Stan about her feelings for Peter.

Stan's expectant face was pressuring her to talk. She'd invited him out to talk. She couldn't very well clam up on him now, could she? Finally she flung herself blindly into the conversation. "Stan, do you think I'm a good cop?"

Stan took a long sip of his beer, and Kara watched as he expertly avoided getting froth on his mustache.

"You asked me out for a beer to ask me this?" he said flatly.

"Not just to ask that. But that's part of the bigger picture."

Stan shook his head. "It's a ridiculous question. We both know you're a good cop."

"Okay, then let me put it this way, do you think I *like* being a cop?"

Stan opened his mouth and promptly closed it again. "Now that, my dear constable, is a different story," he admitted quietly. He regarded her with a suspicious eye. "What prompted all this soul searching, Kara?"

Kara gripped her mug with both hands. She was surprised that he hadn't dismissed the entire topic of conversation. "I'll tell you in a minute, but answer my question first," she insisted.

"Well," he began thoughtfully, "I've told you before that I've never met another cop who lives this job twenty-four hours a day like you do. Sometimes I get the feeling you're looking for something more in your work than the rest of us. It's as if you believe you really can make a big difference with these kids, as if you want to go beyond being a cop."

"Is there anything wrong with that?" she charged, then winced at her own defensiveness.

"Nothing at all wrong with that," Stan was saying. "And I don't know of anyone who's complaining. You do your job and then a whole lot more on top of it—which brings us to this afternoon. Does any of this have to do with your trip to Aiken House?"

She inhaled deeply, then sighed. "Yes."

"So what's the problem?"

Kara traced a small circle in the condensation that had formed on the side of her mug. "Stan, have you ever really needed to believe in something? Needed to believe in it so badly that you're too frightened to even acknowledge that there's any other way of thinking?"

Stan nodded thoughtfully. "I think you're in good company on that one, Kara. Only most people don't admit the part about being scared, either to themselves or others.''

''The really scary part comes,'' said Kara, ''when you do take a look at other ways of thinking and you find they make some sense!''

Stan laughed and looked at her with the affection of an older brother. ''Well,'' he said kindly, ''a couple things that're happening here. First, you could simply be learning something new. Or maybe you've grown confident enough in your own views to be open-minded about viewpoints you don't agree with. Most ways of thinking have some merit. Let's put it this way. If you wind up changing your mind about what you believe, it's probably because you've found something better.''

The way Stan put it, she thought it sounded as if maybe she wasn't unraveling at the seams, but was actually growing stronger. He was a very special friend, she realized for the umpteenth time. ''Sometimes you're pretty smart, for a cop,'' she said, smiling in gratitude.

''And you're a wiseacre,'' he replied pleasantly.

Kara and Stan chatted for a while longer. Then Stan reached around to the back of his chair for his coat. ''If you don't mind, I have a home I'd like to get back to. You're welcome to come, too, of course. We always have room for our favorite aunt at the supper table.''

Fatigue washed over Kara like a tidal wave. ''No, Stan, but thanks. I'm exhausted. I want to say hi to my plants, give my poor aching muscles a hot bath, then go to bed.''

Outside, they found it was already dark, and it was cold. The windows of Kara's car had frosted over and it took the entire ride home for the frost to finally clear. Even with perfectly clear windows, however, she still didn't notice the pale yellow Mercedes sitting in her parking lot. It was when she walked toward her house that she realized she had company.

"Aren't you cold out here?" she asked the dark form seated on her veranda steps.

Peter waited for her to come to a stop in front of him. "Yes," he answered.

"Then why are you doing it?"

"Because we had a deal." And he added to himself, because he knew her well enough to know she'd only have left Aiken House as abruptly as she had if something was bothering her.

"But I came to your session," Kara said. "You can't say I didn't keep my end of the bargain."

"But we're not finished yet, Kara. We still need to talk and decide what to do next. I'm not going to let you run away."

Kara sighed and dropped her shoulders in resignation. "You know, Peter Aiken, for all your redeeming qualities, you can still make yourself quite an effective pain in the butt. If you're going to insist on this, you might as well come in."

Kara thought she heard him chuckle as she brushed past him and unlocked her front door. He followed her through to the living room and sat on the couch while she busied herself in the kitchen.

"I don't know about you but I'm starved," she called out from behind the refrigerator door. She'd let

Stan eat most of the appetizers at Mulroney's because then she hadn't had much of an appetite. "I'm offering an omelette. Is that okay with you?"

"Sounds great."

"Want wine?"

"No thanks."

Kara pulled the bottle out of the refrigerator anyway. The beer with Stan had relaxed her somewhat, but a glass of wine still attracted her. If Peter was going to badger her with questions, at least she could dull the agony of it. "Hope you don't mind if I do."

"Of course not."

Several minutes later, Peter watched from the kitchen doorway as she slid two golden omelettes onto plates. The wineglass on the counter beside her already needed a refill. "Looks great," he said as she added rice and salad to their plates. "Can I get you a refill?"

"Sure," Kara said nonchalantly, breezing by him on her way to the table. "Thanks."

As she settled into a chair and Peter sat down across from her, she was struck by how natural the scene felt, she couldn't help but notice that the mauve of his sweater looked different in the dim light, becoming a deep subdued color that matched his mood. Gone was the pressing manner she'd sensed outside. Now he seemed to be patiently waiting for her to say something. The thought occurred to her fleetingly that she could try to outwait him. But she had the feeling she'd lose. Besides, the wine had given her the bravado she needed to deal with whatever Peter threw at her. "So," she began bluntly, "let's get this over with. What is it you want to know?"

Peter placed his knife and fork down on his plate. "Tell me how you felt this afternoon," he suggested gently.

Kara felt seduced by his caring voice, but his words bothered her. "It's not how I felt that's important. It's what I thought. We don't have to make everyone feel good. We're just supposed to make the right decisions."

Peter saw that her objection was just a shade too strenuous, and he found her strangely attractive at this moment—confused, yet valiantly pressing on. She was trying very hard to be harsh, but the warm lighting overhead brushed highlights of soft amber over her face and hair. He'd never seen her look more beautiful.

"I guess that's true," Peter agreed, managing to get his mind back on their discussion. "But I'm still interested in how you felt."

Kara set her wineglass down heavily in protest. "Feel, feel, feel," she complained. "Why do I have to feel all the time?" When Peter didn't answer, she sighed, realizing he wasn't going to retract his question. "I guess I felt surprised when Mr. Taylor confessed that he had a record. I don't know. How did you feel?"

"I was surprised, too," he agreed. "But at the same time I felt encouraged for Craig's sake. He seemed to be comforted by the news that his own father had made some mistakes."

"It seems ridiculous to talk so much about feelings."

"Feelings have a lot to do with making the right decisions. How do you think Craig feels after what happened today?"

Kara took another sip of her wine and shrugged. "He seemed to feel closer to his parents by the end. But who knows if that will translate into better behavior."

"Do you think it's going to make him act worse?"

Kara felt her chair subtly transform into an interrogation seat. The soft light of the overhead lamp seemed like a bright bare bulb dangling on a cord. "It might." Abruptly getting out of her chair, she moved to a more comfortable seat on the sofa. "Look, Peter," she said heatedly, "what is it you want from me? Your counselling session went better than I expected. Fine. That doesn't mean that another time it couldn't do more harm than good."

Peter stood up and followed her to the couch. "But we're not talking about another time. We're talking about now, and Craig and his parents. You're in the driver's seat, Kara. You tell me if you want another session scheduled or not."

She felt cornered. He wasn't going to let her dismiss what happened with the Taylors as an exception and he wasn't going to let the sessions quietly continue without her eating her words. He'd told her he had something to prove to her and was hell-bent on doing it.

She sighed dramatically. "All right, you want your pound of flesh, so I'll give it to you. I can't deny the session this afternoon was useful. It would be spiteful and irresponsible of me to make you cancel further sessions. Go ahead and schedule another one. You have my support.''

A smile crept over his lips.

''What's so funny?'' she asked. ''Gloating?''

''Not at all. I was thinking that it's very big of you to make such an unequivocal admission.''

Kara folded her arms over her chest and squelched a smile of her own. ''What can I say, it's just the kind of cop I am.''

Peter's smile faded, his face turning sincere. ''I have a lot of respect for you, Kara. All kidding aside.''

They sat quietly for several long minutes. At first the silence was companionable. Then it seemed to go on for too long. At last Kara shifted uncomfortably in her seat. ''I suppose this means that if we're not arguing about some deep philosophical difference, we have nothing to say to each other.''

Peter turned to face her and hiked his foot up to rest on the other knee. ''Is that what it means?''

''Is there anything else you can do besides talk?''

''Have you got any suggestions?'' he asked with a glint in his eye.

''Do you play any card games?'' she asked dryly.

''Card games?''

''Like bridge or gin rummy?''

''Let's see. The older kids play thirty-one. If Stevie's playing, they play fish.''

''Thirty-one and fish?''

''I hate playing cards.''

"No wonder, if those are the only games you know. You should learn a grown-up game."

"Want to teach me one?"

"If you're interested in learning."

"I always thought of cards as a 'make-work' project—"

"I can't *believe* how incompatible we are."

"However, I'm willing to be open-minded and learn something new."

"Progress. All right. I'll teach you honeymoon bridge."

"Honeymoon bridge?"

Kara retrieved two decks of cards from the bookcase. "It just means bridge for two players instead of four."

"Pretty boring honeymoon if you have to resort to playing cards."

"I'm going to change your mind about that. Come on, we need to sit at a table."

"Yes, ma'am."

As usually happened when Kara played cards, the worries of the world slipped into the background. All that mattered was the game, and that relaxed her to the point of no longer being tired.

Peter learned the game quickly, and his distaste for card playing became their standing joke for the evening. As they played they talked about nothing of importance, yet Kara felt they were learning more about each other than they did while debating child-rearing strategies. They compared how they did the laundry and where they washed their cars. They laughed about all the little sayings bridge players have, such as "getting the boys off the street" and "go big or go home" and "it's a game not a science."

It was after midnight when Kara finally announced that she could no longer keep her eyes open and uncrossed at the same time.

"I should go and let you get some sleep," Peter said, responding to her cue.

"I usually have some hot chocolate before I turn in anyway. Can I offer you some?"

"I'd like that," Peter said eagerly. Leaving was the last thing in the world he wanted to do.

Kara prepared the hot chocolate and set it down on the coffee table. She sat beside Peter on the couch, noting that the silences between them didn't make her uncomfortable anymore.

"Well, constable," he said, "you succeeded in changing my mind about cards. I'm willing to make a major exception for the game of bridge. I can even see why people form clubs to play it."

Kara's chuckle was warm. "You don't have to become a fanatic about it."

"No, really. It's definitely more compelling than fish."

Kara rested her head back against the couch and turned toward Peter. The dim lamp was behind him, making him a hazy silhouette. Even with his face in shadow, though, she could tell he was about to kiss her. She could hear his soft breathing, feel the tension in his arms as he reached around her to draw her closer.

Kara lifted her face almost imperceptibly, and his mouth settled on hers.

She parted her lips for him and their kiss deepened as she slipped her arms around his waist, returning his embrace. They kissed long and leisurely, gently and tenderly. She lay her head on his shoulder and he stroked her curls as if it was something he'd been waiting to do all evening. They stayed like that for a long time, drinking in the pleasure of just holding each other. Slowly, enveloped in the warm shelter of Peter's arms, Kara descended into a deep restful sleep.

It seemed like only moments later that a voice reached across a long distance to her. "Kara," it whispered softly but insistently. "Kara, are you awake?"

Groggily she pushed herself up to a sitting position, and when her eyes focused she saw that Peter was massaging his arm as if he doubted life would ever return to it.

"I fell asleep."

"Uh-huh," Peter agreed with a smile. "I didn't want to move you—you seemed so comfortable."

"So you let your arm go to sleep."

"It's almost awake again."

"You have too much patience for your own good," she observed. "And I feel like death warmed over. I have to go and wash my face to feel human again."

Her stiff legs carried her unsteadily into the bathroom, where she gasped when she saw the puffy eyes and disheveled hair in the mirror. With every muscle in her body aching, she was tempted to run the hot bath she'd promised herself earlier, but she couldn't do that with Peter waiting for her in the living room.

Well, at least she could do something about making her face look half-human.

When she returned to the living room Peter was standing as if preparing to leave. "You're leaving."

"You're tired. I was thinking I ought to let you get some sleep."

"It's two in the morning. We're both going to be basket cases for work in the morning."

"But staying up till the wee hours makes you feel young again, doesn't it?"

Her smile faded to a significant stare. More than anything, she didn't want him to leave. Her apartment sometimes provided solace to her, but she knew that tonight, without Peter filling every crevice with his warmth and vitality, her apartment would feel empty. "I'd like you to stay. Just to be with me. Besides, we haven't touched our hot chocolate."

"Cold chocolate," Peter corrected, smiling broadly.

Kara reheated their hot chocolate in a saucepan on the stove, then took the refilled mugs back to the living room where she sat down on the carpet in front of the couch. The warm milk made her feel drowsy again, and by the time she'd drained the cup, she'd settled herself back into Peter's arms.

"If your arm goes to sleep again, you have my permission to move me," she advised.

"I don't want to move you," he murmured into her hair. "I can do without the arm."

He traced an affectionate finger over her face and down to her shoulder, where he stopped to caress the knots of muscles he found there. Kara moaned her gratitude as his strong hands carefully found the pockets of tension across her shoulders, up the vertebrae of her neck, and down each side of her spine.

"What makes you so damned patient and understanding?" Kara asked him suddenly.

He laughed. "What do you mean?"

"Sometimes you seem so patient and understanding that it's disgusting. But with your background you could so easily have hardened yourself to the world."

He paused for a moment to consider her words, and she was afraid he might stop the magic movements of his fingers. But she needn't have worried. Peter wanted to massage her forever.

"In some ways I did harden myself, though," he said. "Don't forget it was you who pointed out my lack of understanding of our dear neighbor, Mr. Brice."

"That reminds me," Kara said with sudden enthusiasm. "I meant to tell you I bumped into Mr. Brice in the supermarket last week. He told me the hole under his fence had been refilled beautifully."

"Glad to hear he was pleased."

"And not only that," she added, "apparently a group of Aiken House kids went over to his property and raked all his leaves. He figured it saved him days of work on his own."

"Nice bunch of kids," Peter commented innocently.

"Mr. Brice agrees. As we were chatting, I noticed a large pumpkin sitting in his shopping cart. This struck me as a little unusual. Not only does Mr. Brice seem like a man who would say humbug to any children's festivity, but Halloween is still a few weeks away. He told me he planned to donate the pumpkin to Aiken House and help the kids carve it out.''

"Lovely man," Peter chuckled, genuinely pleased by her story.

"So you see, even with Mr. Brice, you must have been patient and understanding to get those results."

"Hold on a minute," Peter said, laughing, as he immersed his gaze in her soft brown eyes. "Let's give credit where it's due. My newfound good neighborliness is completely a result of your efforts."

"Glad to be of service," she returned modestly.

"I hope," he said with unabashed intimacy, "that I can also be of service to you."

"You already have been," she answered, tangling her fingers with his.

"Oh? How's that?"

"I have to tell you something else about myself for you to understand," she said quietly. "I was engaged once, when I was eighteen, to a boy from high school. His name was David."

"Did he know Joey?" Peter asked.

Her eyes roamed his face, as if she was discovering him for the first time. "Funny you would ask that," she said quietly. "Yes, he did. I think that was probably the major reason I was attracted to him. He and Joey were friends. I thought that, of anyone in the world, David would be the most understanding of what I'd been through."

"But he wasn't," Peter surmised.

"We kept putting off the wedding for three years. Then he broke off the engagement."

"His loss," Peter commented cheerfully.

"I want you to know something, Peter," she whispered. "I feel I've never been so close to leaving my grief behind as I am now. You're always asking me how I feel. Much as I hate the question, I have to admit I feel scared. I even feel a bit like I would be abandoning Joey or somehow betraying him if I left him behind."

"I know," he whispered back, and held her tight against him until he felt her body relax and heard her breathing become deep and regular as she lapsed into sleep. What was it about her that touched him so deeply? Why did he care so much for her as opposed to any of the other women he had known? Was it her vulnerability, her honesty, the way she laughed with Craig, the angle of her chin, her curls? It could be almost anything about her—or everything. Whatever the reason, though, there was one thing he knew for sure. She was already more important to him than anyone he'd ever known.

Carefully he slipped his free arm under her knees, carried her into her bedroom and put her down on the bed. Then, getting an extra blanket from the hall closet, he lay down beside her and arranged the blanket over both of them. With her close beside him, it took Peter no time at all to fall asleep.

IN THE MORNING LIGHT Kara found Peter beside her. She moved no more than her eyes, yet he knew she was awake.

"I've got to go," he whispered.

"Did you sleep?"

"Like a baby."

She reached her arms around him and drew herself closer. "Thank you for staying," she whispered. Then, without warning, she met his lips with hers. Her pliant open mouth caught him off guard, and he responded instantly with the full force of his passion for her, drinking in her kiss as deeply as she offered it. Her softness was exquisite. Every part of her moved to his touch. Every contour, every curve and recess was opened to him. Her hips called him with gentle undulations as he slid on top of her, pressing closer to the source of her need.

With enormous effort he managed to pull himself back.

"What's the matter?" she asked breathlessly.

"I don't want you to move so fast that you'll have regrets. Only yesterday I was still your enemy."

"You're not anymore."

"Good. But I want to be sure of that."

"What if I told you I was sure?" she asked.

"I'll deal with that when you tell me."

"Okay, I'm sure," she said quickly, moving slowly against him.

"Is that you talking or your passion talking?"

"Both," she answered, running her hands up his sides.

"That's not good enough. Passion is something you can regret later."

"I won't regret it."

"How do you know?"

Kara let her arms flop back against the bed in exasperation. "Let's put it this way. Right now I don't care if I live to regret it."

"That's very complimentary, but a little impulsive, don't you think?"

He didn't move away, but lay on top of her, hiked up on his elbows.

Suddenly she laughed. "You're teasing me! I can't believe it!"

"You're cute when you're being teased," he replied laughing out loud. "You really get quite insistent when you don't get what you want right away, don't you?"

Kara felt herself blush, but there was no use in trying to hide it from him.

She moved her hips against his slowly and felt his grip around her shoulders tighten. "But," she added breezily, "I'm sure I could turn in a good effort in the patience department if I had to. We could get up and have coffee on the patio."

"That won't be necessary," he returned somewhat raggedly.

"No, really," she insisted, her tone friendly as she stepped up the momentum of her hip movements. "I wouldn't want to make a guest feel pressured."

"Okay, I give," he pleaded.

"Say uncle."

"Uncle, uncle, uncle!"

"How long are we going to talk about this?" she whispered working her fingers through his hair.

"The conversation's over," he answered huskily, and quickly slipped her clothes off and then his own.

She moved with him, like a dancer who anticipates the direction of the dance. He caressed her tenderly, gently and Kara felt the exquisite anguish of every nerve ending crying for more attention. When he retreated and rolled onto his side facing her, she felt her own initiative rise. She pressed herself against and over him and took control of their dance. But though he'd given her the lead, he kept close behind her, following up her every suggestion.

She felt like a figure skater, free to leap and twirl with abandon, always sure that her steadier earthbound partner would be there to catch her and offer gentle guiding hands. But as the rhythm quickened, Kara's control slipped away.

"I don't want you to regret anything with me," he whispered heavily, his lips moving against her neck.

"Shh," she ordered urgently.

Kara clasped her arms around him, holding him tightly as she soared to a height she'd never known before.

In an instant he followed her. Then they lay very still, chests heaving softly, skin damp, hands entwined. Sunshine filtered through the white bedroom curtains, infusing the fresh green room with a subdued light.

They stayed that way, neither of them wanting to break the magical silence, the bond of their touch.

"I don't want to move from this spot," Peter said, tightening his fingers around hers. "Ever."

Kara let the silence pass. She smiled and closed her eyes. "I don't think I could go that long without a coffee."

Peter's laughter and bear hug made her secretly wish they really never did have to move from this spot. She watched him draw away from her at last and pull on his clothes. When he kissed her goodbye, she knew already that she was head over heels in love with him.

# CHAPTER EIGHT

THE COOLER AIR of late fall seemed to infuse Kara with new energy. She developed a hunger to discover the world all over again and experience it in ways she never had before. She and Peter developed a fun routine, where one would introduce the other to something neither had ever done before. Kara found she got as much pleasure from being introduced as she did from doing the introducing.

One Saturday night when it was her turn, she drove Peter to Toronto for a midnight horror movie. She didn't usually have the stomach for horror shows, but with the crowd at least as entertaining as the movie, she did enjoy herself—although she spent the last half hour of the show with her head buried in Peter's coat. Afterward, they walked down Yonge Street, Toronto's main drag, until they got hungry enough for a hamburger.

They were back in Guelph in time for one of those breakfasts where you're so tired that no conversation makes sense. They laughed hysterically at nothing as they drank coffee and tried to keep their eyes propped open.

The next weekend Peter signed them up for a bridge tournament at the university. They were the least-experienced pair there, but they had marvelous fun and they met enough bridge players to keep them playing the game forever.

Then, in the middle of the week, they went to the Mannings' for a bridge game. Peter looked perfectly at home carrying Evan over one shoulder and Robbie in his other arm as he helped to put them to bed. Kara and Stan were partners against Sandy and Peter. Cops and robbers, they called it. The robbers won hands down.

Aiken House became a second home to Kara. Even apart from Peter, there always seemed to be a reason to be there. If it wasn't the baseball glove she'd promised to drop off to Craig, it was the history test she said she'd help him study for. Thoughts of Aiken House plagued her at work. She was more interested in the pictures Stevie drew for her than in interviewing witnesses to an assault in a pool hall. Asking Craig how his history test had gone seemed infinitely more important than asking a raft of previous offenders if they'd bought drugs from a trafficking suspect.

She felt like a big sister to Craig, and Craig slowly pumped her for every last detail of Joey's life. She didn't worry anymore about whether it was a mistake to tell him so much. Craig reawakened all kinds of pleasant memories she'd shared with Joey. It was as if Craig had given her back a part of her childhood.

For the first time in years, she wanted to live only for the moment. When she stepped back into the fantasy land of Aiken House, it was easy to leave all her worldly concerns back at the police station. For now, even the conflicts between Peter and her didn't bother

her. For this one precious time in her life, she just wanted to relax and enjoy being in love with a wonderful man and with life itself.

On Sunday, it was again Peter's turn to introduce Kara to something. It was football. She'd never played before, and as she steered her car over to the soft shoulder of the road and parked behind the long line of cars that converged on Aiken House, she wasn't sure she wanted to learn. Peter had told her that Aiken House had won the first annual Aiken House Football Game and that the rival Hanson group home had won the previous year. Today the third annual game was scheduled. The fact that it was a tie-breaking game was an added pressure.

As instructed, Kara wore a red sweater to indicate she was on the Aiken House team. The Hanson players and supporters wore blue. As she strode down the long driveway, it seemed to her she was wading into a sea of swarming red and blue bodies. There had to be well over a hundred people milling about the grounds. The day before she'd helped the kids demarcate the playing field with strings of brightly colored plastic flags, and she was pleased to note that it all looked wonderfully official. She smiled happily. The atmosphere reminded Kara of a country fair. Except these kids weren't with their families.

"Officer Ridgeway!" a familiar female voice called out.

Kara turned to find Marg Hanson's ample form lumbering toward her. She was a stoutly built woman of fifty. Her round ruddy face radiated warmth and good cheer and today, of course, she wore a blue sweater.

Kara recalled the first time she'd gone to the Hanson group home years ago. When she'd knocked on the door, Marg greeted her as a professional, yet insisted Kara stay to sample the vegetable barley soup she'd just made. Kara had gladly consumed a bowl of the delicious soup while carrying on a serious discussion about the home's philosophy. They had never referred to each other as anything but "officer" and "Mrs. Hanson," but suddenly the formality struck Kara as absurd.

"Hi, Marg," Kara returned purposefully, and noted a recognition of the change in the other woman's eyes.

"I can't say I'm surprised to see you here," the woman puffed, beaming. "But I thought you might turn up in a blue sweater."

"It was a hard decision," Kara admitted, laughing, "but the boy I'm working with at the moment is here, and I didn't want to hurt his feelings."

"Ah, yes," Marg said, nodding. "The unmanageable fourteen-year-old. I've been meaning to call you back about him. When I spoke to you last, you were quite concerned about how soon we would have a spot for him. It's been longer than I thought it would be, and now that the boy is settled into Aiken House there's probably no need to uproot him. We do have a bed coming up next week, though, if you still want it."

Part of Kara wanted to agree overwhelmingly with Marg that Craig was best off where he was. Another weaker voice wanted to take Marg up on her offer be-

fore anything went wrong at Aiken House. Her un-
certainty dismayed her. She thought she'd built a
strong confidence in Peter, yet it seemed to be shaken
so easily.

"I—I guess," she stammered.

"That's what I thought," Marg agreed, oblivious to
Kara's discomfort. "But I wouldn't have felt right
about offering the spot to anyone else before you."

"I appreciate it, Marg. But actually I might need
that space for someone else shortly. There's another
boy who's in training school right now. He has agreed
to cooperate with us on a certain matter, and we're
hoping he can serve some of his sentence in a group
home. Aiken House might be all right for Craig, but
Jimmy definitely needs more structure."

Jimmy Chalmers had surprised Kara and Stan last
week by giving them the name of the man who'd sold
him the guns. Stan credited the reversal to Kara's visit,
but Kara was doubtful. The boy had seemed to be at
some crossroads, but Kara hadn't thought he would
take the plunge and help the police. She was encouraged that he had.

Marg started to say something, then stopped, then
started again, then stopped. Then she lunged in one
more time before she had the chance to change her
mind. "I'm curious about something, Kara, and I
hope you don't mind me asking."

"Not at all," Kara assured her nervously.

"I didn't think Aiken House was—how shall I say
it?—exactly your style. Do you remember when you
first came and asked all those questions about how
Hank and I ran our home? I didn't get the feeling you

would have stayed so long if I'd said some of the things I know Peter says."

Kara hoped that Marg would think the flush on her face was merely the reflection of her red sweater. "You're absolutely right, Marg," Kara conceded. "Although your soup made it difficult for me to leave too soon. But seriously, I'm still not one hundred percent convinced about Aiken House. Circumstance forced me to take a look at Peter's program, and so far I've been pleasantly surprised by what I've found."

"Well, well," Marg clucked. She had a curious quirk to her mouth, but she didn't seem disappointed. "Someone must be adding something special to the drinking water over the past month to be making people so agreeable. Just today I've had several people comment to me on how much more flexible Peter Aiken has been. People say he's a lot friendlier. Even Peter's neighbor is now on board."

Marg nodded toward Brice, who was marching about importantly in his black-and-white referee shirt.

"Yes, Mr. Brice has become quite a dedicated supporter."

"It's good to see," Marg said with a smile. "Group homes need all the supporters they can get. I'm glad to see you're happy with Aiken House, Kara. I think most group homes are moving away from the really strict style anyway."

Kara wondered if it was relief she sensed in the other woman. Social-service workers were like police officers in a way, Kara realized for the first time. They were a closely knit group of people who understood the pressures inherent in each other's work. With their problems stemming mostly from lack of facilities and resources, they looked to each other as members of a support network, not as competitors. It felt like a very humane environment.

The two women stood quietly, absorbing the atmosphere around them until Marg suddenly exclaimed, "I love events like this, don't you?"

"Why, yes I do." Kara laughed. "It makes me remember when I was a kid. Each fall when the fair came to town my brother and I would go every day after school and absolutely stuff ourselves with hotdogs. We weren't able to eat dinner at home for the entire week, of course. But anything was worth the ecstasy of hotdogs at a carnival."

"Well, then you absolutely must have a hotdog today, right now before the game gets under way."

"They have hotdogs here?" Kara exclaimed.

Marg nodded enthusiastically. "Peter has barbecues set up on the other side of the house. The kids are cooking up a storm. You go on around there now before it's too late."

Kara accepted Marg's friendly order and made her way over the leaf-laden grounds toward the house. As she rounded the corner the aroma of burning charcoal and the sound of sizzling hotdogs and hamburgers greeted her.

She spotted Peter immediately. He was hunched over a smoky barbecue, demonstrating to Craig the finer points of hamburger flipping. Kara paused for a moment to watch the pair. There was something about the complete concentration both the older and younger man devoted to the task that gave her a twinge of envy.

Her job would most accurately be described as crisis intervention. When the crisis was over, her involvement ended. Peter, however, could build a longer-term relationship and, therefore, could have long-term effects on a young person's life.

Peter must have heard her thoughts. He suddenly looked up in her direction, and his face broke into an immediate smile. He waved her toward him.

Craig greeted her with the voice of a busy nononsense short-order cook. "What'll it be, lady, hamburger or hotdog?"

"Hotdog, please," she said, falling immediately into the role of impersonal customer that Craig obviously expected.

Craig struggled to scoop a cooked wiener into a rather charred-looking bun. But Kara managed by the sheer force of her enthusiasm to divert the dismay that threatened to overtake the secretly insecure cook.

"Just the way I like it," she insisted as she accepted the bun. "Crispy."

"More like burnt," Craig complained with disgust.

"Not at all. Really, Craig, I like it this way. Tastes really barbecued."

Craig watched doubtfully as she heaped on mustard and relish to disguise the burnt taste, then took an enthusiastic bite.

"You'll have to excuse us, Craig," Peter said, placing his hand on the small of Kara's back to steer her away. "We have a few things to discuss before the game starts."

Craig's attention was thankfully distracted by a boy in a blue sweater who had lined up for his lunch.

"Thanks," Kara mumbled through her mouthful of crunchy bun.

"Here," he returned, smiling, and handed her a glass of juice. "This will wash away the taste."

Kara nodded and groaned. She crossed her eyes in painful significance as she popped the last of the hotdog into her mouth and drank thirstily.

"Such a kind-hearted cop," Peter teased. "I hope you get meaner by the time the game starts. We need rough, tough players. Sensitivity is a liability on a football team."

"Hold on a second," Kara said with widened eyes. "I thought you told me this was a friendly game of touch football."

Peter's watermelon-red sweater complemented the outdoor ruddiness of his complexion. The man looked custom-built to spend his time running football games at group homes.

"Don't worry," Peter assured her with a wink. "A friendly game of touch football is all it is. If it were more than that, half my team wouldn't play. But this is still stiff competition. The only way we can get the competitive edge and keep it is if we dredge up some good old killer instinct. After all, this is a grudge match," Peter explained, smiling easily. His hand still rested lightly on the small of her back, and he ached to wrap his arms around her waist and pull her close to him. But that would hardly be appropriate here.

"I'm not much of a football player," Kara said. "Maybe I'd better not take up a place on your team when someone better could fill in."

"Oh, no you don't." Peter said, laughing. "You don't think I'm going to let you worm out of it that easily, do you? I'm absolutely convinced there's no one better to fill that particular spot on the team."

"Why did I know you'd say something like that?" Kara asked, smiling in defeat.

"Because I think you're really starting to know me. Besides, there really is no one better to fill the spot. I need a role model for the female members of my team, and you're it."

"What about Andrea?" Kara asked, thinking of the woman who had been introduced to her as a staff member the day she'd first brought Craig to Aiken House.

"Her sister is getting married today, so she couldn't make it."

"Great," Kara said sarcastically.

"And besides, the Hanson team is matched with ours for males and females, kids and adults."

"Well, I see you have every last one of the angles covered," she accused him good-naturedly. "I guess I'll just have to play."

"That's the spirit," Peter said. "But I'd better get the show on the road or we might be finishing this game in the dark. I'll find the referee and get him blowing his whistle."

"I see Mr. Brice is becoming a bit of a fixture around here."

"I told you before, Kara. You gave me the most constructive kick in the pants I've ever had. He's like having an extra staff person. I owe it all to you." Peter touched her elbow lightly, then disappeared into the crowd, heading in the direction of the playing field.

Kara had gulped down the remainder of her orange juice and taken a few steps toward the playing field when she heard Stevie's distinctive voice.

"Kara, wait!"

"Stevie!" she exclaimed, laughing when she spied the child running toward her with Ketchup, wearing a red doggy jacket, bouncing in his arms. Stevie wore a look of distress. She crouched down to face him on his level. "What's the matter?"

"Ketchup is getting in the way. He's supposed to sit with the fans and cheer for us, but he keeps chasing after the football. Mr. Brice keeps tripping over him." A distant whistle blew, and panic swept across Stevie's face. "The game's going to start without me. Can you take him?"

"You're not going to miss the game," Kara said soothingly. "I can take him for now, Stevie, but don't forget I'm in the game, too. If Ketchup interferes too much, we'll have to put him in the house for his own safety, so don't be surprised if he doesn't watch the game for long," she said, taking the little dog.

Stevie instantly started to run toward the horde of red and blue sweaters gathering on the playing field. Watching him go, Ketchup whimpered and squirmed, but Kara held on firmly, scanning the crowd in search of a baby-sitter for the dog. She needed someone who wouldn't be playing in the game. Marg Hanson probably wasn't a football player, but Kara couldn't find a trace of her. Suddenly she caught sight of an arm waving to her from the area designated for spectators.

"Mr. Taylor!" Kara said breathlessly as she reached Craig's father. He was smartly dressed in his red cap, sweater and coat. "It's sure great to see you," she said with enough enthusiasm to hint at her ulterior motive.

"I thought you were playing in this game," Mr. Taylor said, laughing as Ketchup leaned over to sniff and lick his hand. "Craig seemed sure of it."

"I am playing, but I have to find a brave heart to take Ketchup for me. He's supposed to be a fan, but I think he's a dyed-in-the-wool player. Unfortunately underfoot isn't a particularly safe place to be in a football game."

"I wouldn't think so. Look, I'll take him for you, if he'll stay with a stranger."

"I thought you'd never ask," Kara teased. Gratefully she handed the scrawny black dog to Mr. Taylor. "Right now he doesn't have much choice in the matter. If he kicks up too much of a fuss, just put him in the house. I can't tell you how much I appreciate this."

"It's nothing compared with the appreciation Craig's mother and I feel for everything you've done. If it weren't for you, Craig wouldn't be getting the help he needs. As it is, we're already talking about having him home for a couple of trial weekends. I didn't think we'd ever get our son back. Now, go along or you'll miss the kickoff.''

By the time Kara arrived on the field, Peter had already explained the ground rules. Fortunately, she already knew the general idea was to catch the ball and run with it to the goal line without being tagged.

Peter smiled at her as she arrived and stood behind Stevie. She had the impression that he'd managed to keep track of her movements even while explaining the rules of football to the crowd of attentive faces. She caught a glimpse of Craig grinning at her and winked at him.

Brice blew his whistle to start the game.

Very quickly it became evident that the blue team was intent on winning at all costs. There were four big boys on the team who had obviously played football before and who took the game far too seriously. In almost no time they had bulldozed their way down the field to score the game's first touchdown.

In the first Aiken House huddle, Peter faced ten demoralized faces.

"We're gonna get killed," Randy stated glumly as they hunched shoulders and pressed together.

"Oh no we're not," Peter said firmly. "They've just tipped their hand and shown us their only strength. Their whole team is those four boys. They may as well not have anyone else on the field. That's not a team, and that's not what teamwork is all about."

"They don't *need* anyone else on the field," Randy noted dryly.

"We'll see about that. We still have our secret weapon to unleash," Peter pointed out.

"What secret weapon?" Craig grumbled.

"Have any of you noticed," Peter asked, "how they completely ignore the female players on their team?"

The huddle suddenly erupted into an animated discussion. Peter had struck a chord. The boys complained that girls were useless on a football team. The girls threatened to leave if they weren't appreciated. Brice warned them to hurry up or face a penalty for delaying the game.

"Listen!" Peter whispered loudly, calling their attention back. "I said they're ignoring their girls, not us. But I want them to think that we are, too. So for the first few plays, boys, I want you front and center, acting important and energetic. I'll look only for you when I'm getting ready to throw. Girls, look a little bored, as if you're going through the motions but know you're not going to get the ball. We've got an acting job to do to win this game."

The mood of the huddle changed immediately. Even Randy's face lit up. "All right!" he exclaimed.

During the next few plays, Kara and the Aiken House girls did their best to run lazily in aimless patterns each time the ball was hiked. After a number of attempts, Aiken House had gained only three yards. This was clearly not good enough for a first down unless something changed dramatically. Anticipation was high when it came time to put the final part of the plan into action.

"Okay, team, we've set them up beautifully," Peter said as they all gathered in a huddle looking at each other's flushed faces. "They're expecting a long bomb, but not to the girls. Now's the time for our secret weapon. Kate, I want you to stay close to me to catch the ball, then run deep down the middle. I want the rest of the girls to surround her. Try to look like this is happening by accident.

"Boys, I want you to run like crazy to the sides and drag away their players from the middle. The play goes right down the middle with Kate. The girls will block for her right to the touchdown line."

The plan worked splendidly. The Hanson team, completely duped by their trick, hadn't left a single player in the middle of the field. The female force ran unchallenged to the touchdown line, then screamed with exhilaration as Kate crossed the line. The boys barreled through to receive their share of congratulations for the diversionary tactics. Kara found herself jumping up and down and clapping her hands in excitement.

The Hanson team didn't realize their weakness. As the game progressed, they became more desperate and relied more and more on the same four boys. The Hanson players had far more talent and experience than the Aiken House team, but fatigue became their major weakness. They began to get sloppy and make foolish mistakes. The girls on the Hanson team became more demoralized the more they were ignored, and arguments erupted from time to time in the blue huddle. Kara had to deal with three girls in blue sweaters who asked if they could join the red team.

With only a minute left in the final quarter the score was tied. Both teams became determined to win. Faces had become grim. Kara noticed that several kids had received more than token tags, but Brice couldn't very well have called a penalty on every infraction.

The Aiken House huddle voted unanimously to again try the first play that had worked so well. Peter was doubtful, reasoning that the Hanson team, having once been burned, would recognize the setup as it developed. But the majority ruled, and Kara soon found herself shadowing Kate up the middle of the field.

As the ball came sailing toward them, Kara noticed there were several unexpected blue sweaters close by. Worse, out of the corner of her eye, she caught sight of a pair of blue arms shoving Kate out of the way. Kara jumped high into the air, and felt her hands instinctively clamp around the ball.

Without another thought, she raced toward the goal line so hard she could feel her lungs screaming for air. It didn't occur to her that the roar of the spectators was warning her of something until she felt two hands on her back. The push knocked her forward so that she tumbled headlong into the soft earth. She had the sensation of sliding for a distance, but kept the ball lodged firmly in her arms. A searing pain shot up her right leg as she jolted to a halt, her breath knocked out of her.

Something warm and wet and slightly rough was licking her face.

"Ketchup's trying to help!" she heard Stevie exclaim.

"It's not my face that hurts," Kara complained, pushing aside the furry little nurse.

It was Peter's concerned voice that answered her. "What does hurt?"

"My leg, the right one," she said, grateful that he was there. His mere presence relaxed her.

"I think it's just a bruised muscle," Peter concluded after several quick manipulations of her leg, ankle and knee. "It's going to hurt for a while. You came down on it pretty hard."

"I'm sure it will be fine," Kara insisted as she struggled to her feet. The gathering crowd was making her self-conscious.

Brice, red-faced, with his whistle dangling around his neck, pushed through the crowd.

"You're still holding the ball!"

Brice's voice was half-accusing, half-surprised.

"Well, yes," Kara said, laughing despite her aches and pains. "Isn't that the idea?"

Brice was in no mood for levity. "Did you drop it?"

"Of course not!"

"Anyone see her drop it?" Brice turned to the sea of red and blue sweaters, impervious to her outrage.

No one answered directly, although Kara heard a couple of blue sweaters mumble that they couldn't see her the whole time so she could have dropped it. Happily, Brice at least knew better than that ploy.

"Then it's a touchdown!"

A sea of red sweaters rose into the air simultaneously, and a chant of "We're number one!" welled up around her. Several of the kids grabbed for her legs to lift her up on their shoulders. She pleaded to be left alone with her sore leg. But since they were looking for a hero to carry around, Kara anointed Craig by handing the ball to him.

As the crowd danced away, Kara examined the extent of her injuries. Her jeans were smeared with mud. She pulled chunks of earth from the denim and allowed Peter to fish crumpled leaves from her hair. The boy who had tagged her with enough force to push her over was extremely apologetic, and although Kara could feel her leg beginning to stiffen, she wanted to downplay her discomfort for everyone's sake.

Dusk fell as the football players in red sweaters helped to douse barbecues and the blue sweaters loaded their cars for the drive home. Kara was chilly and aching by the time she and Peter hosed down the last grill and stored it in the shed. Her leg felt rock solid and she limped on it gingerly.

"I ought to get home and out of these clothes," she told him when they finished.

"This is the wrong time to leave," Peter protested gently. "The worst part's all over."

"I'm feeling pretty uncomfortable in all this mud."

"You don't have laundry facilities at your place, do you?"

"No, I was thinking of going home, having a bath, and then taking this stuff to the Laundromat."

"Let me make another suggestion," Peter said, his form becoming a silhouette in the dim light. "Why don't you come to the boat house and have a long hot bath. I'll give you a pair of pajamas and take your laundry to the house to do while you soak. It's the least I can do for all your pain and suffering."

Kara thought about going home and taking care of herself alone. She had to admit Peter's plan was infinitely more attractive. "Sounds like a good deal to me," she said.

## CHAPTER NINE

As PETER WALKED BACK to the boat house with Kara's freshly cleaned clothes in hand, he half expected to find her still soaking her bruised muscles in the tub. When he opened the door to his living quarters, though, he found the stereo playing soft music and Kara curled up in a pair of his pajamas on a pile of cushions in front of the open grate of his wood stove.

She looked uncharacteristically peaceful, curled up on the floor. She didn't jump to sit up and collect herself. There was something about her calmness that triggered the opposite response in Peter. He was tempted to drop to his knees without a word and indulge his craving to touch her. He wanted to show her his need for her, show her how much he cared.

"Aren't you a sight for sore eyes," he said.

She smiled and drew an arm over her face, stretching comfortably and releasing a happy moan. "I'm a lazy bum," she replied sleepily.

"Hardly," he said, laughing easily. He deposited her pile of clothes on the kitchen counter. "How's the leg?"

"Fine," she lied. She'd purposely been ignoring the hard lump in her leg because it didn't fit with the mood of the moment. If she ignored it long enough, maybe it would go away.

"You know, Ms Macho Cop, you don't have to be brave. Your secret would be safe with me. I wouldn't tell a soul."

"Okay, then it hurts," she confessed.

He sat down cross-legged beside her and began to gently massage warmth into her stiff muscles. "I don't doubt it hurts," he said as his fingers worked their subtle magic. "This muscle is so tense it's rock hard."

"You always seem to be massaging me," Kara noted appreciatively. "You're very good at it, but I feel a little guilty that it always goes one way."

"Oh, I wouldn't say that." Peter stretched out beside her and propped up his head with his arm as he looked at her. He placed his other arm around her waist and began kneading the side of her body.

"It was very thoughtful of you to do my laundry," Kara said, quietly enjoying the tingling sensation his touch was producing. "It wasn't necessary."

"I know. It was my pleasure." He did seem genuinely pleased with himself. "It was nice of you to get your body mangled for my group home."

Kara laughed. "Unfortunately I can't honestly say that was my pleasure. But you're unmangling me quite nicely."

"My pleasure once again," he answered. As he watched her face, he realized she wasn't fighting herself or him. Her dark eyes, honest and untroubled, returned his peaceful gaze. Her lips were slightly parted in a smile.

"Actually," he confessed, "I don't feel that I get to massage or touch you nearly as often as I'd like."

"That's nice to hear. Because actually I don't feel you touch me enough, either."

Peter stopped moving his hands momentarily. "Are you trying to tell me something, Kara?"

"I thought I just did."

"I want to be sure I get the message you mean and not just the one I want to hear. Does this mean you're beginning to believe in me?"

"I don't agree with everything you do at Aiken House, but—"

"Then maybe we have more to talk about."

"My God, you're a chatty man!" she exclaimed, giggling. "I've never met a man who liked to talk more than you. What on earth ever made you that way?"

Peter pulled her over to lean comfortably against him as his hand gently ferreted out every trace of stiffness in her body.

"My mother."

"Oh?"

"She used to love to talk to me and hear me talk."

"How do you know that? Surely you can't remember much. You were so young when she died."

His eyes seemed to dance with a light all their own. "I remember a bit. And besides, she kept a journal. Actually, she kept two, one to chronicle her life and one to chronicle mine. She kept them religiously."

Kara turned reflective. "Your mother could never have known how important those diaries would be one day. But what a wonderful idea."

"In my diary she related all the silly stuff you'd ever want to know about me as a baby. But it's *her* diary that's been more important to me. I never got a chance to know her as a person, to know what she thought or what made her laugh. But I get that from reading about her life through her eyes. And it's funny, as I get older, I see the same words differently."

"Did your mother by any chance take a novel, somewhat liberal, view of child-rearing?"

"I don't suppose that would be an inaccurate description. Of course, one would have to be quite conservative to describe my mother's views as liberal."

"I think we have a wiseacre on our hands."

"I think we have two," Peter replied, joining in her laughter. "Kara, tell me something," he said, dropping his voice to a serious tone. "Your being here with me like this, does it mean you've forgiven me for what happened to Joey?"

Kara shifted and fingered a button on his shirt as if it were absorbing her complete interest. "I don't know," she whispered. "When I think about you and Joey and Craig, I still get very mixed up. I'm not sure of what anything means anymore. But I know that when I'm away from you, I miss you. And when I'm with you, I want to touch you."

"But there's something you still fight, too."

Her eyelashes flickered with a silent admission as she raised her gaze to lock with his.

"Kara, I told you I never wanted you to regret anything with me, and I meant it."

"Oh, I don't regret anything, Peter, really. That's the problem. I feel guilty for feeling about you the way

I do. I know you've got what happened to Joey all figured out and put behind you. But half of me feels like I'm betraying Joey for wanting you. And I feel scared for Craig that I'm starting to believe in you.''

Peter glanced up at the subdued shadows dancing silently over the wall. "Joey wasn't something I figured out and put behind me, Kara," he confessed quietly. "I've never forgiven myself for what happened to your brother. I kept thinking there was something I should have noticed in the two weeks he was with us. I have to live with never knowing what might have been.''

Kara's eyes widened.

"You're surprised," he observed.

"Yes. I didn't think you ever doubted yourself.''

"That period of time was the closest I came to getting out of this business.''

Kara was shocked. No matter how much she'd blamed Peter, she'd never thought he should get out of this kind of work. It had been obvious to her from the first time she'd come to Aiken House that it would be a disastrous loss if Peter did anything but what he was doing. She just wanted him to change some of his methods. "But, Peter, at the time everybody agreed that there was nothing you could have done. The police, even my parents, thought you were more Joey's victim than the other way around.''

Peter just shook his head.

She found his hand and entwined her fingers with his. "Why did you tell me this?" she asked softly.

"I'm not sure," he answered, staring at the fingers clasping his. "Now that I've met you and this old nightmare has taken on a new life, I guess I thought I owed it to you to tell you how Joey affected me. I can't change the past, Kara. I don't want you to regret getting involved with me."

She reached a finger up to his lips. "Don't talk anymore. The last thing in the world I feel is regret."

She lifted her head and replaced her fingers with her mouth, feathering light kisses over his lips. His low moan excited something in her that made her press her parted lips against his in search of the passion she had tasted before.

She found it.

Much later, as Peter lay sleeping in her arms, Kara realized that she'd unconsciously hoped Peter would help her rejoin the land of the living. He'd done that. Now she lived life to the fullest. But once again she was at the mercy of fate. She had a winning hand, but tomorrow fate could deal out insufferable agony and pain, as it had before, both to herself and to Peter.

LOVE WAS AN ODD SENSATION, Kara thought the following Friday as she pulled open the front door of the police station. Suddenly everything looked slightly different. It was as if love had a color of its own, and she had it in such abundance that she could afford to wash the world with it. She must look different, too. Each day someone new asked her if she'd dyed her hair or changed her makeup. People kept asking her what she was smiling about.

Unfortunately her work was suffering under the glare of this clearer brighter environment. She went through the same motions as before, responding to complaints, processing warrants, making the odd arrest, but she caught herself thinking about Aiken House most of the time. Instead of her usual single-minded focus, she found her mind wandering to fantasies. She caught herself thinking about helping boys like Craig to learn about themselves and how to handle life. Her role as a police officer felt more restrictive now than it ever had before. She wondered now if a police officer could ever be truly effective with young kids.

As she rounded the corner into the open office, Kara spotted Stan at his desk. He was working diligently on some paperwork, his huge coffee mug in front of him. Kara had bought him the mug as a birthday gift one year. On the side it read Don't Bug Me, I'm Busy Catching Criminals. He didn't notice her until she had hobbled right by him.

"Good morning," she said with a smile as he looked up.

Stan craned his neck to see her walk. "Leg's getting better," he observed.

"Yeah," Kara agreed, feeling awkward. Her leg felt like a flashing neon sign that read Aiken House. "But I'm still surprised it's taken this long to heal. You never realize how much you take a muscle for granted until you can't use it anymore."

Stan nodded and contemplated his coffee for a moment. A trace of a smile seemed to flicker across his kindly face. "You also seem to have shaken your blues from the other week."

Kara shrugged self-consciously and opened her desk drawer to fish around for nothing. "Life seems to give its own kicks in the pants, doesn't it? As soon as you start dwelling on some worry that isn't so important, life seems to deliver something to put it in perspective.''

"Then you're happy with your new way of looking at things," Stan concluded with interest.

"I wouldn't say I'm completely happy. But when I really think about it, I wasn't completely happy with my old way of looking at young offenders, either. Anyway, your advice really helped me to straighten things out in my own mind, Stan, and I appreciate it.''

Stan's broad smile was evident despite his generous mustache. "That reminds me," he said. "What's the latest with your new convert—this guy Brice I've heard about? He's an example of someone who found it downright exhilarating to change his way of looking at things."

"You're not kidding," Kara said, laughing. "He's planning a big film night. It's the premier showing of all his home movies. Apparently he's traveled all over the world, and everywhere he went he took movies. I'm told he's splicing together boxes of films that have been stored in his basement for years. I guess he'd had no one to show them to.''

"He's got no family?"

"He's got absolutely no one. He and his wife came to live here after he retired from the air force. They tried to have kids for most of their marriage. By the time they gave up on the idea of having their own kids and considered adoption, his wife had fallen ill. That made caring for a child out of the question. I think they had a good life together, short as it was. He was stationed all over the world and his wife traveled with him."

"It sounds like there are a few things in that life history that could account for Brice being hostile to a group home setting up next door."

"Sure. For one, he simply wasn't used to having kids around. He thought everything they did was a sign of delinquency—from playing road hockey to climbing trees. I also suspect the kids must have reminded him of his loneliness. His wife's been gone seven years now."

"Are the kids really interested in these films?"

Kara smiled wryly when she thought of all the comments she'd heard about Brice's films. "I'd say that most of the kids will come and watch the films," she explained, "but all for different reasons. Stevie, for example, doesn't care about the movies so much as just wanting to please Brice. This man has turned into a grandfather figure to a lot of the kids, and they're happy with any excuse to be nice to him."

"And the others?"

"The older kids are divided. A couple of them are doing school projects on various countries, and they've got vested interests. They hope they can show some of Brice's films to their classmates."

"Brice must love that. He'd have that much more of an audience."

"He's not sure if he likes it or not. He likes all the excitement, but he's still quite protective of his sacred property. Anyway, Brice has convinced them to leave him alone on the question until they've seen the movies themselves. I think he secretly hopes they won't be appropriate for a classroom setting, but I've got a feeling they're tailor made. As for the rest of the kids, they don't care about the films so much as the popcorn and pop Brice promised to deliver on the big night.''

"So he knows how to stack his audience," Stan said, chuckling. "I guess you don't have to have kids of your own to see what motivates them.''

Kara agreed. "I have no doubt the evening will be a blazing success.''

As Stan and Kara drifted back to their own work, Kara reflected on how good it made her feel to tell someone what was going on at Aiken House. She and Peter had spent much of their time together this week talking about the kids. There were funny comments to repeat and antics to relate that illustrated personality traits. They never tired of talking about the kids, but their time together always seemed to slip away too fast.

Here she was trying to write out a dry police report on a shoplifting case while her mind dragged her back to Aiken House. Stevie had a math test today. Craig had the day off because he went to a different school that had a teacher's professional development day today. But he was still supposed to be working on his project about Australia. She wondered how he was doing.

Then there was Peter. He was the most distracting of all. She couldn't stop smiling when she thought of him.

She tried to shake herself out of this pleasant little reverie, and as she looked up she saw a cluster of three officers near the front counter. They wore the tired but relaxed look of officers coming off shift a little late. The tallest of them, Ed Smithers, a veteran officer of twelve years on the force, caught her eye as she glanced over. He was the epitome of a model cop, strong looking and very clean cut. He finished what he was saying to his colleagues and sidled over to her desk. He nodded first to Stan.

"Stan."

"Ed." Stan nodded in return.

Then Ed turned to Kara. "Too bad you're on days. We could have used you on the midnight shift last night."

Kara felt uneasy. Ed rarely spoke to her, and she wondered what prompted his unanticipated approach.

"Why?" she asked.

Ed was the type of cop who annoyed her. He was perpetually suspicious of everyone. Whenever he told a story, he would skirt the point forever, as if he couldn't stand to give out the smallest bit of information. Perhaps it was just being a good cop, Kara thought. After all, it was an enviable skill to be able to glean more information than you gave. Enviable for a cop, anyway. But Kara realized she preferred to see someone lay out their cards on the table much sooner in a conversation, the way Peter did.

Ed began with his usual indirect approach. "I understand you're quite involved with a group home called Aiken House."

His voice was so heavy with innuendo that Kara felt alarmed for a moment that her personal life was general knowledge. But a little voice of caution advised her that he was more likely just fishing.

"I've investigated the program and placed one kid there," she responded with a hint of defensiveness.

"Right," he nodded as if that was what he'd meant.

"How would that have helped last night?" she asked, trying not to appear too interested.

"You could have helped us identify the punk we picked up in the act of stealing a car. We figured he was from a group home, but he wouldn't give us his name or the home he was from."

"This boy is from Aiken House?" Kara asked, in alarm.

"Sure is," Ed announced on a note of triumph. "But it took most of the night for him to admit it—we finally told him we could call all the group homes and get them to see who was missing. When he told us where he was from, we notified Aiken, but we still thought it would do the kid good to sit in the cell overnight—not that group-home kids ever learn much anyway, but he looked like a runner to us. We figured we might as well keep him in and let a judge decide to let him out on bail."

Kara steadied herself. "What's the boy's name?" she asked with deceptive calm.

Ed turned to go. Clearly the most interesting part of the conversation was over for him. "Craig Taylor," he tossed back over his shoulder.

Kara blinked. It was the name she'd been afraid she'd hear. "Has he seen a judge yet?"

"Naw, he's still in a holding cell. You can see him if you want. Aiken's on his way to pick the kid up."

"Are you sure his name is Craig Taylor?" she asked, wanting there to be some mistake.

She'd never forget the self-satisfied look on Ed's face. "One and the same. He said he was with his girlfriend at a dance at the time the car was stolen. She says he wasn't. This is what you call an open-and-shut case."

Ed gave her a little salute. "Just thought you'd like to know, officer."

Kara watched Ed's blue uniform recede past the front counter and out the front door. She stared long after he'd disappeared.

# CHAPTER TEN

"KARA, ARE YOU ALL RIGHT?" Stan's voice seemed far away.

"Sure, I'm okay," she replied weakly.

"Don't be too shocked, Kara. These things are impossible to predict one hundred percent. I'm always surprised when I see which kids make it and which kids don't. You never know what's really going on inside a kid until something like this happens."

The more he spoke, the more desperately she wanted to be alone. As she listened to Stan's words, Joey's face kept superimposing itself over Craig's face. She felt suffocated.

"It's pretty hard to predict, all right," she agreed as she stood up. She knew she'd won the battle against an emotional display. She had temporarily forgotten her old method of insulating herself, but now she pulled her police officer role around her like a cloak, and her self-control came surging back.

Her stiff leg was now a mere irritation. She didn't bother to favor the leg as she collected her purse and headed for the front of the station. "I think I'll go see him," she told Stan. "See you later."

"Take care of that leg," Stan called after her.

She retreated into the woman's washroom to collect herself. The washroom was empty. Setting her purse down on the floor, she splashed several handfuls of water over her face.

Car theft! That was a serious offense. A training school offense. She'd taken a merely unmanageable boy and seen him through the transition to training school material. Were those the results her brand of help produced? Or had this happened because she'd changed tactics? She'd forgotten all the hard lessons Joey's fate had taught her. Now she was going to pay for her mistakes. And so was Craig.

Her face looked ashen, as if all the blood had drained into her leaden feet. Pinching her cheeks, she tried to persuade the color to return.

She remembered that Peter was on his way to collect Craig. She was responsible for supervising the boy. How did Peter feel now? How could he possibly maintain faith in his methods when they had this devastating effect on another person's life? Did he feel as sick as she did?

She felt he was very far removed from her now, as if he were a person she had never known, had never loved. The Peter she had loved was replaced in her mind by the image of a man who had failed miserably and, in the process, had managed to bring her down with him.

If Peter was on his way, he'd be here soon. She wanted to see Craig, but not Peter. She didn't have the strength to endure his knowing, probing eyes. Quickly she gathered up her purse again and hurried out of the washroom.

When she arrived at his cell, Craig was leaning against the wall, his arms crossed, his face covered by his long, unruly bangs. He looked neglected and unkempt. His clothes were unusually wrinkled, and his skin was a pasty gray, as if he'd been in jail for months. He seemed so young and helpless that Kara wanted to cry for him.

But then she remembered what he'd done, and her compassion turned to anger. He'd had a perfectly good home, caring parents, far fewer problems than many kids his age—and he'd thrown it away for some pointless rebellion. She wanted to throttle him. Kara approached his cell slowly. She had the guard open the door, and as she entered his cell, Craig's eyes instantly locked with hers. His face mesmerized her. His expression wasn't able to alight on one emotion and stay there. It passed from resentment to hope, then anger to fear. Kara could have watched him for hours, reading his face as if it were a map. But the silence was uncomfortable.

"Hi," she said simply.

"I suppose you don't believe me, either," he accused, pacing the cell. His dark-rimmed, sullen eyes told her he'd been awake all night.

Kara leaned back against the bars. They felt cold and hard through her shirt. He was right. She didn't believe him. But she forced herself to allow for a margin of error. "I want to hear it from you," she said.

Craig stopped his pacing and snorted with disbelief. "At least you put on a better act than your buddies do. I don't know how you can be a cop. They're all a bunch of—"

"Craig," Kara snapped, interrupting him. "I get the message. Why don't you just tell me what happened. I know you've been charged with auto theft. I don't know what happened. Tell me."

Craig looked at her hard, then sighed. "Do you know how many times I've been through this already?"

"I have a very good idea, as a matter of fact. But you've been telling your story to cops. Try telling it to a friend this time."

Craig's face softened, but his words remained bitter. "I've already told it to a friend once—I told Peter over the phone last night. He wanted to come and get me then, but your cronies made him wait until morning."

"What did he say when you told him?"

"What do you think he said?" Craig was learning to turn the tables as effectively as Peter did. She didn't like it.

"Craig, this is not a game. This is serious business. I'm sick to my stomach at your being here. Either tell me why you're here or don't tell me, but let's cut the crap."

Craig sat down abruptly on his bunk, as though he'd been knocked down by her words. She was instantly sorry for snapping at him. It showed a loss of control on her part. Underneath those bangs lay a very sensitive boy.

Kara imagined how alone and alienated he must feel. Police expected to be lied to, and they transmitted that message of cynicism and skepticism. She used to think it was good for kids to realize what it was like in the real world. After all, they had to get used to it eventually, like it or not. But this morning, with Craig looking even younger than fourteen, she caught herself wondering if the world had to be this real this soon.

"Have you had any breakfast, Craig?" she asked impulsively.

"I'm not hungry." His voice shook.

"How about a coffee?"

An appreciative smile scooted across his face. "That would be good."

"Cream and sugar?"

"Thanks."

Kara called for the guard, and when he'd let her out, she retreated to the staff lunchroom, where she knew there would be freshly perked coffee. She poured quickly, adding a lot of milk to Craig's mug. Craig might appreciate being treated as a grown-up but he was only fourteen.

Whose fault was it that this child was in a cell? she asked herself. The question plagued her. When she looked at Craig she felt such a jumble of conflicting emotions: guilt, outrage, protectiveness, affection. When she thought of Peter she felt even more confused, but most of all, she felt betrayed.

He'd made her believe in his dreams, his philosophy, his ideals. He'd made her turn her back on her tried-and-true beliefs—beliefs that had seen her through many tough years. Then Peter had taken her supports from under her and offered her his illusions. Now even the illusions were stolen from her. She should have trusted her assessment of him in the first place.

Kara returned to Craig's cell, and the guard let her back in.

"Thanks," Craig said as she handed him the steaming cup of coffee.

"So," she began awkwardly. "I gather your story is going to be different from the one the arresting officer writes up."

"No kidding." He sighed, for the first time not trying to hide the extent of his anxiety. Coffee in hand, he again began to pace the cell floor. It was a habit Kara had seen in many inmates.

"Last night we had a dance at the school. It was a Sadie Hawkins and this girl in my class, Heather, asked me to go."

Kara presumed Heather was the girlfriend Ed had told her about. "Thursday's a funny day for a dance. Aren't dances usually held on Friday nights?"

"Yeah, but today's a professional development day for the teachers, so it's a holiday for us."

"That's right," Kara said, remembering. "You're supposed to be working on your geography project today."

Craig laughed humorlessly. "Right. I wonder how many of my geography classmates would get thrown in jail for walking home."

"Did you walk your date home?" Kara wondered if he knew that Heather had already contradicted his alibi. It was pathetic that he was continuing with a story that had been shot down so fast, she thought uncomfortably.

"Naw, I didn't need to. She was staying overnight with a girlfriend. The girlfriend lives just down the street from the school. But I had a feeling she'd never told her parents about me, and that's why she was staying at her friend's—so that I wouldn't be walking her home. But I told myself that was a dumb thing to think. I figured I was just being paranoid about being from a group home."

"What time did you leave the school?"

"I dunno, eleven or eleven-thirty," Craig answered irritably. "Time means a lot to you cops, doesn't it? Those two last night kept asking me what time I left the school."

Kara wanted to tell him that meaningless details like times and witnesses would be the weapons used to tear apart his story on the witness stand. Instead, she shrugged. "Comes with the training. Tell me, did Peter know you were going to walk home that late by yourself?"

"It's not that far. I would have been home before midnight. Peter said I could call him and he'd come pick me up, but that seemed like a lot of trouble for nothing, so I just started walking."

She wished she could believe him. She liked him, but her feelings didn't cloud her judgment. "Craig, do you know how much trouble you're in?"

"It's not my fault. I didn't do anything wrong. I saw this car parked at the side of the road with its headlights on."

"Was this far from the school?"

"Yeah. It was only about a block away from home. Anyway, the door wasn't closed properly, so the interior light was on, too. I could see nobody was in the car, and I knew the battery would wear down with all those lights draining it, so I decided to give some poor sucker a break and save his battery. I opened the car door and got in to look for the light switch. That's when the cruiser pulled up."

"And there you were, sitting in a stolen car."

"But I *told* them what happened. They just wouldn't listen. I even told them I thought it was kind of weird myself that the door was left open—as if somebody had got out of the car in a hurry."

Kara had heard this kind of story a million times. Every suspect claimed they'd been framed or that they had a witness that couldn't be found. "And did the officers find your observations helpful?" Kara asked, unable to resist the light sarcasm. Police officers didn't take kindly to their suspects trying to solve their cases.

"The tall one was a real jerk about it," Craig answered with sudden animation. "He got sarcastic and told me they were bright boys and could probably solve this case without my help."

"And what did you say back?"

"I told them if they were that bright, they'd have the guy who really stole the car sitting here instead of me."

"I'll bet they liked that."

"I had nothing to lose by that time," Craig insisted. "And I was frustrated. When they first asked me questions, I told them who I was, where I'd been and who I was with. But I realized real soon that it didn't make any difference what I said. Once they found out I was from a group home, they decided to charge me. My story didn't matter."

"You don't think they would have charged you if you didn't live at Aiken House?"

"That's right, I don't."

"Did you tell the officers that?"

"I didn't tell them a thing. Once I saw what they were doing, I clammed up."

"Which probably has something to do with why they kept you overnight."

"Maybe. I don't care why."

Suddenly Craig's face brightened as he looked past Kara's shoulder. "Am I ever glad to see you!" he said with undisguised relief.

Turning around, Kara saw Peter outside the cell. His gray blue eyes were tired. Behind him, she noticed a uniformed officer.

The officer clanked his key into the lock. "The judge will see him now," he advised Peter.

As soon as the cell door opened, Kara seized the opportunity to escape from the discomfort of Peter's presence. When Craig stepped out of his cell, she was already retreating down the hall toward the exit. "Good luck, Craig," she called hollowly.

Craig's amiable wave allowed her to go, but Peter's voice stopped her with the force of a hand clamped onto her shoulder. "Kara, I want to talk to you," he commanded, then added, "after your shift." Her look of defiance forced him to adopt a more moderate tone. "Where will you be after your shift?" he asked carefully.

Kara deliberated. Her mind was flooded with reasons she shouldn't see him. She'd trusted him when she should have known better, and he'd let her down.

She didn't know whom she felt more angry with, herself for believing in him, or him for what had happened to Craig. Still, they had to talk if they were to find a way to help Craig.

She braced herself. "I'll be at home," she half whispered, and bolted out the door.

By the time she finished her shift, Kara had almost decided to avoid seeing Peter after all, but she found him waiting for her on the front steps of the police station. Giant snowflakes fell against a dark sky, leaving a light blanket of snow over everything, including Peter.

"Do you feel like a walk?" he asked softly.

She supposed it was good that he spoke first. She would have stood there staring dumbly at the snowflakes.

"Sure," she said, shrugging noncommittally as she followed him to the sidewalk.

They headed down the short block to Guelph's main street. Already the city was dressed for Christmas. Lamp posts had been transformed into gold and green candles. Strings of lights were woven back and forth over the street, creating a colorful canopy against the night sky. Each store window celebrated the festive season theme, and from some hidden place, Kara heard Christmas music. Could the season really have changed without her having noticed?

They probably looked like any other two perfectly normal shoppers. They blended with others on the sidewalk who also stared into store windows and craned their necks to look up at the outdoor decor. But Peter's and Kara's moods reflected anything but holiday cheer. Their steps took them away from the stores, out past the colored lights until very suddenly night reestablished its dominance.

Peter did not disturb the silence immediately. He felt this was a delicate situation and was unsure how to handle it. Kara was very withdrawn. More so than she had been this morning. More so than when he had first met her. He had to be careful. If he handled things poorly now, he could lose her.

He watched her as they walked. Her hands were thrust into the pockets of her quilted parka. She looked well dressed for the weather, a natural part of the snowy scene. Her fine features were beautiful, and her snowflake-tipped curls were soft, but her brown eyes stared straight ahead out of a face carved in stone.

His voice sliced through the quiet night. "Craig got bail," he said. "I have him home at Aiken House."

"I know. I checked this afternoon," she answered without inflection. "Is he okay?"

"Oh, sure, he's fine," he assured her, then paused. "What about you? Are you fine?"

For the first time, she looked at him. "What do you think?"

Her eyes were clear, but they were a million miles away. He felt he could stretch forever and never reach her again. It scared him.

"Kara, I know you must be pretty upset by what's happened," he said, trying to connect with her somehow, "but I hope you're not blaming me."

Anger surged through her. But the worst of it was that she didn't feel angry with Peter now; she was angry only with herself. Why had she ever left Craig in Peter's care?

Kara answered him determinedly. "You are responsible, Peter, and so am I. We're both responsible for the lives of these kids. But I'm curious. How does it make you feel—since you're the one who's always harping about feelings—that Craig is worse off now than he was before he met us?"

"You're asking the wrong questions, Kara. You're already looking back and asking what went wrong. What if nothing's gone wrong with Craig? What if those cops last night made a big mistake?"

"Oh, come on, Peter. This is hardly the time to be grasping at straws."

Peter stopped in midstep. "Craig told you what happened, didn't he?"

Kara trailed to a stop and turned to face him. "Yes," she answered. "And my big question is: so what?"

"But you know he didn't do what he's accused of."

"What I know," Kara insisted, "is that we've got one boy's word and an empty alibi against the testimony of two police officers."

Peter slipped his hand into the crook of her arm and steered them ahead through the snow. "They know their case is weak," he explained with sudden energy. "Those cops are biased against Craig because he lives in a group home. They know it and you know it. They jumped to conclusions. They charged him before they even thought of investigating the case properly."

Kara felt herself involuntarily buoy to his level of hopefulness, but fought to quash her optimism. Peter's enthusiasm was as dangerous as it was infectious. "This morning I talked to Ed Smithers, one of the arresting officers," she told him. "He didn't seem the slightest bit unsure of his case. Apparently Craig says he was at a dance with a girl. The girl denies it."

"That doesn't surprise me," Peter allowed. "But I talked to the Crown Attorney after Craig got bail. The Crown is willing to recommend the sentence be served at Aiken House if Craig pleads guilty."

A flicker of hope stirred in Kara. "Well, that *is* a bit of good news," she agreed. "At least then Craig could avoid training school."

"That's not why it's good news. It's good news because it shows the Crown is nervous. Otherwise you can be damned sure they'd be recommending training school. Kara, the only important fact here is Craig's innocence. He says he was just turning off the lights in that car. I believe him one hundred percent. Do you?"

"What he did or didn't do isn't the point. It's what happens to him that's important."

"That's where you're dead wrong, Kara!" Peter said, and his vehemence took her aback for a moment. "What he did or didn't do is completely the point."

"Not if he has no case to back him up. He's got no witnesses. Ed caught him in the car. He had the time and opportunity. Craig doesn't have a chance. At least the Crown is offering a way to cut our losses."

"And what does that tell Craig about life, Kara? And about your justice?" Peter challenged. He stopped again and jabbed his finger at her. "What does that say about telling the truth and being trusted and trusting others? Are you really willing to counsel Craig to plead guilty to something he didn't do because you don't happen to have any faith in the criminal justice system?''

They stood staring at each other, chests heaving with the intensity of their convictions. She knew that no matter how frightened she was for Craig, she could never counsel him to lie. She'd have to tell him straight out she thought he was lying to get him to plead guilty. Maybe that was her best course, anyway.

"You're cold," Peter noticed sympathetically. "Look, there's a doughnut shop across the street. Why don't we run over for a coffee and warm up?"

Kara accepted his hand and followed him across the slushy street. Inside the doughnut shop, delicious smells of perking coffee and freshly baked doughnuts assailed them. Kara picked out a table in the corner and Peter brought two mugs of coffee over.

Stirring their coffee in silence, they watched people come and go. Condensation fogged the windows, and a feeling of laziness washed over Kara. Peter relaxed as he watched her.

"You couldn't tell him to lie, could you?" Peter asked with a smile.

"Don't think it's such a victory," Kara replied. "Look at the choices Craig faces. He can plead not guilty and ruin his life in training school. Or he can plead guilty and continue to get the help he needs. I'm sorry but I don't find the decision quite so cut and dried as you seem to."

Peter sipped his coffee. His ruddy cheeks had flooded with color in response to the warmth. "You missed one option. He could be found not guilty."

"I suppose," Kara conceded doubtfully.

"Kara," Peter said slowly in a low patient voice. "I know how you feel about the possibility of Craig's going to training school. If I didn't believe Craig was telling the truth, I'd probably be saying something quite different. But I do believe him, so I can't turn around and tell him he has to lie to see justice done. That's like saying it's all right to do anything just as long as you don't get caught. There has to be some connection between how you act and what happens to you."

Kara drained her coffee cup. "This just happens to be the real world we're living in," she answered soberly. "And neither you nor I can make it perfect for Craig. He needs to learn to deal with it the way it is, not just the way it should be."

"Do you believe Craig, Kara?" Peter asked. "Do you believe he had nothing to do with stealing that car?"

Kara hesitated. She began to twist her napkin into a knot. "I know Craig isn't beyond lying to save his own skin," she answered haltingly. "I suppose few of us are. Back when I put him in the Children's Aid shelter he stole some cash from his parents and tried to lie about it later."

"That's hardly as serious as this!" Peter objected.

Something about his defense of Craig struck her as curious. How could Peter be so sure of the boy's innocence? She wondered if his vehemence was hiding his doubts. "I suppose," Kara allowed diplomatically, "but the circumstances with the car are pretty suspicious. It's hard to believe that the minute Craig claims he was in that car is the same minute Ed happened along."

Peter narrowed his eyes. "It's not impossible."

"True, it's not impossible," she sighed, "but I find it highly improbable. But what do I know? What I think doesn't matter anyway."

"What you think is all that matters to Craig," Peter insisted. "He'd be devastated if he knew you doubted him this much, Kara. He's going to want to know he has your support on this, and if he doesn't, he still needs to know where you stand. It's only fair. You owe him at least that much."

She did owe Craig her honesty, and at least if she could get him to tell the truth and plead guilty, she could help him stay out of training school. "All right," she said heavily. "I'll talk to him."

"The trial isn't that far away. He needs time to make a case, and I know he wants to ask for your help."

"What kind of help?"

"I think it's best you talk about it with him."

Kara sighed. "Okay, this weekend. Sunday."

They walked back to the police station in an uncomfortable silence. As far as Kara was concerned, there was no reason for them to say any more to each other. One event had destroyed everything between them.

When they reached her car, Kara mumbled goodbye as Peter closed the door for her. She turned the key to bring the frosty car to life, and he quickly dusted the powdery snow off her windows. As she watched him she was thinking that if not for Craig she never would have fallen for Peter Aiken. As she waved her thanks and pulled away, she realized that if not for Craig she might have devoted her life to Peter, too.

What a mistake that would have been.

## CHAPTER ELEVEN

THE PREVIOUS NIGHT'S SNOW had persisted relentlessly until morning. Now a bumper-high drift across
the Aiken House driveway forced Kara to abandon her
car and cover the last two hundred yards to the house
on foot along a narrow, freshly shoveled path.

"It's going to have to be a lot wider than this for a
car to get through," she called to Craig, whom she
found at the end of the path, hunched over a shovel.

"I saved that job for you," he called back,
straightening up.

Kara studied him as she approached. Craig could
never be described as an outdoorsy type. Even with his
bulky Nordic jacket, earmuffs and shovel, his pale
face gave him away. Even sub-zero temperatures didn't
bring a rosy flush to his cheeks.

"Where's my shovel?" she offered breathlessly as
she reached him.

Craig plucked an upright shovel from the snowbank and handed it to her. "It's all yours. I figured
you could dig out the road from your car to here," he
suggested.

"That was very generous of you."

"Thought you'd appreciate it," he said with a grin.

They were both doing their best to maintain their usual rapport, despite the obvious strain between them. But Craig's uneasiness showed in his unusual clumsiness. And he avoided her eyes. There was no doubt in Kara's mind that he was worried.

For her part, she tried to act naturally, which made her unmistakably stiff. She was actually relieved to grab a shovel. The physical labor at least provided a temporary diversion.

After a while, though, she noticed that Craig had stopped digging, and she followed his gaze out over the river. There was snow along its banks, but the water with its fast-moving current hadn't frozen over yet.

"When I was little I used to dream about living beside a river," he told her.

"How come?" she asked, stretching to get the kinks out of her back.

"I dunno." He shrugged and thought for a moment. "There's so much to do around a river, I guess. In the summer you can fish in it or paddle a boat on it or swim in it. Little kids can catch tadpoles and frogs."

"I like to just dangle my feet in the water and cool off," Kara added.

"Uh-huh, and in the winter you can skate on it. Peter says that by mid-December the river will be frozen and we can play hockey. We've already picked our teams."

"Sounds like fun," Kara said, smiling, and leaned on the handle of her shovel. "It also sounds as if you like it here well enough to want to stay for a while." If

Craig needed an entry into their discussion, she'd just given it to him.

"I like it here," he said, then abruptly changed the subject. "Randy said you wouldn't show up today," he stated, as if the information was weighing heavily on his mind. "I bet him five bucks you would."

"Then you're five dollars richer for your wisdom."

"But I was worried about it," Craig went on, "because once or twice I think you've almost switched sides. But I still believe in you. And I'll believe in you until you show me that I can't anymore."

"Craig," Kara said, lowering her voice from her previously breezy tone. "What is it you're trying to tell me? Don't talk in riddles. Tell me straight out."

Craig gave her a steady, brutally frank look. "You don't believe me. You think I'm lying about not stealing that car."

Kara floundered. "I wouldn't say that," she stammered. "But there are big problems with your story." She couldn't just devastate him with how she did think when there was a chance—however slim—that he could be telling the truth.

"If I'm not lying about stealing the car, then you must agree that I should plead not guilty, right? Who cares what the Crown offers if I'm innocent, right?"

"I wouldn't say that, either," Kara hedged. "I just think that the Crown has offered an option worth considering."

"Then you think I should lie and plead guilty?"

"No, of course I don't think—"

"Then you don't believe me."

He'd caught her in her conflicting story more effectively than a cross-examining lawyer. "I'm not sure what I believe," she admitted carefully. "I haven't had a whole lot of practice believing in things. It's my job to be suspicious."

"Is that all you are, just a cop? Am I just another screwed-up kid who's broken the law?"

"You know I think of you as more than that, Craig."

"I thought so until today. Now I'm not sure I can believe in the things you tell me."

Craig's words sliced through her defenses. The reality therapy she'd served up to juveniles over the past three years seemed like a collection of empty cliches to her now. How could she tell him her thoughts didn't matter? A judge's opinion would determine what would happen to him next. Yet, she knew it was her opinion that would live with him forever. "I guess I'm used to working with kids who are guilty," she confessed.

Kara was startled by the anguished cry that escaped from Craig as he heaved his shovel into the snowbank. It was as much a cry of frustration as it was despair. She stared at his back and noticed he was trembling with stifled sobs.

She approached him slowly and lifted her arm to put around his shoulder. But she changed her mind and let her arm drop to her side.

"Craig?" she said softly as she stood beside him.

A stream of renegade tears raced down his cheeks. He crushed the back of his hand against his flushed face to wipe it dry. "I thought you were different."

"What do you mean, Craig? Different from who?"

"Different from everybody around me who's so afraid of making a mistake that they don't have the guts to do what's right. My parents should have trusted me, but they were too afraid that what happened to my dad would happen to me. Your two cop friends who arrested me should have dropped the charges—or never should have charged me in the first place—but they're too afraid of losing face. And Heather. She should be testifying for me, but she's too afraid of her parents' reaction.

"And now there's you. You're no different. You know I should tell the Crown Attorney to shove his offer because I'm innocent. But you're too afraid of what might happen to believe I'm not guilty."

Kara wondered if he was right. If she was doubting him merely to protect herself, that would be just as damaging as believing in him when he was lying.

Would he be so insistent about her believing him if he was guilty? His eyes looked too direct and clear to be hiding anything. He didn't seem to doubt himself for a second. He wasn't acting the way guilty kids usually did.

What if he was telling the truth? She'd come today to tell him she couldn't, in good conscience, help him with his case. But suddenly she didn't feel so absolutely sure he was lying.

"Tell me what you want from me, Craig," she said.

"Are you serious?" Craig returned suspiciously.

"I'm serious but I'm not promising anything," she cautioned. "I just want to know what you think I could do to help."

Craig seemed to debate with himself whether or not her request was reasonable. He glanced at her a couple of times before he exhaled a long heavy sigh.

"I'm starved," he stated.

"All this turmoil works up an appetite," Kara agreed with a tentative smile.

She warmed to his sheepish mood. Sometimes it was easy to forget he was only fourteen.

"Andrea left a bunch of sandwiches in the fridge," he suggested. "You feel like something to eat?"

Kara handed him her shovel. "What I really feel like doing is shoveling another twenty-three tons of snow. But since you're not up to it, I guess I could see my way clear to a little break."

"Admit it, you're pooping out," Craig joked as he took her shovel and started up the path to the house. "We've got the place to ourselves," Craig continued. "Everybody else went tobogganing today."

"Oh yeah? Where?"

"There's a farm Peter knows about someplace between Elora and Fergus," Craig explained over his shoulder. "It's supposed to have a fantastic tobogganing hill. It's so steep it's practically like a mountainside."

That was the general area where Peter lived with his parents, Kara recalled. She wondered if that was the farm he lived on until their deaths.

"If it's that great, why didn't you go along?" Kara wondered aloud. She stepped through the front door and kicked off her boots.

"Because you were coming, and this was more important," he said casually as he led the way down the hall to the kitchen.

Kara smiled. Lately she'd been noticing a budding maturity in him. His nonchalant acceptance of priorities made her feel she was catching a glimpse of the man he might become. Odd that she would feel such a personal sense of pride.

"Besides," he added, "we needed some time alone to talk, and that's impossible when everybody's here."

She watched Craig's lanky adolescent form as he rattled around in the refrigerator, shifting jars and containers to find what he wanted. Finally he emerged with two ham and tomato sandwiches and a container of carrot sticks.

"Okay?" he asked as he set the food on the table. "And we've got coffee, tea, milk and juice. What'll it be?"

"Tea sounds good, thanks."

Kara settled comfortably into her seat at the long rectangular table. The huge bay window provided a panoramic view of the back yard. She could see a half-built snowman in the distance and, behind it, a corner of Brice's house.

It seemed impossible it was only a couple of months ago she'd sat here eating tortellini. So much had happened since then that she felt she'd been involved with Aiken House a much longer time—or perhaps it was the emotional distance she'd traveled since then that made it seem so long ago. Now it was difficult to visualize her life without Peter or Craig in it.

"I guess I'm a little hungry, too," she admitted after she had devoured the first half of her sandwich.

"I guess so," Craig agreed, laughing as she took another ravenous bite.

When only crumbs remained on their plates, Craig retrieved a cookie tin from the counter. "You can't have a decent pig out without cookies," he declared as he opened the lid.

"They look kind of funny," Kara observed as she peered in.

"They're carob jobs," he explained as he pulled the plug on the boiling kettle and poured a pot of tea. "Kate found the recipe for them in a health food cookbook," Craig added. "So you can eat as many as you want."

"Is that what health food is?" Kara laughed. "Even cookies become nutritious?"

"Sure thing," Craig said, grinning. "That's what we decided."

"Well then," Kara said as she selected a cookie. "I'd better get started." She was pleasantly surprised by how tasty it was. "Not bad, considering the way they look."

They munched in companionable silence for several minutes before Kara noticed the return of Craig's serious mood. She braced herself for a turn in their conversation.

"There is something you can do to help," he said quietly. "But you're not going to like it."

"I was afraid you'd say that."

"My lawyer says we have to try every angle to build a case," Craig explained.

"That makes sense," Kara agreed, taking another cookie from the tin.

"What we have going for us is that we just have to raise a reasonable doubt about me stealing that car. It's the police who have to prove beyond a reasonable doubt that I'm guilty."

"But two officers can testify that they caught you practically red-handed, Craig. That's pretty strong evidence."

"They didn't catch me red-handed at anything but turning off lights," Craig corrected her. "I have an explanation for what they saw. I didn't steal the car, so there's got to be some doubt!"

"Tell me something," she said as she dunked a cookie in her tea. "Explain to me again why the girl who asked you to the dance won't help you."

Craig dropped his head and studied his folded hands before answering. "Heather's parents are super strict. She told them she was staying over at a girlfriend's house that night. And she did, only she didn't tell her folks she was going to the dance first. If she'd told them, they never would have let her go—at least not with me."

"Did you know that at the dance?"

"No or I wouldn't have given her name to the cops. When they called her parents and asked if their daughter had been at a dance, her parents freaked out. They called her at the girlfriend's, and luckily she was there by then. She denied everything.''

"You're more understanding with Heather than a judge is going to be with you," Kara said sternly, then stopped herself. "What about other kids at the dance? Could they say they saw you two together?"

"Some people might have seen *me* at the beginning of the night. But I met Heather at a side door of the school, and we spent the rest of the night just sitting and talking in the stairwell. We left by the same side door when I walked her back to her girlfriend's place. I'm sure no one saw us."

"And Heather's too deep into her lies to be able to help you," Kara concluded.

"I suppose that's one way of putting it."

Kara picked up another cookie and broke it in half. "Suppose I talked to her, Craig," she suggested. "She's got to understand that a bit of trouble at home for her is nothing compared to what you're up against."

"She knows that already and she feels bad," Craig reported with resignation. "But Paul Brewster, my lawyer, already tried. Now she's in deep with her parents and the cops and the Crown Attorney. It's gone too far for her to turn back and tell the truth."

"Great."

"But try if you want," Craig suggested without enthusiasm. "Brewster says we should try every angle."

"She can't perjure herself," Kara said. "Has she any idea how serious a crime that is?"

"Who's to say she's lying except me?" Craig argued. "We might try putting Heather's girlfriend on the stand, but so far she's backed up Heather's story. We don't need yet another witness contradicting me. As it is, we don't even want Heather to take the stand. If she does, it will be my word against the cops' word about the car, plus my word against Heather's about the dance. I wouldn't stand a chance. My lawyer figures the Crown might not put her on the stand if we don't mention her first as an alibi, so naturally Mr. Brewster doesn't want to chance it."

Kara stared bleakly out the window at the snow. She wished she could find his explanation more convincing. "So where do I come in?" she asked. "You said I could do something to help."

"Without Heather, we don't have any hard evidence," Craig said carefully. "So all the judge has to go on is his impression of what kind of kid I seem to be."

"We call it credibility," Kara supplied.

"Yeah, that's what my lawyer called it. Anyway, Brewster thinks it would help my credibility if you were a character witness for me."

Kara reached for another cookie. "What would you want me to say?" she asked weakly.

"Only what you think," he returned with renewed hope. Perhaps Craig had thought she'd reject his suggestion out of hand. He seemed encouraged that she was even considering his proposition. "If you think that basically I'm a good kid and not likely to get into this kind of trouble, that would be good to say. Believe it or not, my parents want to go on the stand and say all this stuff.''

Kara had wondered how his parents were handling this crisis. ''That must have been a nice surprise for you. A few months ago you might not have been able to count on that.''

''Yeah, I know. It's been hard for them. It was really hard for my dad at the beginning. He was a space cadet for a whole day, wouldn't talk to anyone. Just when he thought we were getting things straightened out in our family, this blew everything apart.''

''That's not bad, though,'' Kara pointed out, ''if your father was upset for only one day.''

''Well, he did some thinking that day, and it helped him to realize that this wasn't a case of history repeating itself. There's a big difference between what happened to him and what's happening to me.''

''Like what?''

''Well, like he was guilty,'' Craig answered, spreading his hands out on the table. ''He did what that crowd of kids told him to do. But I didn't steal that car. That's a big difference, and my parents believe me.''

He paused then, and the significance of his pause wasn't lost on Kara. ''That's good,'' she said and reached nervously for another cookie.

''But there isn't much parents can do in a situation like this,'' he continued, clasping his hands together. ''They can get up on a stand and tell the judge that their son is a fine boy. And that would help a bit. My lawyer says some parents would get on a stand and tell the judge to go ahead and put their kid in jail—it would teach him a lesson. But most parents would say what my parents would say, and the judge would figure they were just saying that because they were parents."

"What about Peter? He'd be seen as more objective, wouldn't he?"

"He'd be better than my parents," Craig agreed, "and Brewster says he'll use him if he has to, but Peter says himself that he's done this sort of thing a millions times. He doesn't think it does much good."

"He doesn't?" Kara asked, surprised.

"Let's put it this way," Craig explained. "It's Peter's job to help kids. So the judge would expect to hear the same sort of stuff a parent would say."

"But the judge doesn't expect a cop to want to help kids," Kara concluded with a touch of sarcasm. "Is that the theory behind putting me on the stand?"

"Well," Craig said, "your job isn't completely devoted to helping kids. I mean, maybe you help some, but sometimes in a pretty roundabout way."

Kara felt her dander rising. "You may think it's roundabout, Craig. But for most kids it's the most direct way."

"I know, I know," he said, hastening to smooth her feathers. "I know you think that your brother might have straightened himself out if the police had caught him at the beginning."

"That's right," Kara said, with unnecessary emotional force.

"What I'm trying to say," Craig returned quietly, "is that it would mean a lot to my case for a cop to testify. And it would mean a lot to me if that cop was you."

For a moment, Kara hesitated, and in that moment she told Craig more about how she felt than a thousand words could have done. "A year ago I never would have even considered such a request," she offered by way of sheepish explanation. "It's not the sort of thing cops generally do. It's our job to build up the prosecution's case, not tear it down."

Craig's chair scraped loudly across the kitchen floor. He began to pace again, as he had when he'd been locked in the holding cell at the station. Suddenly he stopped and looked at her with fury in his eyes.

"You know," he said hoarsely, jabbing his finger at her. "This may not be nice to say about someone who's dead, especially since I didn't know him, but your brother drives me nuts. I'd throttle him if I could. I never met him, but I can't stand him."

"Craig!" Kara said, flabbergasted. "What a thing to say!"

"Well, it's true," he insisted stubbornly. He jutted his jaw forward, setting his features in a defiant expression. "If your brother hadn't been such a con artist, you'd be giving me a break right now. It's crazy, but your brother, Joey, is messing up my life!"

"What do you mean? Joey has nothing to do with what's happening to you."

"It's only because Joey died that you've gone weird on all this 'be tough for their own good' stuff. If he hadn't been so good at conning everyone around him, then someone could have called his bluff and my life would be easier right now. I wouldn't let you down like your stupid brother did."

Kara sat back in stunned silence. She couldn't believe what Craig had had the audacity to say to her. It was even more unbelievable that she was allowing him to get away with it. Only she couldn't think of any way to refute his argument.

Most likely her testimony wouldn't make any more of a difference to Craig's defense than Peter's would. Judges were generally impressed only by hard evidence, like what witnesses saw, not what so-called experts thought. Yet the mere fact that she would testify would have an enormous impact on Craig. That in itself was something to think about. Whatever her decision, whether to testify or not, and regardless of how the case turned out, her decision would be significant in Craig's life.

"Looks like the tobogganing expedition is back," she noted, nodding out the window to where she could see Peter arriving with a station wagon full of kids.

"Yeah." Craig gave her a resigned sigh.

In a moment they heard the thunder of footsteps on the porch, then voices as the crowd burst through the front door.

Kara's thoughts were in a turmoil. Was he innocent or guilty? That was the real question, because if he was innocent, she had to stand up for him. It was funny.

One fourteen-year-old boy had stolen her faith in people many years ago. Now another was challenging her to reinstate it.

A stream of kids rushed down the hallway, calling out greetings to Kara and Craig as they whipped by the kitchen doorway. Only Peter paused at the entrance and entered the room to join them.

To Kara, he was a welcome sight. Fresh air had brought his face alive and heightened his complexion. His blue eyes glistened. In his down parka and jeans he looked strong enough to withstand the harshest elements, physical or emotional, and Kara craved his reassurance.

She wanted to run to him and bury her head in his shoulder. She wanted them to review all her choices again, with their heads bent close together over doughnut-shop coffee. But deep down she knew that the reason she wanted so badly to sit and talk with Peter was that it would protect her from having to decide for herself what to do. It would delay her having to commit herself.

Peter and Craig chatted about the tobogganing expedition, and Kara noticed how natural they were with each other. She felt on the outside right now. They were a team, and lately their mission had been to assail her first line of defense.

Craig laughed at something Peter was telling him, and Peter smiled, too, as he finished his story. Suddenly Kara felt ashamed. Craig was the one directly affected by this ordeal, yet she was the one demanding kid gloves. Watching Craig, realizing how brave he was being, she was inspired to let her fears dissipate.

What did her heart tell her? Ed Smithers could very well be frightened that he'd made a mistake, and she couldn't picture him ever admitting to making one; and Heather could very well be boxed in to her story. But for herself, Kara thought, if she just concentrated on Craig and didn't worry about anything else, how did she really feel?

"Any tea left?" Peter asked, glancing at her for an invitation. She could sense him reading the atmosphere, trying to interpret it like a bloodhound sniffing the air.

"There's more left, but I don't know how hot it is," she replied.

"I see you left us a couple of cookies," he noted as he pulled out a chair from the table. "How thoughtful."

"To tell you the truth," Kara said with a groan, "my stomach hurts."

"But they're supposed to be health-food cookies," Craig protested.

Peter laughed. "I guess it just goes to show that too much of anything can be dangerous."

"I have a health-food stomach ache, and I think I'm going to take it home to get better."

She noticed Craig's face drop, but he offered no objections.

"Craig," she added, "maybe you'd better give me your lawyer's telephone number."

"Why?"

"It's been my experience that lawyers like to know what their witnesses have to say before they go on the stand."

"You're going to testify."

"I'm going to make you put your money where your mouth is," she corrected. "You made me a promise you weren't going to let me down."

"And you believe me!"

"Yes, I believe you." Kara stood and tugged on her coat. "Does this win you five bucks from anybody?"

Surprise soon melted to embarrassment as a crooked smile erupted on Craig's red face. "Ten bucks this time."

Kara stopped at the doorway and shook her head. "You're too much, you know that? Just don't let me down on this."

"I won't," he answered resolutely. Kara wondered fleetingly if it was the reassurance of an innocent or the fervent hope of a guilty party. But she'd committed herself, and already a tremendous weight had been lifted from her shoulders.

Peter touched her elbow as she turned down the hallway. "I'll see you out," he said quietly.

It dawned on Kara that something was different about Peter today. Superficially he still seemed natural and nonchalant, as he had been when he'd joked with Craig and bantered about the tobogganing trip. But Kara could sense an uneasiness beneath his controlled surface. It was odd to see in Peter.

He had been consumed by his worries about Craig. Since his discussion with Kara in the doughnut shop he'd lost sleep, which hadn't happened in years.

He fixed his eyes on the back of Kara's brown winter coat as he followed her out the door and along the snowy footpath. She turned to face him when they reached her car. Her face looked warm and tanned against the stark white background of the snow.

"Want to get inside for a minute?" she invited. "You look like you're going to self-destruct if you don't say something."

Peter glanced back at the house. He was on duty today, but Andrea could handle things for a while. He pulled the passenger door open and dropped heavily into the seat.

Getting in her side, Kara started the car and switched the heat on to high. "You look depressed. I hope there's no more bad news."

Peter looked at her soft questioning face. "No, love, no more bad news."

"Then what is it? You seem upset."

Peter gazed out through the windshield over the grounds of Aiken House that stretched down to the frozen river. He'd built all this on so much hope. He wondered now if he'd been naive.

"I've been thinking about what you were saying about Craig stealing that car."

Kara sighed and placed her hands on the steering wheel. "Peter, let's not go into that again. You won your point. What do you want, a signed confession that I changed my mind, that I was so messed up I couldn't see that Craig's become an honest kid? I just hope I really do have things right now, because for better or worse, I'm going to testify for him."

Peter shook his head. "That's not what I wanted to say. I've been thinking about everything you've been saying about Craig—and about Joey, too—and I'm starting to think you've been right all along."

Peter's words sank in slowly. It was as if he'd spoken in another language, and Kara had to repeat them over and over in her mind before she really understood them. Then the dam broke, and she was flooded by feelings of betrayal, panic and confusion. "You what?" she breathed.

Peter drew in a long even breath to steady himself. "You've always thought that what happened to Joey was my fault. I thought you were wrong because it was an isolated incident. But now I look at what's happening to Craig and I wonder if what I'm doing here is helping anyone after all. Maybe you were right. Maybe Craig is guilty. Maybe what I'm doing causes more grief than it prevents. Maybe I should be laying down stricter rules and changing my approach—or getting out of this business."

He studied his boots, watching the snow slowly form rivulets of water on the car floor. He couldn't bear to look at her face and see the shock he knew must have been registering there.

"I can't believe this is happening," she said quietly.

"Believe it," Peter answered sullenly, then risked a quick glance at her. She was staring out the windshield toward the river.

"I should be happy you're saying this," she said as if arguing with herself. "I should feel vindicated, just hearing you say those words."

Peter looked at his feet again. There was a pool of water under each of his boots.

"Go ahead, you deserve to feel vindicated."

"But I don't," she said, and turned to look at him. Her eyes were distant and cloudy. "I feel betrayed. All this time you've been trying to convince me to trust what you're doing. Now you pull the rug out from under me. Again."

Her condemnation was more than he could stand. "I'm sorry," he mumbled. "That's all I can say."

He pulled open the car door and stumbled into the snow. More than anything he needed to be alone right now, but the sound of Kara's car backing out of the driveway was enough to make a grown man want to cry.

# CHAPTER TWELVE

CAPTAIN BANNON'S OFFICE was on the second floor. A reasonably pleasant room, it had large windows and clean, if Spartan, furniture. Floor-to-ceiling flags lent the room an appropriately institutional air of importance.

"Come in, constable, I've been expecting you," the squat man Kara knew as Captain Bannon invited, not rising from his seat at the desk. "Please, sit down."

Kara perched herself uncomfortably on the straight-backed leather chair that faced him. She watched him adjust his glasses as he flipped through several papers in the file that lay open in front of him.

Gord Bannon was not the sort of man Kara would easily have guessed was a high-ranking police officer. She would have pictured a tall solidly built man with a strong square jaw and enough gray streaked through his thick black hair to signify maturity and give an air of authority.

But middle age hadn't treated Bannon kindly, and Kara doubted if he'd ever possessed those distinguished attributes, even in his youth. He was shorter than her, a curiosity considering the department's height requirements of days gone by. Perhaps he'd squeaked by or worn shoes with extra layers of sole and built-up heels. His hair had thinned, revealing a definite shiny spot at the back of his head, and his body had settled into a pear shape. He carried himself with authority, but had more the aura of a street-smart cop than of a statesman. He cleared his throat several times before he spoke.

"You've been with the Youth Bureau for how long now, constable? Three years?" he asked.

"That's right, sir. It was three years this past September."

He nodded while he shuffled through the rest of the pages. "Shown yourself to be quite committed to helping out young offenders, I see."

Kara couldn't be sure from his tone of voice whether he meant the observation as a compliment, so she kept quiet.

"I've been hearing some interesting reports about you lately, constable." He closed the file and looked at her directly for the first time. There was a calculating intelligence in those eyes, but Kara could detect little in the way of compassion. "They were interesting enough," he continued, "that I wanted to follow them up in person. Regrettably I don't get down to the Youth Bureau often, although, as I frequently tell people, young offenders are a special interest of mine," he went on. "And this case of yours was one I wanted to look into personally. I am, of course, referring to the Taylor case. Craig Taylor, I believe, is the boy's name."

Kara had a vague feeling she was being toyed with. "Yes, sir," she confirmed. "That is correct."

He interlaced his fingers on the desktop. "I understand you've offered your services as a character witness for the defense. Is this true?"

"Yes," she answered steadily, keeping her eyes on his face, even though he appeared to be scrutinizing his fingers. "That's true."

"You don't regard this as somewhat unusual police procedure?"

"I regard this as an unusual case," she answered.

This conversation was a police officer's nightmare come true. Yet Kara knew she would not waver from her duty to Craig. To her mind, this wasn't a simple question of the police department defending one of its own. Ed should have been the one sitting in this chair, defending the charge. She shouldn't have to defend her attempt to keep an innocent kid out of training school.

"I see. And may I ask why you regard this as an unusual case?"

"I've worked with Craig Taylor for the past eight weeks, since the Bureau was contacted for assistance. I've come to know the boy quite well and I don't believe he is guilty of what he's been charged with."

"Don't you think that's a matter for the court to decide?"

"Absolutely," Kara agreed. "But first it requires a careful investigation, and I don't believe Craig has been given that."

"I see," Bannon nodded, his mouth quirking into a sarcastic slant. "You're planning to right an injustice before it happens."

"I am planning simply to tell the truth."

Bannon took off his glasses, laid them on his desk, then rubbed his eyes and sighed. "I've been with the force for thirty-seven years, Constable Ridgeway. That's a long time."

Kara dropped her eyes. This sounded like the beginning of a patronizing lecture.

"And there's one thing I've learned over and over again," he continued. "Police officers must stick together and work as a team. When we don't, it hurts us all. Sure, sometimes we're wrong. The odd time we get a little overenthusiastic and charge the wrong man or cut corners on procedure. We're human. But most of the time we're right about what we do. Kara, what I'm trying to tell you is that police officers do not testify against each other in court. Surely you must have learned that in your time on the force."

His words were tempting. They offered camaraderie, a sense of belonging, an unquestioning support group.

"With respect, sir," she countered gracefully, "I thought that we were all on the side of seeing justice done."

"That too," he agreed, shrugging, as if his concession proved he was a reasonable man. She hadn't given him the answers he was looking for, and Kara sensed that his next step would be to flex his muscles. She didn't have long to wait.

"There's one more thing," he said slowly. "I've also had reports that you've been spending a lot of your time at a group home—Aiken House."

Kara blanched. How intricate was his reporting network? She prayed it wasn't so elaborate that it included details of her personal life.

"That's the home where I placed Craig Taylor," she explained. If Bannon had heard rumors, he would have to be the one to raise them.

"There is only so much a police officer can and should do with a juvenile delinquent," Bannon directed her. The stern undercurrent in his voice had risen closer to the surface. "Social workers have a noble profession. I'd be the first to admit it. But they have their place, and it would be disastrous if cops tried to act like them. Maybe that's something worth thinking about."

"Sir, I don't think that's what I'm—"

"Let's face it, constable," Bannon said, cutting her off. "It's damned difficult these days to convict kids for anything. You know yourself how much we go through to catch these kids and build cases against them. As it is, half the time, some defense lawyer convinces the judge the kid just made a silly mistake. We know this offense is probably just the tip of the iceberg, but we have to watch the kid walk out of the courtroom scot-free. I shouldn't have to tell you that after you've been on the Youth Bureau three years. You know what it's like to be a cop."

"I know the frustrations," Kara agreed. "And I've always maintained that the sooner a kid bumps into the police, the sooner he's going to get some down-to-earth help. But that doesn't mean we shouldn't worry about the innocent kid who gets dragged into the system. That kid's life could be ruined because of his contact with the police."

"I see," Bannon concluded. "Well, I appreciate you being so candid with me, constable. It throws some light on this rather sticky situation."

"Sir, I can't in good conscience refuse to testify," Kara said frankly.

"I realize that. And I can't order you to do what I think is appropriate. But one thing I can do is make sure that from now on you are doing your job and only your job. I see no reason for you to be at Aiken House anymore. You can do your job from the station like all the other police officers."

"I do volunteer work at Aiken House on my own time," Kara protested.

"Then I suggest you keep the two worlds separate," Bannon advised her coldly. "You can leave it up to the social workers and judges to find the right services for your offenders. There's no need for you to have contact with Aiken House on police time. You've had a good record on the force until now. You've been recognized as promotion material. Now I hope you recognize that only team players are going to get promoted in this force. I'd like you to consider that very carefully. That will be all, constable. Thank you for your time."

Kara walked out with her head up, maintaining the illusion of self-control and dignity. But her face was burning with humiliation.

Everyone was squeezing her. Whatever happened to respecting a person's integrity? she asked herself.

Whatever happened to doing something just because it was right?

PETER HAD EXPECTED open hostility when he'd called Kara at the station. Maybe he'd been selfish to call. He'd hurt her enough already. Maybe a nobler soul would have let her be. But he couldn't. He'd told her he'd made dinner reservations at the Elora Mill and had been vastly relieved she'd had enough sentimental attachment to the mill to waver and then finally to agree to come.

Actually he'd been surprised she'd consented so quickly. But now, as she sat facing him across the candlelit table, he wondered if his optimism had been wishful thinking. She looked beautiful, soft curls framing vulnerable eyes, but her manner was matter-of-fact. He couldn't find the special glow she used to reserve for him.

She recreated her conversation with Bannon vividly, and he felt he'd been right in the room with her. Of course, if he had been in the room, the conversation would have taken a drastically different course. Peter could never have matched Kara's self-control.

As he listened, he glanced around the dark dining room at the sprinkling of other off-season customers. The relative emptiness of the place made it seem all the more private and intimate. They were together, hidden away in a small remote village that would be mercifully forgotten by the outside world until spring. Through the window, Peter could see the Tooth of Time blanketed in snow, illuminated by floodlights.

White water roared around the tiny island, the thunderous sound muffled by closed windows. The gorge looked cold, with patches of snow and ice hugging its banks.

Peter smiled as he stared out the window. Anyone looking at them from across the room might have concluded he and Kara were lovers. Few would have guessed their topic of conversation was the Guelph Police Department.

Kara poked at her melon balls *au porto*. "So," she concluded, "the captain has more or less slapped a restraining order on me. This is the way the police department deals with its sinners."

"It sounds like you've really stirred things up."

"Yeah, and frankly I'm not used to it. I'm usually commended for the extra work I do. It helps with community support when cops are involved with community groups. I've never done anything to step on anyone's toes before."

Peter struggled to assess just how serious these challenges from Bannon and Smithers really were. "It's funny that this controversy reached right up to the captain without even Stan hearing rumors about it."

Kara had already wondered about the same thing. "I think it's because everyone knows Stan and I are friends as well as partners. Around a police station that's like a blood relationship. But back when I told Stan I'd agreed to testify, he warned me that a higher-up would have something to say about it. Making another officer look bad even if he *is* bad, is a no-no."

Peter thought that it didn't seem fair that Kara had to pay so personally for her convictions. It would disappoint him if she couldn't follow through on her promise to Craig. But he felt he had to offer her the option of a graceful way out.

"Is it worth the pressure, Kara? I think Craig would understand if you decided not to testify."

Kara shook her head stubbornly. "It's too late for that now."

They sat back to allow the waiter to serve Peter's sirloin and Kara's sweetbreads.

"At least things are going well on one front," she added with a self-deprecating laugh. "Stan told me today that Jimmy Chalmers was granted a few day passes. He's going to look for a job, so he can help make a case in court that he should serve his sentence in a group home. He's already started correspondence courses to upgrade his education. It would be great if things worked out for Jimmy—and right now, I've more hope for him than for Craig."

"You can't make up for the Ed Smithers of the world," Peter reminded her gently. "Craig's lawyer will work on building a defense."

"He's going to have trouble doing that," Kara returned. "Craig's lawyer can subpoena Heather, which he still might do. But then he has a hostile witness testifying for him, and the judge would accept her testimony as binding on the defense. She could do more harm than good to the case. Let's face it, you and I are both afraid she just might be telling the truth."

Peter poured what wine remained in their carafe into Kara's glass. "Why did you agree to testify for Craig?" he asked curiously.

Kara twirled the long-stemmed glass between her thumb and forefinger. "It's bad police procedure to jump to conclusions," she explained. "That's what Ed Smithers and his partner did."

"I'm missing something here, Kara. You said yourself that the evidence against him is quite damning."

"It is," Kara agreed. "But Craig deserves a defense, weak as it is, and I'm part of it. I can tell a judge I think he's a good kid and still keep a clear conscience. Sure, it's possible he stole the car, though I don't believe he'd do something so serious. His offenses to date have only been spiteful ones against his parents. Besides, on Sunday I saw how much he'd grown up. He's no longer the same kid who stole a hundred bucks from his father, then tried to lie about it."

"Why did you accept my invitation tonight, Kara? Feeling betrayed is pretty serious stuff."

Kara didn't hurry to answer. "I did feel betrayed." She started to say more, then stopped as if searching for the right words. "I felt the floor fall out from under me the other night, Peter. For one awful moment, I was utterly convinced that Craig was guilty. I was sure I'd made a horrible mistake. It's a terrible thing when your worst fear comes to life right in front of you."

Peter nodded reluctantly. He knew his confession must have sent her into a tailspin. That hurt worse than anything.

"But by the time I got home," she continued, "I'd realized something important. Even if Craig is guilty, you, Peter Aiken, are not the one responsible for it."

Kara smiled affectionately. "I know that sounds ludicrous coming from me, but I mean it."

Peter tried to talk, but for once in his life, words failed him.

"Don't tell me I've left Peter Aiken speechless."

He nodded.

"Incredible," she said in mock awe, and Peter laughed out loud.

"You can laugh, but don't talk," she ordered. "I want to explain this to you all at once."

Peter folded his hands on the table to indicate patience. Then he lifted his head to listen.

"You know all this yourself," she said with confidence. "You really don't need me to be saying it to you. If the situation were reversed, and you were talking to someone else who stood in your shoes, you'd have no trouble seeing the situation for what it is. You'd tell that person these kids make their own decisions. You'd remind them not to delude themselves into thinking they can make decisions for anyone else. Don't lose faith in Craig, Peter. His case is weak, but there's nothing to be gained by jumping to conclusions."

Peter felt delirious, not so much because of her vote of confidence, but just because everything was obviously all right between them. He noticed how her cream knit sweater drew out the golden highlights in her skin and wanted to reach across the table to run his fingers over her freckles. He half expected they would have a special feel all their own. "I love you," he murmured instead.

His statement robbed her of breath. "Boy," she finally exhaled. "I must really be finding the magic words."

Peter's gaze was dead serious. "Everything about you is magic."

A tingling sensation began at the base of her spine and moved up. "Peter, nothing means more to me than to be loved by you. I—I admire you, Peter," she confessed shyly. "I've seen how the kids at Aiken House look at you. You're their hero. To them, Peter Aiken is a caring man who lives a straight, happy life. You had the same hardships in your youth as they're coping with now, and you still managed to make your life work. You're an inspiration to them. They try harder for you. I think of a kid like Jimmy Chalmers, and I wish he could know you."

"I love you," he murmured again.

A warm blush of pleasure suffused her face.

"Peter, if Joey could have known you, just held on for another three or four weeks, I'm sure things would have turned out differently. I don't think training school would have helped him. You're not responsible for what happened to Joey. I don't blame you anymore. I can't."

"There's nothing you could have said that would mean more to me," he answered quietly. An awkward silence ensued as they stared intensely at each other. Peter tilted his head to one side, curious. "I don't understand why a woman like you doesn't have a brood of your own children already, and someone who's been nuts about you for years."

His gaze was soft yet intense. She reveled in the knowledge that it was her reflection in his eyes.

"I could ask you the same question," she returned in a low voice.

Two slices of lemon cheesecake were silently deposited in front of them. Peter pressed his fork through the soft cake and looked at her. "You're looking at me squinty-eyed," he accused. "I know that means trouble. What are you thinking?"

He feigned dread, but nothing could keep his newfound happiness down. He'd be happy just sitting, drinking red wine, talking and laughing with her until they fossilized. He didn't care what they talked about; he just never wanted it to end.

Kara laid down her cutlery and folded her hands under her chin as she concentrated. "Tell me why you fell apart on me the other day. It's not like you to change your mind about your whole life like that."

Peter drew his hand over his eyes and squeezed the bridge of his nose with his thumb and forefinger. He could feel the tidal wave of anxiety he'd bottled up flowing out of him. It was a relief to be able to tell her.

"You're right, it's not like me. But I've never been in love before. It's as if I have two switches inside me—on and off. My whole life, the switch has been off. I channeled every bit of my energy into the kids. They gave me so much satisfaction that, for a while, I thought I'd never have to turn my switch on and love somebody. I didn't need anyone else. I treated everyone over the age of seventeen the same way you saw me treat Brice.

"Then I met you. Suddenly it wasn't me judging the world anymore. You actually had the audacity to judge me back! And for ammunition, you had the one event in my life that had really made me question myself."

"Joey?" she offered, and he nodded.

"I guess I was afraid history was repeating itself," he said, "that I'd somehow failed Craig, just as I felt I'd failed Joey all those years ago. And just for a moment I lost faith in Craig and in myself."

Kara shook her head. *Joey,* she thought, *you may be my brother, but it's time your ghost was buried forever.*

"Peter," she said aloud, "I love you, too."

Peter closed his eyes. "Say it again."

Kara laughed gently. "I love you, too."

"I never thought I'd hear you say that. I thought that this whole thing was just too big for us."

"Peter, it was too easy for me to blame you for everything. But I'm not fourteen years old anymore. What you do with kids is so overwhelmingly positive, it's a crime that I ever made you question yourself. When you fell apart on me, I fell apart, too. But then I realized that I love you for exactly who you are."

Peter clasped her hand and creased his face in mock pain. "I'm going to die in about thirty seconds if I can't kiss you."

"You're easily satisfied," she teased.

Peter glanced across the room. "I could see us quickly making a spectacle of ourselves."

Kara squeezed his hand. "It's too cold for one of your nature walks."

Peter laughed and nodded. He thought for a moment. "I'll be right back."

Kara watched him cross the dining room and disappear around the corner into the main hall before she realized she was grinning. He returned minutes later, key in hand and wearing the same grin, to lead her to a third-floor room overlooking the gorge.

"That took way too long," she whispered as his arms circled her waist and tightened until he'd almost lifted her off the floor. He walked with her over to the window, which was deeply recessed in the pale limestone wall.

They peered out the window into a night illuminated by a cold moon in the winter sky. "It's hard to believe that water rushes along all night, too," he whispered in her ear.

Kara sighed happily and turned to face him. His face looked contented in the silvery light. Impulsively she reached up her hand to gently explore his familiar features. He captured her fingers with his lips just before he looped his fingers through the beltloops of her skirt and pulled her tightly against him.

"I can't get enough of you," he breathed, nuzzling her neck.

She felt his warm hands against her skin as he lifted her sweater up over her head. She kissed and nibbled at him teasingly as she undid the buttons of his shirt and felt the softness of his chest hair as it pressed against her. "You can have as much of me as you want," she answered.

His breathing deepened and he lifted her from the window ledge and lay her down gently on the bed. "I can't believe this is happening," he said, drawing his hand down between her breasts and splaying his fingers over her abdomen. "I was afraid you'd walk out of my life tonight. Are you sure that's not going to happen?"

Kara smoothed his shirt back over his shoulders. "You just happen to be in love with someone who takes a terribly long time to change her mind. That can be good and bad."

"It's worth the wait."

She reached up around his neck and pulled him down, melting under his weight.

## CHAPTER THIRTEEN

PAUL BREWSTER SIGHED heavily as he rummaged through his briefcase, which lay open before him on the large mahogany table. Peter didn't like to see resignation on the face of the man who would defend Craig in less than an hour. He glanced at Kara and Craig. Obviously they were thinking the same thing.

Brewster's voice matched the look on his face. "All we can do is go ahead with what we have," he said. "It's a good thing we have you, Constable Ridgeway, or we'd be in even worse trouble." They sat in a small anteroom near the courtroom.

Peter studied Kara's body language. She sat very still, struggling to win the war she was undoubtedly waging to keep her emotions under control. Her face, however, was beyond her control. Perhaps if she'd had a mirror in front of her, she could have banished the telltale furrows from between her eyebrows and the vulnerability from her eyes. But they remained as visible symptoms of her anguish.

It was clear Kara couldn't yet accept defeat. "I really thought that Heather might change her mind in the end. I had the feeling she really did want to testify for us."

The tired-looking lawyer shook his head slowly. "There's only so much anyone can do in a situation like this. We gave it a try. That's all we can do. Now we have to accept that Heather will be testifying for the prosecution, not for us."

"It's just that she seemed so close. I thought if she had a little more time to herself to think..."

Peter, too, had hoped Heather would change her mind. He'd gone to see her only last week at her school, hoping that away from her parents she might be a little more candid about what really happened. The school principal had allowed them to meet privately in the teacher's lounge.

The petite dark-haired adolescent had been very nervous. She'd expected him to pressure her with threats about what would happen to her on the witness stand. But in the place of threats he'd issued appeals to her sense of fair play and reminded her how important the outcome of this trial would be for Craig's future.

When Heather had started to cry, Peter had hoped it meant she'd finally accepted that she had to do the right thing. Now, in retrospect he realized that had been wishful thinking. She'd been crying for herself and her own fears.

"She wants to help," Craig said, "but she's too scared. She wasn't allowed to go to that dance, at least not with me. She locked herself into that story."

"You're far more understanding and sympathetic than I'd be, Craig," Kara said. "Sure, she stands to get into a little trouble if she tells the truth. But you stand to get into a lot more trouble if she doesn't. Anyone with a shred of courage would realize what she had to do.''

Peter was inclined to agree with Kara about Heather, but he still couldn't help but feel sorry for the girl. She must be feeling very isolated, confused and guilty. Besides, Craig was a bit defensive on her behalf, so it wouldn't do to be too critical.

Peter nodded to Craig. ''There's no doubt she's scared. I get the impression she's also worried about what the police might do if she did change her story. The Crown Attorney or the police themselves might have told her they have the right to lay charges of public mischief and obstructing justice in such circumstances.''

Kara looked at him appreciatively. Peter knew it was because he'd subtly pointed out that Heather was busy saving her own skin at the expense of Craig's.

Kara turned to Brewster. ''Didn't you tell her that by getting on the stand and not telling the truth, she's committing perjury? Does she know how serious that is?''

''She knows,'' Brewster replied wearily, hiking one elbow up over the back of his chair. He was a tall lean man who sincerely wanted to help his young client. His boyish face made him seem an adolescent himself. ''I tried browbeating her with that, but it didn't work. It just frightened her more. Peter's right. She's really in a no-win situation.

''She's afraid of what the police will do if she tells the truth and she's afraid of what we'll do if she doesn't. Unfortunately there's nowhere for her to run, so she just sticks to her story. It may not be fair or far-sighted, but this is what we have to deal with in the real world of witnesses. They're human beings with their own motivations and limitations."

"But surely you're not going to let her get away with it," Kara insisted. "You can cross-examine her and show the court what's really going on."

"Now wait a minute, Kara. Where would that get us? She knows very well the position she's in. She knows she's our alibi. But she also knows that it's her word against Craig's. I could cross-examine her aggressively. I could ask her to tell the court what would likely happen to her if she ever admitted she was at the dance with Craig. We might be able to cast some doubt on her story by showing the judge just what a bind she's in, but it's not worth the risk."

"Why not?" Kara asked. "That sounds good to me. At least then the judge would know to suspect her testimony."

"Slow down, though, and think this through. Let's say I really challenge her on the stand and wear her down. Chances are I'll see the girl in tears and still sticking to her story. The three of us have tried unsuccessfully to get her to change her mind. There's no reason to believe I'd be more successful this time. If I have her in tears, I don't look like the purveyor of truth and justice. I just look like an insensitive boor grasping at straws. I'd do it if I thought it would help our case, but we can't forget that it's our word against Heather's as well as our word against the cops'. Those aren't great odds. And I'm sure Ed Smithers has pointed that out to Heather.''

Peter shared Kara's exasperation, but he knew Brewster was right.

"What do we do then," Kara complained. "Just give up?"

"No," the lawyer returned patiently. "What we do is present Craig in the best light possible. We're depending on you to do that, Kara. I want the judge to be so impressed with Craig by the end of your testimony that he just can't believe such a fine young man could ever steal a car. That impression would leave a reasonable doubt in the judge's mind."

Peter watched as Kara digested the news that there would be no last-minute miracle to rescue their case. He felt for her as she shifted restlessly in her chair.

"It just seems so flimsy..." Kara said.

Brewster looked at her grimly. "I'm not going to kid you. It is flimsy. Your testimony will be the strongest card we have, next to what Craig will say for himself."

The people around the mahogany table fell silent. Peter knew that Paul Brewster had done his best to build a case out of nothing. But the man would never feel satisfied if Craig was convicted, no matter how good a job he'd done. Peter knew the frustration of not being able to solve someone's problems. Even if the responsibility wasn't yours, you still felt the burden on your shoulders.

Peter stole a look at Craig. He'd been strong and steady this morning before they left Aiken House, but now he looked a little shaky. He had to be wondering about his future. Craig wouldn't do well in training school. He was too interested in right and wrong, fairness and unfairness, to make the necessary adjustments.

Finally Peter shifted his gaze to Kara. What was she thinking? He found it difficult to predict her thoughts. He knew she felt frustrated and anxious. They all did. But he didn't know if she might still be tempted to blame herself or him for Craig's trouble.

"I'll tell you something else," Paul Brewster added in a quiet tone. "Even if Heather changed her mind at this point and told the truth, it probably wouldn't do us any good. The judge wouldn't believe her. Judges are highly suspicious of witnesses who change their testimony."

"So," Kara said lamely, "we're in a no-win situation, too."

"I wouldn't paint the picture quite that bleak," Brewster replied, glancing at Craig. "Don't get me wrong, Kara. If Heather came pleading to testify for us, we might have a shot at it. But things don't look too good right now."

Peter noticed Kara's eyes widen. He intercepted her gaze, but she looked away quickly. What was she up to? he wondered.

Brewster stood up and clicked his briefcase closed. "I think I'll go and pay an eleventh-hour visit to my colleague in the Crown Attorney's office."

Kara looked up hopefully. "Is there something more you think you can do?"

"No, I just want to ask him how he slept last night."

Craig asked the question on Peter's mind. "Why? He's the one with the great case. He probably slept like a baby."

"I'm sure you're right, Craig. But I want to follow that question with another one. I want to ask him how he thinks he'll sleep tonight if he convicts an innocent kid. It's just a last-minute thought I want him to take into the courtroom. It won't change anything, but we need any psychological edge we can get."

Brewster strode out of the room without a word, and Kara strode out after him.

Peter started up out of his seat to go after her, then checked himself. Maybe Kara needed some time alone. Besides, Craig was still here and he needed him the most.

The boy looked as if he didn't know what to do with himself. It was difficult to just mark time during a crisis. Peter knew Craig felt the need to do something, preferably something that would help save the day. Unfortunately the most productive thing he and Craig could do right now was to forget about the court case until it started.

Peter pulled his spirits up for Craig's sake. "Well, partner. Can I buy you something out of one of those disgusting machines down the hall?"

A smile tugged at Craig's lips. "You trying to poison me?"

"I'll take the first bite of whatever you get."

Craig cocked his head to one side as he considered the offer. "It's a deal."

They shuffled to the door, and Peter dropped an arm over the boy's shoulder. Together, they left the safety of the small stuffy room.

Twenty minutes later, Peter swallowed the last bite of his dry roast beef sandwich and regretted having eaten it. It sat lead-heavy in his stomach. He couldn't get his mind off Kara. Where had she gone? Craig had already followed his parents into the courtroom. Why was she cutting it so close? The trial was due to begin in less than five minutes.

Suddenly he spotted her at the far end of the hallway. He watched her familiar brown curls as they bobbed their way toward him down the hall.

"You okay?" he asked when she reached him.

Her face was flushed as if from anger or some other intense emotion. But her expression was inscrutable, her voice cool and distant. "I'm fine."

"You were gone a long time. I was starting to worry."

"No need to worry." She seemed to falter for a fraction of a second, but quickly resurrected her composure. "I just had a bit of work to clear up."

Peter looked skeptical. The Kara Ridgeway he knew wouldn't have been doing her paperwork. More likely she would have been making a last-ditch effort to get Heather to tell the truth on the stand.

Whatever she was up to, though, she apparently wasn't about to divulge it to him, and he saw no point in pushing her.

Just then there was a flurry of activity as people hurried to enter the court before the doors were closed.

One of the crowd was wearing a dark blue uniform and came to a halt as he passed Kara.

"Ed," she said, surprise in her voice.

Years of cynicism had etched his forehead into a permanent frown, and when he spoke, Kara knew instantly that his intentions weren't friendly.

"I thought you'd be interested in hearing the latest on another one of your rehabilitation projects."

When Kara didn't answer, Ed stared into her eyes with a fierce intensity. He looked as if he held her personally responsible for everything that had ever gone wrong in the world.

"You and Stan have been playing social workers to one James E. Chalmers," he said, "trying to get him day passes and into a group home. You ought to stick to police business, Ridgeway. You're batting zero with the social work."

"What about Chalmers?" she asked weakly.

"He was busted today for sticking up a convenience store on Speedvale Avenue. He was out on one of his day passes. Must have paid another visit to his friends because he had another gun. You won't be involved with this case, of course. He's eighteen now. No more juvenile stuff. He's ours now," Ed said, sounding pleased with himself.

Peter took Kara's elbow. "I believe we're late," he said with a threatening undertone.

Ed glowered at him, then grunted and turned his attention back to Kara. "Just thought you'd be interested in the news, officer."

Kara kept her head down as Ed strode off and Peter led her to her seat in the courtroom.

As she waited for proceedings to begin, Kara struggled to put the pieces of her shattered confidence back together. Jimmy had been telling her and Stan that he really wanted to get his life on the right track. He'd known all the right things to say, even the right words to use.

She'd been fed a line just as surely as if Jimmy had served it up for lunch. She'd believed he was going to make all those changes. She'd been excited to help him make arrangements for school and to get into the Hanson group home.

What did that have to do with Craig? She didn't want to be paranoid, but if there was ever a story she wanted to believe, it was Craig's. He knew exactly what she wanted to hear. He knew her vulnerable spots better than ten Jimmy Chalmers ever could.

Craig was in a perfect position to lie to her and benefit from it. She'd never gone this far out on a limb for anyone before.

Maybe Ed Smithers was right. He knew the Jimmy Chalmers types of the world better than she did. Maybe it was a big mistake for a police officer to dabble in social work.

Looking out at the courtroom now, Kara had the sinking feeling she knew what was to come. She sensed that Peter was trying to reach out and console her, but she was too nervous to be consoled. All she wanted was to get this ordeal over with. She wished Paul Brewster could present his case before the Crown

Attorney. To have to listen to the witnesses for the prosecution give their damning evidence was sheer agony.

Actually Peter's mere presence seemed to make everything that much more painful. When she looked at him, she couldn't help but feel overwhelmed by her love for him. His eyes meant understanding; his arms, comfort. Yet a little voice inside her still plagued her with doubts. She had resolved her feelings about Joey, but a shrill and irrational voice rose up in her mind from time to time, telling her this was all Peter's fault. Try as she might to stop it, the little voice persisted. She could never openly admit it to Peter, yet she was certain he knew.

It hurt to feel so close to Peter and yet not allow her guard to fully drop. Her mind flashed to their love-making. No guards were up then. Why did the guards always return?

Ed Smithers and his partner were the first witnesses to be called. They quoted their evidence from the meticulous notes they'd made on the night Craig was charged. They remained unflappable, absolutely sure of every detail, despite Brewster's challenges.

Several of Craig's classmates testified that they were at the dance until midnight and didn't recall seeing Craig after seven-thirty. No one, it seemed, recalled seeing Heather at all.

Kara had to admit an unpleasant fact. If she were sitting in judgment of this case and she didn't know Craig personally, she'd be convinced of his guilt by now.

It made sense that the Crown Attorney would save Heather until the end of his case. The Crown had introduced into evidence Craig's statement that he was with Heather on the night of the charge. All the other witnesses couldn't say whether or not Craig's alibi was true. Only Heather could blast a giant hole through his story. It was more dramatic to save her until last.

Heather's name was called, and Kara felt a chill climb to her shoulders and up the back of her neck. She turned with everyone else in the court to watch the attractive young girl respond to her name. Heather's bent head and stiff shoulders reminded Kara of a prisoner walking to the gallows. Or a sailor walking the plank. Kara stared at the girl's face, hoping to catch her eye and send a reminder of Craig's need for the truth. But Heather kept her eyes averted.

In regular court protocol Heather would have proceeded directly to the witness stand. She would have been sworn in, and the Crown Attorney would have posed his first question. But instead, the girl detoured to the Crown Attorney's table. She stooped and whispered something in his ear.

The man snapped up his head at Heather's words. But Kara couldn't tell if his action signified shock or decisive decision-making. Heather may have caught him off guard, or merely reinforced something he expected. The Crown Attorney was experienced in a courtroom, so his acting ability was undoubtedly strong. He could mask everything except what he wanted the court to see.

To Kara's surprise, the Crown Attorney indicated that Heather take a nearby seat. Clearly she was not going to the witness stand. Then the Crown Attorney approached the bench. He held the rapt attention of everyone in the courtroom.

His voice rang out confidently. "Your Honor, the prosecution wishes to rest its case at this point in the proceedings."

The judge, a serious-looking man in his late forties, took off his glasses and set them down in front of him.

"You're not questioning that last witness, counsellor?"

"No, Your Honor, we are not. The prosecution has completed its evidence."

The judge thought for a moment, then reached for his gavel. "Very well," he announced to the assembly. "Court will recess for thirty minutes, then resume with the case for the defense."

People all around Kara whispered to each other excitedly. They were all asking the same questions. What happened? Why hadn't Heather taken the stand?

Peter ended a brief conversation with Brewster and glanced back at Kara, signaling for her to follow him. With Craig in tow, Peter led them back to the room with the mahogany table.

"Peter, what's going on?" Craig asked even before the door clicked shut behind them.

"We don't know yet, Craig. That's what Brewster stayed back there to find out."

As if the mention of his name was an introductory cue, the young lawyer burst through the door and slammed it behind him. "Damn!"

"Bad news?" Peter asked.

"Worse than that. It's no news."

"What's that supposed to mean?" Craig insisted.

"It means the Crown won't tell me why he pulled that last-minute stunt. He just says he decided not to call her because he's got enough evidence in to convict. Something's going on."

"It doesn't make sense," Peter said. "Heather was his most important witness. What could he possibly gain by not questioning her?"

"It's simple," Craig offered. "Heather must have told him she was going to tell the truth."

The three adults in the room looked at him.

Brewster was sympathetic. "I wish that were the case, son."

"Why are you so sure it isn't?"

"I can't be completely sure. But I can tell you it's the riskiest possibility for us to believe. I would bet it's exactly what the Crown wants us to believe."

"Why would he want that?"

Brewster hoisted himself to sit on the table. "To get us to make fools of ourselves. He'd love us to call a hostile witness to the stand. I don't need to tell you that the cops and the Crown are especially hungry for a conviction in this case. I think they're a little nervous about Kara's testimony."

"I don't get it," Peter said doubtfully. "If they're so hungry, you'd think they'd present their strongest witness."

"Right now the Crown doesn't need her. We need her. It's our job to establish the alibi. Anybody here have any doubts about how this case is going?"

Kara kept her eyes glued to the table, and she didn't hear a sound from Peter. She didn't want to discourage Craig, but there was no doubt that their backs were against the wall.

"As it stands," Brewster continued, "we're claiming that Craig was with Heather at the dance. The Crown has already established that no one saw them there together. We don't have any witnesses to contradict that testimony. We have two options. One, if we don't call Heather, it looks like we can't substantiate the alibi and support Craig's statement to the police. Two, if we do call her, we risk having her blow us out of the water."

Peter's face was grimly intent as he folded and refolded his arms several times. "Is that the only explanation, Paul?"

Brewster pushed himself up from the table and began to pace. "No, I suppose there are other possibilities. We all saw how pale Heather looked. Maybe she told the Crown she'd faint if he put her on the stand. Or maybe he was worried about how aggressively I would cross-examine her. You'd think he'd be suspicious that she was hiding something and that she might break down and tell the truth on the stand if I pushed her hard enough. But these possibilities are all long shots."

Craig's voice was plaintive. "Why don't we just go ask her?"

Brewster smiled indulgently. "That makes the most sense, Craig, and in the twenty-odd minutes we have left we'll try to do that. But any Crown Attorney worth his salt would make sure we couldn't get anywhere near her. With us not knowing what Heather plans to do, the Crown Attorney has us exactly where he wants us."

Peter looked at Kara, but she gave no indication she was about to say anything.

"What do you think, Kara?" The others turned to look at her now. "Do you think Heather is ready to tell the truth?"

She seemed caught off guard by his direct question.

"I wouldn't know. We've all tried to get her to change her mind and so far it hasn't worked. I don't know any better than you what she plans to do."

Craig looked from one adult to the other. "So what do we do?"

Kara was relieved when Brewster outlined Craig's choices. "If we call Heather to the stand, she could make you look like an out-and-out liar, Craig. The judge could decide to make an example of you. The possibility of serving a sentence at Aiken House could go right out the window. That would mean training school."

"And if we don't call her?" Peter's voice was grim but steady. Kara didn't think she could manage the same feat.

"If we don't call her—" Brewster repeated, then paused. "We could lose the only possible break we've had in this case."

Peter spoke for all of them. "It has to be your decision, Craig. We'll go with whatever you decide."

Kara was aware she was holding her breath. What a monumental decision to leave to a fourteen-year-old!

There was a sheen of perspiration on Craig's forehead. "I say we call her."

The decision sent an instant jolt of energy through Brewster. He jumped to his feet. "All right, my man. Let's go for it. We're with you the rest of the way."

Kara stared after Craig as he marched out the door after his lawyer. He was so vulnerable, so young. Yet he was making adult decisions, and no adult could protect him from the consequences.

She turned around to face the eyes that were boring into her back. "Are you going to ask me how I feel?" she asked.

Peter's eyes were bright. "Yes."

"Let me explain it this way. If someone was trying to think up the worst, most fearful and perverse thing they could do to Kara Ridgeway, this would be it."

Peter dropped his head and nodded, his smile one of resigned recognition rather than happiness. "I've got to admit I'm worried."

"You've never seemed much like the worrying type."

"I'm not. But I seem to be getting more so for some reason."

"My bad influence?"

His face softened, and something deep inside Kara was relieved that he could still look at her that way. "There's nothing bad about your influence, Kara. Maybe it's good for me to be a little more aware of how things can go wrong."

"It wouldn't change what you do."

"That's true. I don't think it would. But it doesn't have to, to be a good influence all the same. Look at you. I know what you're feeling. But it's not stopping you from doing what you promised to do."

"I'm not so sure that's good."

He looked into her eyes steadily. "No, I suppose you're not."

Kara leaned forward and melted into his arms. He was the only person who could know the extent of her fears. He was the only one whose arms could comfort her in the way she needed most.

THE COURTROOM WAS INFUSED with drama. For Kara, it served to heighten her anxiety. She stood as the judge returned to the bench, then sat numbly as the defense was asked to present its case and Heather's name was called once again. She watched as the frightened girl retraced her steps up the center aisle and this time continued to the witness stand.

The court attendant recited the words that only seem real in the movies. "State your name."

"Heather Crawly."

"Do you swear to tell the whole truth and nothing but the truth, so help you God?"

"Yes."

Heather was dwarfed by the witness box. Her pale complexion seemed snow-white against the backdrop of her dark hair. Kara noticed a stubborn look about her pursed lips.

Brewster stood at his table, then paced back and forth several times in front of Heather. Kara wondered if he did that for dramatic effect or if he really was considering how to pose his first question.

"Are you a classmate of Craig Taylor's?"

"Yes, we have the same homeroom."

"How long have you known him?"

"Three or four months. Since he came to the school."

"Do you like him?"

"Yes."

"There was a dance at your school on the Thursday night in question in this case. Do you remember it?"

"Yes, I was staying at my girlfriend's place that night."

"Is that what you told the police?"

"Yes."

"Is it true?"

"Yes."

Brewster rubbed his hand over his chin. "Is it true you were at your girlfriend's house for the entire evening without leaving?"

Kara was sure that Heather's eyes alighted on her for a split second.

"No."

Kara sat back in the hard wooden pew. Had she heard what she thought she'd heard?

Brewster stopped pacing dead in his tracks. "Let me rephrase that, Miss Crawly," he said quickly. "You *did* leave the house?"

"Yes."

"You were at the dance?"

"Yes."

"For how long?"

"From about seven-thirty to just after eleven o'clock."

"Who were you with?"

"Craig Taylor."

"Did you and Craig dance?"

"No. We sat in the stairwell, talking."

"Isn't that an unusual place to be during a dance?"

"We wanted to talk. We wouldn't be able to hear each other in the auditorium. The music was too loud, and the band was awful."

"Did you see anyone else while you were at the school?"

"No. I came in through the side door. Craig was waiting there for me. We both left by the side door, too, and Craig walked me back to my girlfriend's."

Kara couldn't believe these words were coming out of Heather's mouth. The girl had found her courage.

Brewster gained confidence. "Tell me, Miss Crawly. I have here in my hand a statement signed by you and given to the Crown Attorney in which you claim you were at your girlfriend's residence doing homework for the entire evening. Did you understand the seriousness of your signing these statements?''

"Yes, sir, I did.''

"And now you are saying that those statements are not true. Can you please explain to the court why you are doing this?''

Heather drew back a lock of her black hair and tucked it behind one ear. She seemed determined to get through this examination. "Well, sir, I was afraid I'd get into trouble for being at the dance with Craig.''

"In trouble with whom?''

"Well, my parents. I told them I'd asked Craig to go—it was a Sadie Hawkins—and they got mad and said I couldn't because they thought a boy from a group home was bad news. But my girlfriend was going to the dance, so I decided I'd go, anyway, and just not tell them.''

Heather paused, blushing with embarrassment, but Brewster encouraged her to go on. "The police came to my girlfriend's sometime after midnight," Heather continued, "and asked me if I'd been to the dance with Craig. I panicked and said no. I didn't know what had happened to Craig then, and when I did find out, I was too afraid of the police to tell the truth. They'd warned me I'd be charged if I changed my story. They really seemed to want to get Craig.''

"And what was it that finally convinced you to risk the wrath of the police?''

Heather looked over at Kara. This time there was no mistaking it. "I don't know exactly. It sort of hit me all of a sudden today. I kept thinking, what if I change my mind and tomorrow I want to tell the truth? Well, then it would be too late. This whole thing would be over with."

The silence in the court tempted the sob that had lodged in Kara's throat, but she fought it.

"No more questions, Your Honor."

The judge scrutinized Heather carefully. When he finally spoke, his voice was skeptical and unsympathetic. "Changing your testimony at the last minute like this, Miss Crawly, is a very grave matter. There is no objective reason for me to believe this story is any more accurate than the first one you told. I am aware that you have taken a considerable risk by changing your testimony, but I'm not sure how much good that will do your friend."

Kara watched her last vestige of hope evaporate before her eyes. Brewster had been right.

The judge turned to the Crown Attorney. "Do you wish to cross-examine, counsellor?"

"No, Your Honor."

"Very well," the judge said with finality. "Mr. Brewster, please call your next witness."

Kara responded to her name as the court attendant called it out. But her spirit was broken.

## CHAPTER FOURTEEN

ON THE SURFACE, Mulroney's appeared the same as always. The soft lights, warm pine furniture and plants still worked together to produce a homey atmosphere. But below the surface, in the guts of the place, there was something decidedly amiss.

Even as she and Peter walked through the front door and found a private table by the far wall, Kara could sense how drastically the mood of the place had changed. Perhaps she should have predicted that the dark cloud hanging over the station was big enough to cast its shadow here, too.

On the way to their table, Kara extended a routine hello to a fellow officer. The man ignored her. Again, when they were seated, Kara greeted another officer who caught her eye. Again, no response. Now she kept her eyes lowered. Her hurt and embarrassment were impossible to hide from Peter.

"If this is how these guys treat each other, they must be ugly on the street," Peter noted dryly. "Why don't they argue with you? Or ask you what was so important to you that you'd break ranks in this case? I tell the kids to debate these kinds of issues with each other. At least then you can respect each other for your differences. If you don't talk, you never understand each other."

"That would be the mature way of handling it." Her voice sounded sarcastic even to her own ears. Kara was bitterly disappointed with her fellow officers. It was made even worse because Peter was there to see it. She felt completely exposed to him, vulnerable to his judgments. She suddenly felt very protective of herself and her kind. "I imagine social workers would act much the same way," she snapped.

Peter let her defensive comment pass. "Well, for what it's worth, I was proud of you up there on the stand."

Kara looked up, grudgingly appreciative of at least one sympathetic face in the room. "I don't know that it did Craig any good. That judge seemed pretty unconvinced about Craig and his story."

"You convinced *me* that Craig was a good kid."

Kara scoffed. "Big deal. Convincing you is just preaching to the converted."

"I'm being objective," Peter protested. "You gave a very compelling character reference. I think you did exactly what Brewster wanted."

"Well, thank you. At least that part of the ordeal is over. Now there's just tomorrow's sentencing to deal with."

"The verdict comes first, Kara. There's still a chance we won't have to deal with a sentence."

Kara kept her retort to herself. Even Brewster would admit that a "not guilty" verdict was only mathematically possible at best.

Peter was looking at her steadily. "I figure you had a whole lot to do with Heather finally testifying. I saw how she looked at you when Brewster asked her why she'd changed her mind. That's where you were before court, wasn't it? You weren't clearing up police business like you claimed. You were talking to Heather."

"I could argue that was police business."

"I don't think your argument would go over very well around here, do you?" he said, and Kara winced. "I just want to ask you one thing. What did you say that finally convinced her?"

"I'm not sure, because she didn't seem convinced when I left her, but I told her about Joey. I told her he'd haunted me for all these years because there was no longer anything I could do to help him. I told her to grab her chance to help Craig now while she still could. After today, her chance would be gone forever."

"Obviously you hit home. But you didn't do it as a cop, Kara. That's too personal a thing for you to call police work."

"I suppose," she answered, and her voice trailed off.

"What about this campaign to freeze you out around here? Will that end with the trial?"

Kara sighed. "I don't know. I've broken a pretty serious unwritten code. Probably if Craig is found not guilty, most of the cops would think there must have been a good reason for my testifying. But they still wouldn't approve of what I did."

"Does it make you regret what you did?"

"No, not at all. It makes me furious. They should be freezing out Ed Smithers, not me. They should be mad about his sloppy police work, because it reflects badly on all of us. Now an innocent boy is about to be convicted. They should be lining up to offer their support."

"It's nice that we're in total agreement on something," he said as he surveyed the place. "How long do you usually have to wait in here for a waiter?"

"They're usually very quick," she answered sadly. "We might have to order from the bar."

Peter got up from his chair and stalked toward the bar. He didn't need to say a word to communicate his contempt.

In a minute, he was back with two draft beers and a basket of nachos balanced in his arms. He had a half smile on his face. Kara thought he looked pleased with himself, like a hunter who had pitted himself against the dangers of the jungle and returned the victor. He seemed smug and self-satisfied and totally insensitive to her fragile emotions.

He sat down and passed her a napkin.

"You're enjoying this, aren't you?" she charged.

Peter looked startled. "Of course not. I don't enjoy seeing you get hurt."

"Maybe not that part, but you're glad I'm getting disillusioned with cops. They're doing what you thought they'd do all along. Well, maybe it's all very blasé and predictable to you, but it's still a bit of a shock to me."

Peter felt confused. She'd turned on him, redirected her pent-up anger from her coworkers to him. This was the wrong day to do it. He felt testy and overstretched himself.

"Okay," he snapped, "you want the truth? I think it's good for you to see cops acting like vindictive children. And I don't think social workers, on the whole, would be so idiotic and immature. It's about time you realized that."

Kara's emotions shifted to overload. "I knew you were glad about it. You like to see anything that puts cops down."

She could feel herself spiraling out of control, but she couldn't put a stop to it. She felt completely alone, shut out by everyone.

Peter softened as he detected a quaver in her voice. "That's not quite true, Kara. I look at someone like Stan, and I'm glad that he's out there. But you're different. As long as I've known you, you've always had much more to give than your role as a police officer allows. That's all I've ever said."

Kara clenched her jaw and looked away. Her life had been fine before Peter came along. She'd never been in trouble at work. She'd never had anything but approval from Captain Bannon and the other men. She'd dabbled in social work and tried to place her juveniles in the homes she thought would do them the most good. But it had never taken over her life the way Aiken House had.

Peter seemed to think he was giving her compliments, but in fact she felt criticized and undermined.

She felt confused, too. Here she was defending being a cop and yet her heart hadn't been in it for weeks, especially tonight.

"Kara, let me ask you something. Before Craig, was there any kid you were able to help more than you've helped him?"

She thought hard. "I think I've helped to turn a few kids around." Why couldn't she think of any examples when she needed them?

"I'm talking in a more personal way. Did any of those kids look at you the way Craig does? Did any of them care as much about what you thought as he does?"

"You know the answer to that."

"That's right. And let me ask you something else. Have you ever been able to change a young person's mind about right and wrong more dramatically than you did Heather's?"

"I did that as a police officer."

"By telling her about a personal event in your life that was more painful and more significant than any other."

Kara sighed. Being a cop was all she knew. It was what she'd always wanted, ever since Joey. Had she really outgrown being a police officer? Had that happened because she'd fallen in love with Peter?

Bannon told her she was a cop, not a social worker. Peter was telling her she was a social worker, not a cop. She felt isolated. Both Bannon and Peter knew who they were and where they fit in. She was the one who no longer fit anywhere.

Suddenly she felt overwhelmed with the perverse desire to see how far Peter was prepared to go with his little employment counselling session. "So what is it you suggest I do with this extra special talent for social work?"

Peter scrutinized her before answering. "I think you ought to believe in it and see where it takes you."

Kara stared at his intent face, aghast. "What's that supposed to mean?"

"I don't want you to feel insulted when I tell you this," he warned, "but I don't think you're cut out to be a cop."

"You don't," she repeated quietly.

"No, I think you should do what you wanted way back in the first place. I think you ought to make a career change. You'd make a great social worker."

A look of rage registered on Kara's face. "Do you think that yours is the only noble profession? Sure you've seen some jerk cops today, but there are jerk social workers, too. I dreamed about being a cop and I worked hard to get where I am today. And you think I'm not cut out for it? You think I offer nothing as an officer of the law?"

Kara slid her chair back from the table. "Thank you for your grand insights, Peter. If you'll excuse me, I think I've had enough. You don't need to concern yourself with my life any longer."

She hadn't expected Peter to follow her, but he did.

He stopped as they reached her car, his hands jammed into his jacket pockets. She looked at him as he spoke and saw real anger there for the first time since the night she'd stayed at the house for tortellini.

"I don't know why you're doing this, Kara. Maybe you're frightened about what will happen tomorrow when Craig's trial winds up." He paused, anger and frustration churning inside him. It had been a long day, too long. He felt punch-drunk and didn't care anymore about being diplomatic. "All right, that's just fine with me. Maybe you're cut out to be a cop after all. You're certainly acting immature enough. You fit right in with all your buddies back there. I had you figured all wrong. I thought you were stronger, but go ahead, run. I've run after you long enough," he said, then turned on his heel and walked away.

MORNING SUNSHINE STREAMED into the courtroom, its warmth making Kara sleepy. She'd had a restless night. She sat alone, close to the back where it would be easier to make a quick getaway after the judge's verdict and sentence.

From her seat, Kara had a view of the entire courtroom and could watch people without their being aware of her scrutiny. Ed Smithers and his partner sat together, backs erect, faces front. Kara wondered how they felt right now. Were they smugly waiting for a conviction or were they nervous, wondering if they'd been wrong about Craig?

Mr. and Mrs. Taylor were toward the front near the defense counsel's table, sitting close together for mutual support. It was nice that they had each other,

Kara thought. She wished she could be sitting that way with Peter.

Craig was seated in front of his parents. Although he was cleaned up, with an ironed shirt and his hair combed out of his eyes, his distinctive posture was still recognizable. His shoulders and head were slumped forward at the precise angle that said to the world he was expecting to be disappointed. Kara's heart lurched in her chest. It was likely he was about to get exactly that.

Heather was on the other side of the courtroom. She didn't need to be here today. She'd given her testimony. Only two days before, Heather had been hostile to Craig's case. Now, Kara had a warm feeling toward her, as if they were all part of the same group of well-wishers standing behind Craig.

Kara's eyes wandered over to the part of the room she'd been trying to avoid. There was Peter. She could only see his back from the shoulders up. But every inch of him was familiar. So achingly familiar.

She'd hoped for too much with Peter. It broke her heart to realize it now, but she had to face facts. She had been inspired by him to open herself up to more than she'd ever dared before. She must have been distracted by the exhilaration of self-discovery, because she hadn't noticed his growing lack of respect for her.

He had no right to turn himself into a know-it-all do-gooder and run down everything that was important to her. Maybe she hadn't been too graceful the night before at the bar, either, but she hadn't been telling him his vocation was wrong or his coworkers useless. Kara sighed. She and Peter just had too much to argue about.

The door at the front of the courtroom opened, and the judge strode in, his black robes flowing behind him.

The court attendant's voice betrayed no interest in what was about to transpire. "All rise."

Kara studied the stern look on the judge's face. Did he appear perturbed? she wondered. He sat down and organized the papers in front of him. His manner was brusque, as if he was anxious to get on with business.

"I am about to render judgment in the case of the Crown versus Taylor."

He reviewed the formal charge and related the relevant facts as they had been presented by each lawyer. He had the quiet authority of someone accustomed to making decisions. As Kara listened to him, her hands turned cold with fear for Craig.

"There are a few things I'd like to say about this case," the judge said. He broke from his notes and addressed the assembly as if he was having a conversation with them.

"Auto theft is a very serious charge, one that should meet with swift and uncompromising consequences. And precisely because it is a serious charge, it requires serious investigation in each and every case. Serious investigation requires two things: an open mind and attention to detail on the part of the investigators. I believe that both of these ingredients are missing from the investigation of the charge against Craig Taylor."

Kara drew in a sharp breath. She glanced over at Peter, but his attention on the judge was unwavering. Even Ed Smithers remained motionless. She dragged her attention back to the judge's words.

"When I look at the Crown's case, what I see is a collection of evidence that would routinely convict an accused person. What I also see is an attitude. I see police officers who decided they had a suspect they could convict. I don't sense an urgency to uncover the truth. I don't believe Craig Taylor's alibi was taken seriously. I do not believe his alibi was thoroughly investigated. I have to ask myself why this was not done. Was it mere laziness on the part of the police, or might there be another reason?"

Kara continued to tremble.

"What I also see," the judge was saying, "is the exceptional effort shown by certain individuals in the courtroom who stood by this young man when he most needed help. Peter Aiken of Aiken House group home obviously has a great deal of faith in his young charge, and I was impressed with his testimony. I can see that this kind of support is especially meaningful to a youngster in a group home.

"Society must be careful not to alienate its youth or to allow them to learn disrespect for the legal process. Mr. Aiken represents an arm of the criminal justice system because he works with young people who have been in conflict with the law. I sensed Mr. Aiken believed justice would ultimately be done. Every youngster—whether guilty or not—should have the same faith that he will receive a fair hearing, in accordance with due process of law."

Kara keyed in on the words, "whether guilty or not." That didn't sound good. She appreciated the truth of what the judge was saying, but felt frustrated that he wasn't really giving any clues to his verdict.

"The second individual who stands out in this case is Constable Ridgeway."

Kara's attention snapped away from Craig.

"She has taken a lonely path for a police officer. I imagine she has already paid substantially for her integrity. I admire her fortitude. She somewhat makes up for the shoddy performance of her colleagues who initiated this charge."

Kara dared not relax. The judge's compliment didn't mean anything, either. Judges had a habit of highlighting the strengths of a losing case just before passing judgment. She waited for him to say "nevertheless" or "but" or "however." One of those little words would herald Craig's demise.

"Now to the matter of Miss Heather Crawly and her rather surprising testimony. Miss Crawly was attempting to keep herself out of trouble with her parents when she told the police she was not at the dance with the defendant. By changing her story here in this court, she stands to get herself deeper into trouble. She knew this and still testified, despite what might have amounted to veiled threats that she would be charged if she changed her testimony from her previous statement.

"I am always suspicious of a witness who provides conflicting stories at different times. We must therefore examine very carefully the reasons for the change in testimony. I am satisfied that this young lady took a risk here because it became more important to her to tell the truth than to keep herself out of trouble. I do not approve of the way she did it. She should have told the truth from the beginning. But recognizing human frailty, I applaud the action she took to right the wrong. I am encouraged to see one of our young people take such courageous action, and I am satisfied she has learned something important from this experience."

Surprise rippled through the courtroom. Kara forced herself to avert her eyes from Peter's general vicinity. It would be too easy to meet his eyes and smile. She would know his look that gently reminded her he'd told her so. It would be difficult to look at each other and not express their relief that something had gone in Craig's favor. But the verdict was still to come.

"There is one final matter I wish to address before I pass judgment. As noted earlier, I find the shoddy performance of the police in this case very disturbing. I find it disturbing because it says to me that the police presumed that a boy from a group home is guilty by virtue of being at the scene, regardless of his explanation. I've been asking myself if the police might have been more energetic if the boy they had found in the car had been the mayor's son or the police chief's son or my own son.

"When I ask myself these questions they lead me to more questions. I ask myself if young people in general know that this is the police attitude toward young people from group homes. Does this have anything at all to do with why a stolen car was abandoned in the vicinity of a group home? Would the police automatically harass the inhabitants of the home and neglect thorough investigation elsewhere? I sincerely hope this is not the case, but it certainly appears to have been the case here.

"Now, in the case of the Crown versus Craig Taylor, I find there to be a reasonable doubt as to the whereabouts of the accused at the time the offense occurred. Therefore, I find him not guilty of the charge."

A groundswell of excitement rose around Kara and threatened to engulf her. This was so different from what she had envisioned!

Kara walked quickly across the back of the room, out the courtroom doors and into the hallway. Craig was swamped with well-wishers, and it seemed to take him forever to progress down the aisle. Kara saw him crane his neck every so often to make sure she was still there. The shy smile he reserved for her touched her too deeply to allow her to indulge her need to slip out the back door. This was his moment, his vindication, and she had to share it with him.

Peter stayed discreetly in the background, and Kara appreciated the courtesy. She was having enough trouble holding back her tears.

Craig reached her, and she could see in his vulnerable face that he was bombarded by feelings of triumph, relief and thankfulness. "This is something else, huh?"

His boyish grin inexplicably decimated Kara's control. Tears spilled over as she hugged him and whispered in his ear that she was proud of him. She had to turn and run before her sobs made their inevitable way into the open.

## CHAPTER FIFTEEN

WHEN KARA SPOTTED CRAIG and his parents at the front counter of the police station she scrambled to her feet. What a welcome sight they were! In the three days since the trial, Kara's desk had seemed like a prison to her. She'd been preoccupied with thoughts of Aiken House and all the kids there. Without them, she felt as if she'd lost her family.

She thought of Kate and Randy and Kyle, little Stevie and even Ketchup. They all must have been jubilant for Craig. She wished she could have been there to share in the celebration. Most of all, of course, she'd been thinking about Peter. She wondered if he thought about her, too. Probably not. He had plenty of distractions. He had everyone he cared about around him.

Mrs. Taylor looked as if she hadn't stopped smiling for three days. "We're on our way home, but we felt we had to stop to say goodbye," she said.

"I'm so glad you did. I've been thinking about all of you," Kara replied, then turned to Craig. "This must feel like a big day for you, to be going home."

Craig shrugged sheepishly. "I've been having so many big days lately they don't feel different anymore. They just seem normal."

"I guess so," Kara agreed. "Let's hope things settle down a bit for you now."

"They will," Craig pledged. "I guarantee it."

Mr. Taylor shook her hand warmly. "I want to thank you for everything, Kara. I'm sure I don't need to tell you how much you've meant to Craig. We feel we have a clean slate now. This time we're all going to work together. We have a few errands to run while we're downtown, but Craig wanted to stay and visit with you for a short while, if he wouldn't be bothering you. I told him we'd have to make sure it wasn't interfering with your work."

"Not at all. I'd love a little time to visit, and my shift ends in five minutes anyway. Come on, Craig. We can go for a coffee."

Kara led Craig down the long hallway to the lunchroom. As they entered, Stan greeted them with a wave.

"I thought you might be hiding back here," Kara teased him.

"Back here, I keep out of trouble," he replied, and offered Craig his hand. "Good to meet you, Craig. Kara has told me all about you and the trial. Congratulations."

"Thank you, sir."

"I have to say it's pretty impressive that you can come for a coffee with a couple of cops after what you've been through."

"It all worked out okay, I guess," Craig answered charitably. "But to tell you the truth, it does make me kind of nervous being here. I keep expecting somebody to come along and tell me I have to go back to the cell. I know a lot of people around here didn't exactly agree with the judge.''

Stan pulled up a chair and straddled it backward, so that his arms rested over the back of the chair. ''I don't think you have to worry about that anymore, son. The boys who really stole that car were arrested this morning.''

''They were!'' Kara exclaimed. ''Who were they?''

''Two boys from the other side of town.''

Craig stared intently at Stan. ''How'd the cops find the guys who did it?''

''By using the usual procedures. The new officer who was assigned to the case pulled the names of everyone who had been in trouble with us for similar offenses in the past couple of years. Then he started interviewing them, asking where they were on the night the car was stolen. When the officer showed up at this one kid's door, he confessed and implicated a friend along with himself.''

''In other words, the guilty parties were there to be discovered all along if Ed hadn't presumed that Craig was guilty.''

''Yes, ma'am.''

''So was it just a joyride?'' Kara asked. ''The car wasn't involved in a holdup or anything?''

''Nope,'' Stan answered and drained his cup. ''Apparently they did it on a dare. They didn't even know that someone else had been arrested for it.''

Stan and Kara both glanced at Craig. He seemed a bit shaken as he looked back at them. ''All that for a stupid joyride.''

"Pretty stupid, eh?" Stan said.

Kara filled the ensuing silence by fixing coffee for herself. "Coffee, Craig?"

Craig twisted his face into a grimace. "I've had so much of that stuff in the last two months, I don't think I could keep down another drop."

"Good. The stuff's bad for you anyway."

"Rots your insides," Stan agreed happily.

Kara turned back to Craig. "I hope you're not going to have a chip on your shoulder against the police after all this."

Craig paused, apparently assessing the likelihood. "Naw, I guess even cops make mistakes. I'm just glad that some cops aren't afraid to stand up and defend innocent people."

Stan answered him seriously. "I think very few cops would go out on a limb like Kara did. You're lucky, Craig, that you bumped into someone who cares so much."

"I know I'm lucky, sir."

"Anyway, I have to get back to my desk. I'm glad it all worked out for you, Craig."

Craig stood to shake Stan's hand again as they said goodbye. Kara was pleased to see Craig looking so relaxed. But she felt saddened, too, knowing that very soon she would have to join the line to shake his hand goodbye.

They sat quietly, avoiding each other's eyes.

"So," she offered at length. "How do you feel?"

Craig's chuckle was familiar. "You sound like Peter."

"I suppose I do with that question, eh? But how do you feel?"

"I dunno. Kind of funny, I guess."

"Funny how?"

He shrugged. "To be in a cell and have the world against me one day, then be everybody's hero the next. It's kind of weird."

"I can see that."

"At least you and Peter never changed. You were never against me. I could count on you all the way."

Kara dropped her voice to a whisper. "And you didn't let me down, either, just like you promised."

"Peter told me that it was you who finally got Heather to change her mind about testifying."

"Heather made her own decision."

"But you told her about Joey. You didn't have to do that."

"Yeah, well, I guess we all have things in our lives that are difficult."

"You really do care an awful lot about what happens to me, just like you said when I first met you."

"I do."

"So, what happens to Heather? Will she get charged for changing her story?"

"No, they've decided not to bother. I think the two cops who arrested you would like to erase the names Craig Taylor and Heather Crawly from their memory banks."

Craig laughed. "Good. I'm going to do my best to forget about them, too. Heather did the right thing. It would have been wrong for anyone to punish her for that."

Craig looked around the lunchroom. "This might sound strange, but it seems weird to see you here."

Kara giggled. "This is where I work."

"Yeah, but I'm used to seeing you at Aiken House. You look like you belong there. You don't belong here."

"I won't have much reason to be at Aiken House now that you're going home. You're just more accustomed to seeing me there than here."

"What about Peter? Aren't you going to see him?"

The question was a logical one, one she should have expected. But it still caught her off guard.

"Not if I have no juveniles in his home," she stammered.

Craig slouched back in his chair and folded his arms. "You sure do some funny stuff sometimes. When you're here you aren't happy, and when you're with Peter at Aiken House you are happy, yet you want to stay here."

"Now, wait a minute, Craig," Kara protested, then stopped. "All right, I'll admit it. I am happy at Aiken House. I'm not so happy here. There, I said it. So what do I do about it? Aiken House is Peter's place, not mine."

"How can you say that? You ask any kid in that house and they'll tell you they look up to you just as much as they look up to Peter."

"That's very nice of you to say, Craig, but it doesn't change things. Peter has not extended an invitation for me to be there, other than to see you, and as of now you're history."

"Since when did you need an invitation? That's crazy!"

"And you, Craig Taylor, are venturing beyond the bounds of what you can call your business."

Craig laughed warmly. "I was wondering when you were going to say that."

"Now you know."

"I remember when you came to Children's Aid I thought you were a real tough lady. But you're not really, are you?"

"It's just that you're a bad influence on me," Kara replied, smiling. "It's a good thing I don't run across guys like you every day."

Footsteps sounded down the hallway. Kara and Craig turned to see Stan pop his head in.

"Call for you, Kara. Line one is holding."

Craig stood to leave. "Go take your call," he said. "I'll just rinse these cups. My parents are probably waiting for me by now anyway. I don't want to keep them too long."

"Okay, Craig, thanks. That's sweet of you."

Craig seemed to become suddenly self-conscious. "You're the one who deserves the thanks. I owe you a lot."

All at once, Kara felt overwrought by her own emotions. Craig and she had been so important to each other, such significant players in each other lives, that she didn't want to let go of him.

Peter must have felt the same way, she realized, and somehow she felt comforted by the knowledge that he, too, had found this business of saying goodbye distressing.

"I figure it's been pretty nice knowing you, too," she returned.

"Can I come back and visit you sometime?"

"I'd like that very much."

"Good," Craig said, his voice thick with emotion. Kara blinked back tears as he leaned forward and gave her a quick kiss on the cheek.

"Joey was a lucky guy," he said. "His sister is something else."

She whispered goodbye and hurried down the hallway.


"Constable Ridgeway here."

Her voice sounded shaky to Peter. "Kara, it's me," he said. "I just wanted to see how you were."

Peter heard a faint moan and ragged breath.

"Craig was just here," she answered. "Was it hard for you to say goodbye?"

"Yeah. I never thought I'd miss any particular kid when I had a house full of them. But Craig was different."

"He sure was."

Peter hastened to fill the ensuing silence. "Everything back to normal around there?"

Kara laughed mockingly. "Captain Bannon actually called me into his office to apologize. The guys are talking to me again, except, of course, Ed."

"You must be thrilled."

"You'd think I would be, wouldn't you?"

"But you're not?"

"No."

"Why not?"

"I don't know. Nothing seems to mean a whole lot anymore. Maybe I'm just worn out."

"Kara, I was a jerk that night at the bar, and I'm sorry. I had no business sticking my nose in your affairs. There's nothing wrong with being a cop and you're a good one. Kara, I love you. I need you. Nothing around here makes sense without you."

He thought he heard a muffled sob from the other end of the line. "Kara? Are you there?"

"I'm here."

"Are you all right?"

"If you really mean what you're saying—"

"Of course I mean it. Don't ever doubt it."

"You know what's really crazy? I don't want to be a cop anymore. I didn't want to tell you that. But the only place I feel completely myself, really feel happy, is with you at Aiken House."

"Kara, you're what makes everything else worthwhile. I want to share Aiken House with you. That's what I was trying to say to you. I think you could be happy here."

"I know I could be happy there. Deep down I knew it all along, but I couldn't tell you."

"No wonder. I was being such an obnoxious moron."

"I don't suppose I was being my most rational, either."

"Kara, I should have been more sensitive to how everything was affecting you. You've been through so much in the past few weeks. I should never have dumped more on you—especially about something as important as your work. You didn't need me to run down the police force. You needed me to ask you to come here. So I'm asking you now, Kara. Please come and share Aiken House with me."

He could hear sniffles at the other end. "Are you sure?" she asked.

"Absolutely, one hundred percent. If I had you here, I'd sweep you off your feet to show you. Kara, it's ridiculous to have this conversation over the phone. Can I come and get you?"

"No, not here. I'm starting to make a spectacle of myself as it is."

"Then come here. I'm at the boat house."

"I'm on my way."

Stan was watching her gather up her things. "You look like you're in a bit of a hurry," he observed.

It was just like him to mention her haste rather than the tears that streamed down her face.

"Stan, I never told you this before. I'm in love with Peter Aiken. Isn't that ridiculous?"

He laughed indulgently. "It is, if this is the first time you've realized it." If he wondered why she was crying, he didn't say.

Stan was not given to emotional displays, but still he got up from his desk and came over and hugged her. "Go for it, Kara," he said with brotherly affection.

She squeezed him one last time and tried not to break into a dead run to the parking lot.

No ghosts haunted her today. She felt released from the dark clouds that used to rise from thoughts of her past. She craved to hurry into the sunshine and bask there, feel its warmth seep through her skin and into her bloodstream.

Another layer of snow had fallen since she and Craig had shoveled out the driveway, and the new drifts reached up to her car's axle. She barreled through the white powder until she buried her car deeply enough to have to stop.

She threw open the car door and broke into a run across the snow toward the boat house. The crusty snow would not hold her weight. Each step was echoed by a quiet thud that landed her knee deep in snow, and from time to time, she lost her balance and fell over, patiently picking herself up each time.

Laughter gurgled up in her. She laughed for the sheer delight she took from everything around her. If she hadn't been in such a hurry, she would have stayed lying in the snow, staring at a sky so brilliant that it reminded her of Peter's eyes.

She caught sight of Peter as he rounded the corner of the boat house. He ran in the same jerky fashion as she did. He laughed, too, as his feet dropped through the crusty layer of snow. He wore no coat over his red plaid shirt and blue jeans and his boots weren't laced. He was the most beautiful thing Kara had ever seen.

They met and his arms closed around her. "I love you," he moaned.

"I love you, I love you, I love you," she returned, closing her arms around his neck.

"I'm never letting you go."

"I'm not going anywhere."

Her legs swung out from under her as Peter hoisted her into his arms. He carried her the short distance to the boat house steps, then set her down. He was puffing.

"Much as I love you, Kara, I don't think I can carry you up all those stairs."

"Some Prince Charming."

"Well, I probably could get you up the stairs, but I'd have no energy left once we got there."

"Oh, I wouldn't like that," she said and ran quickly up the steps and opened the door to his tranquil blue living room. It felt like home. Her home with Peter.

Peter closed the door behind him and drew her to him. He kissed her, at first slowly and languidly, then deeper and more intensely. She pressed herself along the length of his body and warmed to his response.

"I was afraid you wouldn't come," he breathed between kisses.

"I was afraid you wouldn't call."

"I wasn't sure you wanted to be here."

"I wasn't sure you wanted me here."

"Well, that was pretty dumb on your part. I want you to know something. I'm knocked out, crazy in love with you. You'd have to be blind not to notice that."

"I have a short memory. I need lots of reminders."

His face was soft and loving, and he kept gently touching her face and hair as if he couldn't touch her enough to satisfy him.

"I've never felt this way about anyone," he breathed.

Kara was so happy she could have cried. She battled the waver in her voice. "Is this the beginning of another speech?"

"No speeches."

"I just wanted to know how long it was going to last."

"It's over."

"Good. Now show me how much you love me."

"My pleasure."


KARA LAY WATCHING rays of sunshine work their way across the bedroom wall.

"Peter, are you awake?"

"Mmm."

"We've been in this bed for fifteen hours."

"Mmm."

Kara smiled as she felt his arm tighten around her waist and his legs entwine with hers.

"I'm afraid I've got something to tell you."

She giggled as his eyes popped open and his head lifted from the pillow.

"Your bed's lumpy."

He smiled and dropped his head back down. "I'll get a new one."

"Is that what you're going to do with me when I get old and lumpy?"

He drew her closer. "I'm not complaining about the bed. I like it old and lumpy."

"Then you haven't changed your mind?"

"Of course not. Have you?"

"No."

Peter hiked himself up on his elbows and looked at her. He drew a gentle outline of her face with his finger. "I love you, Kara. That isn't going to change."

"Your wanting me could."

"Let me tell you about what I want. I want to spend the next fifty years at least helping kids at Aiken House. I want to do that with you. I want those kids to see us like parents who love them and love each other. I want us to teach them how to love. Some of them never learned in the first place. Some of them have never been loved.

"And I want our own kids. I want to look at you as the mother of some little tyke who sees you as the center of the universe. Just like I do. That's what I want. Kara, I love you for things that don't get old and lumpy. Now, you tell me what you want."

"I want exactly the same things. Only I want to start a program that specifically recruits police officers as volunteers. I want the Ed Smithers of the world to learn to see these kids as they really are. And I want to expand Aiken House like you told me you wanted to when you first gave me my tour."

"We'll dedicate the new section to Joey."

Kara kissed his nose.

# Harlequin Romance

# ATTRACTIVE, SPACE SAVING BOOK RACK

Display your most prized novels on this handsome and sturdy book rack. The hand-rubbed walnut finish will blend into your library decor with quiet elegance, providing a practical organizer for your favorite hard-or soft-covered books.

**Only $9.95**

*Approximately 16" x 8" when assembled*

*Assembles in seconds!*

---

To order, rush your name, address and zip code, along with a check or money order for $10.70* ($9.95 plus 75¢ postage and handling) payable to *Harlequin Reader Service*:

Harlequin Reader Service
Book Rack Offer
901 Fuhrmann Blvd.
P.O. Box 1396
Buffalo, NY 14269-1396

*Offer not available in Canada.*

BKR-1A

*New York and Iowa residents add appropriate sales tax.

# PAMELA BROWNING

. . . is fireworks on the green at the Fourth of July and prayers said around the Thanksgiving table. It is the dream of freedom realized in thousands of small towns across this great nation.

But mostly, the Heartland is its people. People who care about and help one another. People who cherish traditional values and give to their children the greatest gift, the gift of love.

American Romance presents HEARTLAND, an emotional trilogy about people whose memories, hopes and dreams are bound up in the acres they farm.

HEARTLAND . . . the story of America.

Don't miss these heartfelt stories: American Romance #237 SIMPLE GIFTS (March), #241 FLY AWAY (April), and #245 HARVEST HOME (May).

HRT-1

# *Harlequin American Romance*